A Lady's Guide to Etiquette and Murder

A Lady's Guide to Etiquette and Murder

Dianne Freeman

KENSINGTON BOOKS
http://www.kensingtonbooks.com

KENSINGTON BOOKS are published by

Kensington Publishing Corp.
119 West 40th Street
New York, NY 10018

All Kensington titles, imprints, and distributed lines are available at special quantity discounts for bulk purchases for sales promotion, premiums, fund-raising, educational, or institutional use. Special book excerpts or customized printings can also be created to fit specific needs. For details, write or phone the office of the Kensington Special Sales Manager: Attn. Special Sales Department. Kensington Publishing Corp, 119 West 40th Street, New York, NY 10018. Phone: 1-800-221-2647.

Library of Congress Card Catalogue Number:

ISBN-13: 978-1-4967-1687-3
ISBN-10: 1-4967-1687-6
First Kensington Hardcover Edition: July 2018

eISBN-13: 978-1-4967-1689-7
eISBN-10: 1-4967-1689-2
First Kensington Electronic Edition: July 2018

10 9 8 7 6 5 4 3 2 1

Printed in the United States of America

In memory of Elaine Freeman,
who always believed in all of us.

Acknowledgments

There are so many people who helped bring this story from idea to finished book and I offer my most sincere gratitude to each of them

To Brenda Drake for the time and effort you give to Pitchwars and making writers' dreams come true.

To E.B. Wheeler, my mentor and friend, thank you for guiding me through my first ever round of edits.

To Melissa Edwards, Agent Extraordinaire. I'm so grateful to have you in my corner.

To my editor, John Scognamiglio and everyone at Kensington who played a role in making this book shine.

To my Pitchwars peeps, writing partners, and beta readers, especially Mary Keliikoa, for all your support, encouragement, and invaluable feedback.

To my husband, Dan for loving me, believing in me, and sharing this journey with me. I am one lucky lady.

Chapter 1

~≈~

April 1899

Black—no. Black—no. *Black crepe?* Oh, heavens no! I bundled the offending gowns and dropped them on a bench for my maid to dispose of, then glanced around my dressing room. One word described it—*mourning.* In my wildest imaginings, I never would have dreamed I'd find myself a widow at the age of twenty-seven. Though for me, the difference from marriage was barely discernible.

While I'll confess to a foolish infatuation, Reggie and I hadn't married for love. My mother instigated the match when she brought me from New York to London. I suppose love had something to do with it. Reggie loved my money, and my mother adored his title. When we married, I became Countess of Harleigh. My family gained the consequence of that title. The Wynn family gained me, Frances Price, commoner. Oh, and a little over a million U.S. dollars.

True aristocrats that they were, to this day the Wynns acted as though they'd been swindled.

I'd endured a whole year of mourning with them. Miserable,

yes, but at first I had no desire to show my face in public. While only two people besides myself knew the circumstances of my husband's death, I'm sure many more had their suspicions. You see, my husband died just over a year ago—in his lover's bed.

At a house party.

At our home.

Delightful man.

I eyed the gown I'd be wearing tonight, a rich royal blue. Ah, color in my life again. Mourning period over.

With a warning knock, Bridget, my maid, slipped into the room. "Are you ready to change for dinner, my lady?" Her eyes brightened with excitement when she saw the gown on the bed. "Are you wearing the blue?"

I smiled. "My first strike for independence."

"Well, I'm all for that." She turned me around and began unfastening my dress. Under her skillful hands, I was in the blue gown in a matter of minutes—a good thing as evening had brought the inevitable chill to the room. Bridget handed me a shawl for my rather bare shoulders and ushered me to the dressing table to do my hair.

"I don't remember seeing that picture before," she said, removing hairpins and shaping curls.

"I've been gathering things for packing." I picked up the photograph from the dressing table. "We sat for this one a long time ago. Must have been seven years as Rose was just a baby." I smiled down at the familiar faces. A family portrait, including Reggie's parents. I did have some pleasant memories of this family, and I'd tried my best to be a credit to them. I wasn't such a bad bargain. Reasonably attractive, I had my father's height and dark hair, coupled with my mother's blue eyes and fair complexion. No overly prominent chin, nose, or teeth. And I certainly knew how to act like a countess. My mother had been grooming me for this since my tenth year. Why, I'd even added a child to the family. Yes, Rose was a daughter, but I'd have been happy to try for an heir if Reggie had cared enough.

But pleasant memories aside, day-to-day life with this family had become intolerable. It was time to move on.

"Will that do, my lady?"

I placed the photograph back on the table and took a quick glance at the mirror. Then a much longer look. "Goodness, that's quite a sculpture you've created."

Bridget pursed her lips. "You're wearing a fashionable gown and you need a fashionable hairstyle to match." She gave me a firm nod that told me I'd better not argue.

"It's just so—tall."

"The extra height will give you courage."

That clinched it. "Thank you, Bridget. It's perfect." I glanced at the clock on the dressing table. "It's too early for me to go down, but you should go to your dinner. I'll just stay up here and gather some more belongings."

With a curtsy, she left. I let my gaze travel over the room. What should I take with me when I move out? And what would my in-laws insist belonged to the manor? Considering I'd been dreaming of this move for almost a year, I'd done little actual planning. In the back of my mind, I feared living on my own might be just beyond my financial reach and I'd have to give up the idea as a foolish dream. Bridget alone knew of my plans as she'd traveled with me to London last week under the vague guise of business. In my three-day trip I'd met with my solicitor, who scheduled appointments with an estate agent, who showed me five homes—four of which were definitely out of my reach.

But one was perfect. And in that moment I realized I could actually do this, assuming I could get past my in-laws' objections. I'd sworn Bridget to secrecy but wouldn't be at all surprised if several of the servants already knew, so Graham and Delia would have to be told before someone let it slip.

I blinked a few times. Heavens, it was dark in here. Stepping over to the bedside table, I turned up the wick on the paraffin lamp. Better. Between the lamp and the fire in the grate, the room now had a warm glow.

Hmm. Obviously my personal things would come with me, clothing and jewelry. I scanned the dressing table—silver-backed brush, comb and mirror, crystal bottles and atomizers. Their ownership was indisputable. I turned around and gazed at the large four-poster bed, and its beautiful carved rosewood head- and footboards. I'd miss it, but trying to lay claim to this bed—which I'd paid for—would cause far more trouble than it was worth. I ran my hand across the smooth silk coverlet. That was coming with me.

The sound of voices interrupted my inventory. Someone was speaking in my brother-in-law's study, located directly below my room, and the volume was increasing. I stood still as I waited—listening to the muffled words—for the sound of my name. There it was. Of course they were talking about me. They were always talking about me.

I moved to the other side of the bed and drew back the corner of the ancient Aubusson carpet along the wall, revealing a six-inch hole in the floor. This hole led to a corresponding one in the wall of Graham's study, complete with metal tubing. The holes were left from an attempt at installing gas lines to the family rooms of the house, aborted when the workmen learned Graham would be paying them late. If ever. As a result, the house retained its chill, but the holes made for an excellent listening device. Graham had hung a picture of his sons over that hole, but it made little difference to the quality of the sound.

It was quite an accomplishment to lower myself to my knees in the narrow skirt of my gown. Yes, I know, a lady has no business eavesdropping on the conversations of others, but I looked on this as a method of self-defense. Over the last year, Graham and Delia, my brother-in-law and his wife, had hatched an endless number of schemes, which always involved the use of my funds. So when they spoke about me, I listened. Fore-warned is forearmed. I leaned closer to the hole, wrinkling my nose against the musty air in the tube.

"The balconies on the north wall are crumbling, Graham." That was Delia's voice. "We can't have guests here until they're replaced."

Graham muttered something about mourning and I pictured Delia rolling her eyes.

"Honestly, Graham, do you never consult the calendar? Our mourning period is well past. Now if we don't get workmen out here soon, we won't have the balconies repaired by summer."

A chair squeaked, and I assumed Graham had finally put down whatever he'd been working on to attend to his wife. "My dear, we cannot afford repairs. We can't even afford guests. Not now. Not this summer. You must be patient."

"I will not. If you're saying we have to wait for your invest-ments to pay off, the manor will fall to rack of fruit by then."

I raised my head from the floor and mouthed her words. Rack of fruit. That couldn't be right. Delia must have walked away as she spoke. Well, I never said this device worked per-fectly. I tried to puzzle out what she might have said while mas-saging a sore spot in my neck. Sometimes I wondered if listening to them was worth my aches and pains. Wait! The house would fall to wrack and ruin. That must be it. I huffed. As if it weren't already well on its way.

I placed my ear back on the floor and tried to catch up with the conversation. "She has the money, Graham." That would be me to whom Delia referred. "And should she ever run out, all she need do is ask her father for more."

"Yes, but I already plan to request some funds. It wouldn't do for us both to ask."

Heavens, they spoke as if I were a bank. Graham went on to

explain some agricultural innovation he wanted to test on the home farm. Poor Delia. All she ever wanted was to be the grand lady, but fate thwarted her at every turn. First, she wasn't wealthy enough to marry the oldest son and was pawned off on the second. Then, when she finally became a countess, the old manor was falling apart and the coffers were nearly empty.

"Surely I can ask for a little money for the house. How else can we make the repairs?"

"You know my solution to that." Graham spoke so softly, I could barely hear him. Unfortunate, as I was truly curious to hear how he planned to ease their financial woes.

"Don't say it." Delia replied in a sharp tone, as if poking him with each syllable. "You know how I feel about *your solution*."

Oh, my. If Delia didn't like Graham's plan it must involve some restriction on her spending while he continued to sink money into the estate.

I heard a door creak followed by footsteps, then a swish of skirts near the bed.

Heavens, it was my door! I jerked my head up and tried scrambling to my feet. Instead I fell to my side in something of a sprawl on the floor. Jenny, one of the housemaids, dropped the linens she'd brought to my room and scurried over to assist me.

"Sorry to disturb you, my lady," she said, offering her arm so I could pull myself up. "I saw Bridget downstairs and thought you'd already gone to dinner."

How humiliating. With my ear to the floor and my posterior in the air, I must have looked like a worm inching across the room when she'd walked in. I stood and tried to compose myself—and some sort of explanation. When I looked at Jenny, her gaze was on the hole in the floor. Oh, dear. No chance of explaining that away. The maid was young, cheerful, and something of a chatterbox. How would I keep her from talking about this?

"Jenny, you may have heard some whispers below-stairs

about my moving to town. Would you be interested in coming with me? I can promise you a good wage."

Her eyes widened as she bobbed her head.

"Excellent." I gave her a smile as I assessed her qualifications. I could do worse. "Why don't you roll that rug back into place and we'll talk tomorrow. Until then, don't breathe a word about my move."

As she bent to her task, the dinner gong sounded. I smoothed my skirt and stepped over to the dressing table to see if I'd mussed my hair. I took a deep breath. This move would come as something of a surprise for my in-laws and I anticipated resistance. No cozy family dinner for us.

Delia noticed my gown immediately. She gave me a nod of approval as I entered the drawing room where the family traditionally gathered before dinner. "Frances, what a lovely new gown. It's good to see you out of mourning. Isn't it, Graham?"

I took a quick glance over her head at my brother-in-law, busily pouring drinks, determined to ignore his wife's hints. Not only was the family's mourning period over, but I was spending money on myself.

With a blink, I looked back down at Delia. She was an inch or two shorter than I, which always took me by surprise, as her thin-as-a-whip frame gave her the appearance of height. In the same way, her heart-shaped face, blond curls, and ready smile camouflaged the backbone of a warrior. She intimidated our tenants and the local villagers, but she also stood as my ally back when I first came to this family and tried to make a place for myself. I quite liked her, despite the conversation I'd overheard, and her unwavering attachment to both my money, and this white elephant of a house. She was just trying to make the best of a bad situation.

"I'm glad you approve." I gave her hand a squeeze and waited for Graham to join us.

The drawing room boasted gas lighting, but was still rather dim. The dark, heavy furnishings and carpets, well into their dotage, only added to the gloom. After a significant battle, I'd been permitted to change the draperies. Lighter, they allowed sunlight in during the day, but as soon as evening set in, the room turned dismal.

Graham stepped up and handed me a glass of sherry. As I turned, I noted a section of scaffolding outside the window, and wondered if Delia had already hired the workmen for the balconies. Poor Graham.

Shaking off that concern, I smiled at my in-laws. "I feared it might shock you both that I cast off my mourning, but it has been over a year. I thought it time, so I had a few things made up while in London last week."

"A few things," Delia echoed, giving her husband a significant look. I took a sideways glance at him myself. His bland face showed no reaction. There was nothing unattractive about him, but Reggie definitely had the looks in the family. Graham was a toned-down version of his brother, hair more sandy than blond, average height, average build. On the asset side of the ledger though, he was far more responsible than Reggie, and seemed truly to care about his wife. I gave him high marks for that.

We didn't bother seating ourselves, but rather stood near the doorway making small talk, as the second gong would sound shortly, disrupting any relevant conversation. When it did, we processed into the dining room like well-trained hounds, responding to the sound of the horn.

"I suppose you noticed we're preparing for another round of construction," Delia said, as a footman seated her at one end of the massive table. He then scurried around to the center, where I stood at my chair, waiting for him to perform the same service for me.

"Scaffolding does tend to herald construction." I spoke in a strident tone in order to be heard at either end of the table, then waited a beat as my words echoed off the high coffered ceiling. How ridiculous to dine in such formality when it was only the three of us. The nine-foot mahogany table, candle-lit, and laden with floral arrangements, was lovely, but who on earth were we impressing? "Is it to be a large project?"

Delia placed a hand to her chest, releasing a false sigh of regret. "They are always larger than we expect, but an honorable old structure such as this demands a great deal of maintenance."

"Over two centuries old, you know," Graham added from his end of the table.

I was well aware of the age of the house, and intimately familiar with the amount of maintenance it required. I smiled in acknowledgment. The footman served the soup course so we left off conversation for a moment. The only sound was the tapping of his heels on the marble floor as he rounded the table with his tray.

"Well," Delia continued, through sips of consommé, "Graham and I wish to restore the manor to its original splendor."

"At some point in time, my dear." Graham scowled at his wife. "Right now the home farm requires an infusion of cash." He turned to me. "As the elder countess, I'm sure you'd agree. After all you are still a member of this distinguished family."

I forced myself not to cringe at the epitaph. Elder countess indeed! Another bit of misery Reggie had left me to endure.

Once I got past the denigrating title, I realized they were still fighting over my money. As the only member of the family who had any, of course the useless elder countess would pay for everything. Of all the devious tricks! My gaze drifted over to the sideboard where Crabbe, the butler, decanted wine for the next course. The footman stood nearby, waiting to clear the soup course. It would be unseemly to discuss finances in front of them, but if I ignored these hints, they would assume my consent. I'd intended to wait until after the servants had withdrawn before giving them my news, but now they left me with no option.

"There is nothing dearer to my heart than assisting the family, but I'm afraid my funds are committed elsewhere."

Delia's ingratiating smile faded. "Whatever do you mean, dear?"

I'd been bursting to tell them for a week now, and foiling their little trick made it all the more thrilling. "Well, I have some rather exciting news." I paused, glancing from Delia to Graham and back. "When I was in London last week, I leased a house."

Delia's jaw sagged, and I heard Graham choke at his end of the table. When I turned toward him, he was mopping his mouth with a napkin. Clearly breathing, so all was well. "Do you mean you're leasing a house for the Season?"

"No, indeed. I bought the leasehold. There are eighty years left on the lease, so it required a significant down payment, but my solicitor negotiated splendidly, and, well, it's mine." I nearly sang out the words.

Graham stared at me as if he still didn't quite understand. "A *house*, you say? *A house?*"

"Yes!" I clutched my hands together, trying to contain my excitement, but on second thought, why should I? I leaned toward Graham. "Now before you say a thing, you dear man, I know you'd put up with my presence, and never allow me to feel I was in the way. But you are the Earl and Countess of Harleigh now. I no longer serve a purpose here and should move on. You've been wonderfully kind during this past year, but I refuse to impose a moment longer."

Take that, Graham.

"But a house. The cost!"

"Graham." Delia chided him with a frown. "*Pas devant les domestiques.*"

I dipped into my soup, hiding my smile behind the fragrant vapors of steam. Not in front of the servants. Exactly why

Delia started this conversation in the first place. I was happy to turn the tables on her. They could hardly say what they really thought about my leaving—at least not yet.

"You needn't worry about me, Graham. My father provided for me well enough to set up a household for my daughter, which is what I should be doing. After all, I must get on with my life, and let the two of you get on with yours."

My smiled faltered as I saw how red Graham's face had become. Goodness, I'd forgotten he had a weak heart. I should have considered that before giving him such a shock. I certainly had no intention of making him ill.

His brow furrowed as he watched the footman remove the soup bowls. He was working up an argument, but Delia's voice broke the silence first.

"Are you sure moving to town is the best idea for you and Rose? Not that I want to change your mind, of course."

Of course she didn't. No lady of the house wants the former lady of the house hanging around for years on end. I'd been a thorn in Delia's side since she and Graham moved in here a year ago. It had taken ages for me to earn the loyalty of the staff at Harleigh Manor and now they were reluctant to hand that loyalty over to Delia. No matter how many times I publicly referred the servants and tenants to her, they still came to me with their questions and problems. And I admit, in private, I encouraged them.

There was a battle taking place in her mind between her twin desires—status and money. I had hoped she'd be my champion in this endeavor as I knew she'd be thrilled to be the only countess in residence, and therefore the lady of the house by default. But she had to know it would be much more difficult to wheedle money out of me if I weren't on hand.

As her decision could go either way, she needed a nudge in the right direction. "I'll only be a short train ride away, Delia. I'll see you when you come to town for the Season."

The footman leaned in at her side, with the main course. She studied my innocent smile as she took a portion of beef. "I must say I'm quite excited for you, but I'd be terrified living on my own. You've chosen a good neighborhood, I hope."

I could have jumped from my seat and cheered. The battle might not be over, but I'd won the first skirmish. "It's in Belgravia, on Chester Street. Far away from any criminal element. We'll be moving next week, right after Easter, which reminds me, there are some pieces of furniture I'd quite like to take with me."

"Of course. You'll want familiar things in your new home. Why don't you give me a list and your direction, and I'll arrange to have them delivered."

At this, Graham's complexion seemed to turn from red to green, but he made no further protest. In fact, he said nothing through the rest of the meal, though he never stopped glaring as Delia and I carried on our conversation. I had the niggling feeling this might have been too easy, but right now I was too happy to care.

Chapter 2

A word of advice—when planning an escape, do not alert the guards. I only wish someone had counseled me on this before I opened my mouth. Graham and Delia had a full week to work on changing my decision to move out on my own. I would be losing the protection of the family, they told me, and placing myself into God-only-knew what danger. I would be shunned by good society and bring shame to the family name. Ladies would label me "fast." Gentlemen would take advantage of me.

I listened to their concerns, but the simple truth was if they lost control of me, they'd lose control of my money. But they were no match for my resolve, and eventually, moving day arrived, and I found myself ensconced in my very own home.

I loved it. It may well have been the smallest house I ever lived in, but it belonged only to me. I found it perfectly cozy, and cleverly designed to contain everything one would need. The third floor held a spacious nursery-schoolroom, and two bedchambers; one for Rose and one for Nanny. A large reception room, dining room, and library made up the main floor, with four bedchambers and fitted bathrooms above. It even had electric lighting. Very modern. And best of all, I was situated on the end of the row, with Wilton Mews to my side. Therefore, I had an abundance of windows, making the house light and airy. And rather empty. Furnishings were meager. As I glanced around the reception room, I made notes of what I might need to buy, and my list was growing quite long.

My staff was a bit sparse right now too, but I wasn't quite sure what my needs would be yet. I had Mrs. Thompson, a housekeeper who doubled as a cook. Jenny, the housemaid from Harleigh, came to work for me along with Bridget, my personal maid, and of course, Nanny. Mrs. Thompson brought on a scullery maid and a kitchen boy. No butler, no footmen. Did I need them? It might be handy to have a man around the house for heavy lifting but I could always hire someone on a temporary basis if the need arose, as I'd done with the movers. Time would tell.

"Shall I put the knocker on the door, my lady?"

I turned to see Jenny in the doorway, brass knocker in her hand, and a new rush of excitement made me giddy. "I know this is silly," I said, my hands making little flutter movements, "but I'd like to place it."

Jenny flashed her friendly grin. "Not silly at all, my lady. Being as it's the first time going up on your new house, it makes everything official-like. I'd want to do it myself if it were my house." She preceded me into the hall, and opened the front door for me. Stepping outside, we came to a halt, and waited, as if the knocker would simply affix itself. The door wore a fresh coat of paint—a deep forest green, which looked well against the white stone façade. On closer examination, I found a peg had been painted over. Aha!

I turned the knocker around, looking for some sort of indentation to fit on the peg, when I heard footsteps coming up the walk.

"What-ho! It looks as though I have a new neighbor."

I glanced over my shoulder to see who belonged to the low-pitched drawl. Oh, no. This could not be possible.

"Lady Harleigh, what a surprise."

Surprise didn't begin to describe how I felt as I looked into the face of the Honorable George Hazelton. *Horror* was more appropriate. And did he just call me *neighbor?*

I suppose this would be as good a time as any to recount the story of my past relations with him. Only two people have all the facts of my husband's death. One of them, of course, is the lady in whose bed he died, Alicia Stoke-Whitney. The other is George Hazelton.

Reggie and I were hosting a shooting party in the country. We'd prepared a joint guest list. Some of my friends, some of his, as well as Graham and Delia. The events of that day were not particularly memorable except for the rain, a downpour that flooded the streams and washed out the road. The shoot was cancelled. Left without a scheduled activity, Reggie and some of the other men played countless games of billiards, and drank rather a lot. By dinner Reggie was sloppy and unpleasant, and most of us went to bed shortly thereafter.

What I will never forget is Alicia Stoke-Whitney shaking me awake in the middle of the night. I blinked several times before bringing into focus the face that belonged to the figure in the white dressing gown, bending over my bed.

"Alicia? What's wrong?" As I pulled on my own wrapper, she just stood there, mute. Once my eyes had adjusted, I could see she was quite shaken. Alicia was a fair-skinned redhead, and even in the dark, her red nose and eyes told me she'd been crying. I swung my legs over the edge of the bed and stood, taking her arm. "What is it, dear?"

"It's Reggie." She looked at me in horror. "I really don't know how to say this."

Something in her voice chilled me. "What happened to Reggie?"

"Try to stay calm," she said, patting my arm. "And keep your voice down."

If she thought that would calm me, she was mistaken. I took hold of her shoulders and gave her a shake. "Alicia, what is it?"

Her lips opened and closed a few times. Then she spoke. "He's dead."

The words acted like a dousing of cold water. While definitely wide awake, I was incapable of any sound save a gasp, and a few inarticulate gurgles that were meant to be "Where?" and "How?" My vision blurred. My ears rang. I must have looked as if I were about to faint, because Alicia pushed me back to the bed, pressing my head down uncomfortably into my lap. Her voice shook as she whispered, "I'm so sorry. I'm so sorry."

It took a few minutes, but finally the room stopped spinning, and I could hear again. I raised my head to see her tears were now streaming. The first hint of suspicion struck me. Why was she the one to bring me this news? "How did you find him, Alicia? Is someone with him?"

"Frances," she sobbed. "I can't tell you how terribly I feel about this." She sniffed. "He's in my room."

I stared uncomprehendingly. "In your room?" I don't know if I was that naïve, or if the shock was making me particularly dense, but the confusion on my face made her cry all the harder.

"Oh, God, you didn't know. He was with me, Frances. I'm so sorry."

It's not that I didn't know my husband had affairs—many affairs—but I'd never had the fact so blatantly pushed in my face before. Neither had I ever run through so many different emotions in so short a time—confusion, fear, shock, grief, and finally anger. Good Lord! In our own home? And then he had the nerve to die in her bed. I grew cold at the thought. Damn him!

"Frances." The urgency in Alicia's voice brought me back to the moment. "We have to do something."

We? *We* have to do something? The two of them had carried on as if marriage meant nothing. How had I become part of the equation again? I took a calming breath. However unfair, I had to admit she was right. We had to do something.

"Take me to him," I whispered.

We slipped around the corner and down the hall, our dressing gowns swishing against the carpet as we passed the main staircase, and turned into the guest wing to Alicia's room. I waited while she unlocked the door. My thoughts turned sour. Too bad it hadn't been locked earlier.

The room was dark, but the hall sconce sent a weak shaft of light across the four-poster bed, where Reggie lay on his back, one arm trailing off the side. I inched toward him, tears welling in my eyes. He did indeed look lifeless. I lifted his wrist and felt for a pulse.

Nothing.

The tears came harder. I blinked them away and choked back a sob. Damn! What was I crying for? For what might have been? I was a fool, an idiot. He would never have changed. He never saw a reason to change. He was lying in another woman's bed, naked for goodness' sake.

Oh, my! He was naked, wasn't he? Well, I suppose if he could have chosen a way to die, this would have been it.

I turned to Alicia, hovering behind me, and whispered, "What exactly happened?"

"I think he must have had a heart attack. After we . . ." She shrugged, and I suspect she might actually have been blushing, if you can imagine that. My brows rose as I awaited her explanation.

She continued in a hushed voice. "Well, after we were done,

we fell asleep. I woke a little while ago, and tried to rouse Reggie, to send him back to his room. But I couldn't wake him." She raised her hands to her cheeks, and drew a deep breath, as if trying to calm herself. "I can't believe he did this to me."

"I hardly think he died to spite you," I hissed.

"Yes, yes, but he should have been back in his own bed. Then I would not have to deal with this disaster."

I turned to her in utter disbelief. "I've been cheated on. Reggie is dead. You have a long way to go before I'd consider you as the injured party in this."

In disgust I turned for the door, but she clutched at my arm. "Frances, don't leave me." In the dim light, I could see her shaking with panic, and put an arm around her shoulder to calm her, marveling how our roles had just reversed.

I looked over her head at Reggie. "You're probably right about the heart attack," I said. "He and Graham both have arrhythmia but Reggie was never good about taking his medication." And a lifetime of cigars and alcohol didn't help either.

Drawing a deep breath, I pushed Alicia away. I should thank her for making me so angry. It seemed to clear my head. "I suppose we'll find out what it was, when we send for the doctor, but we have to move him back to his room first. And we should probably put on his nightshirt. If he'd gone to bed in his own room, he'd be wearing it."

Alicia scurried around and found his nightshirt trailing from the chair. It took both of us to dress him. I climbed around behind, pushing him to a seated position, while she struggled to get his arms into the sleeves. It was an exhausting business as Reggie was not exactly cooperative. No surprise there. When we'd finished, I fell back against the headboard while I caught my breath and fought another flood of tears. I glanced at Alicia, standing beside the bed, one hand resting on the post. She was only of middling height, and of slim build. A wave of dread spread through me as I realized the truth. "We are not going to be able to move him ourselves. We'll never get him down that hallway."

Alicia nodded her agreement. "Whom do you trust then?"

She looked up at me with watery eyes. Was it fear, or did she actually care for Reggie? Either way, it was clear the irony of that question escaped her. Whom did I trust? I hardly knew. "Since we both have a stake in keeping this a secret, I suppose I must trust you, but we need a man." I considered our options. "Formsby, Reggie's valet perhaps?"

"No!" Even in the dim light I could see the alarm in Alicia's face. "Don't you think I would have called him, rather than you, if I thought he could be trusted? This is too large a piece of gossip to place in the hands of a servant. And now, Formsby is a servant without a master. He will talk," she said, emphasizing the words with a bob of her head. "He has no reason not to."

She made a good point. I struck Formsby from the list and considered the other possibilities. "The only man here with a good reason *not* to talk is your husband."

She gaped in astonishment. "Are you mad?"

With a gesture, I reminded her to keep her voice down. "Who else is more likely?" I was becoming more than a little irritated with her again. She helped to create this situation; why couldn't her husband help us now? I pushed Reggie off my knees, and climbed down from the bed. "Think about it. If any of Reggie's friends knew of this, they would hold it over our heads forever. We'd be hearing from them anytime they needed money, or a favor. Your husband is our best choice."

Alicia brushed that idea aside. "Our marriage is hanging by a thread, Frances. He'd use this as evidence against me in a divorce, dragging your family name through the mud as well," she added, jabbing a finger at me. "There has to be someone else."

Good Lord. This would be laughable if it weren't so horrifying.

"Well, we must perform some magic then," I said, my frustration making me snap at the woman. "We must find a gentleman in this house who is so chivalrous, he would move a dead body for a lady, and has so much integrity, he would never use that favor against her. Is there such a paragon on this earth?"

I looked down and found myself wringing my hands. Forcing them apart I came to a decision. It had to be George Hazelton, my dear friend Fiona's brother. I knew him socially but not well. He only attended this party as escort to Fiona as her husband was occupied with estate business. When she and I met during our first season, he'd been away at school. Since then he was always at his family's seat in Hampshire or out of the country on some sort of business.

When I did finally meet him, I took him for a typical man about town; younger than Reggie and his friends, perhaps in his thirties, impeccably dressed, tall, dark, and though not quite handsome, he had a natural come-hither expression few women would ignore. But I also sensed something both kind and courageous in him—the very traits Alicia and I needed at the moment. Perhaps that was why I trusted him. Perhaps it was pure instinct.

"I think we can trust Mr. Hazelton. I'm just not sure if he'll do it."

Alicia bit her lip as she considered my choice. "If you trust him, we'll simply have to convince him."

We could hardly knock on Mr. Hazelton's door without waking guests in the surrounding rooms so we slipped inside. As bed-hopping was one of the primary entertainments at a house party, I sent out a silent prayer he'd be alone. The light from the hallway was bright enough to see only one figure slumbering in the bed before Alicia closed the door quietly behind us, throwing the room into darkness.

We waited at the door until our eyes adjusted and I gave Alicia a nudge with my elbow. She widened her eyes and mouthed the words, *Why me?*

Good heavens, she'd chosen this moment to be shy? I pointed at the bed and pushed her forward.

"Ladies?"

We both jumped at the unexpected sound.

"While I'm honored to find you fighting over me, something tells me I won't like the reason."

The sleepy drawl emanated from the bed. I turned to see Mr. Hazelton, or at least the head, bare shoulders, and arms of Mr. Hazelton. The rest was just a shadowy outline under the coverlet. He cocked a brow in question and it dawned on me how this must look to him. Two women in his room, in their nightgowns and wrappers would normally be looking for a favor far different from what we planned to ask.

I had to set him straight. "Forgive me for interrupting your sleep, Mr. Hazelton, but I'm afraid a tragedy has happened. My husband has . . . has passed—" I could get no further as my body convulsed with sobs. I clapped my hands to my mouth to quiet them but there was no holding them back. Now? I couldn't control myself for another thirty minutes?

"Attend to her." Hazelton whispered the order at Alicia as he pulled the coverlet off the bed and rushed into the dressing room.

Alicia wrapped an arm around me and seated me on the bed. "Good work," she whispered. "He'll do anything for you now."

I turned to her in horror. Good heavens, if the woman was serious, she and Reggie truly deserved one another. The shock of her comment had the fortunate side effect of stopping my ridiculous bout of crying. With a few deep breaths I was once again in control of myself, just in time for Mr. Hazelton's return, now dressed in trousers, slippers, and dressing gown.

He gazed down at me with sympathetic eyes. "I'm so sorry for your loss, Lady Harleigh. How can I be of service?"

I explained the situation to him as delicately as possible, watching his expression change from concern to surprise with a tinge of censure. I'm sure most of it was for Alicia but some might have been directed at me. A proper lady should never find herself in such a situation, though I have no idea how I could have avoided it. Whatever his opinion of me, I was both amazed and gratified that he agreed to help us move Reggie's body. And I've felt guilty about involving him in my horrible drama ever since.

Imagine my chagrin at seeing him walk up to my new home.

"Mr. Hazelton. Are you visiting your brother?" As I spoke, I had to fight the urge to flee. George Hazelton is the last person I'd want to see today—no, make that ever. I was certain he felt the same.

"My brother?"

"Your brother." I raised my brows. "The earl. Does he not have number nineteen?" I nodded to the house directly next to mine. I knew very well the earl held the lease on that house but left it empty now that he'd inherited the family townhome in Mayfair.

"Ah, yes. This was Brandon's house but he no longer has a need for it. Since I'm finding myself in town more and more these days I decided to take it off his hands."

"So, you live there now?" Leave it to me to lease the house next door to George Hazelton.

He nodded. "Indeed. And you must be the new number eighteen." His lips curved upward, and I saw a hint of a crinkle around his green eyes. A genuine smile? Directed at me? I couldn't be sure. And that was the trouble with him: I was never sure.

I could well believe his manners were far too polished to snub me completely. In fact, his impeccably good manners had driven me to distraction in the few times we've met since Reggie's death. He was always kind and polite, but behind that façade was he remembering how he had to clean up my mess?

Just now he simply could have nodded, or tipped his hat to me as he walked by. Instead he approached me on my very doorstep, and welcomed me to the neighborhood. Me, the woman who'd imposed on him to remove her dead husband's body from a scandalous scene. Just what was he about?

I forced myself to recover my senses, and smiled back, hoping he couldn't see mine was not genuine. "I've just taken occupancy this week in fact. We were about to do the ceremonial hanging of the knocker."

"By all means, please proceed." He waved an elegant hand at the door.

I'd completely forgotten about Jenny, and when I turned, I would have coshed her with several pounds of brass knocker if she hadn't ducked quickly. Once it was hung, both she and Mr. Hazelton applauded. I felt rather silly, especially when I saw a man on the pavement near my steps pause and glance our way. A working-class man in a shabby brown coat, he looked out of place in this genteel neighborhood. As he merely tipped his hat and moved on I didn't give him another thought.

"Well done," Hazelton said. "Glad I was here to mark the occasion." He extended a hand, which I took instinctively. "Welcome to the neighborhood, Lady Harleigh. Please feel free to call on me if I can be of any service."

Was it my imagination, or had he left with a particularly wicked grin?

Chapter 3

The next day started a blur of activity as my household of females set about putting my new home in order. I delighted in the work. For the most part, I only compiled lists of future needs—a change to the paper in my bedchamber, a few new pieces of furniture. But in the nursery, Rose and I splurged. I knew she'd be missing her cousins at Harleigh, so I tried to involve her in decorating the nursery. I gave Nanny the day off, and Rose and I spent a long day at the shops. And I do mean a long day. My mother never took me shopping with her when I was a child. Now I know why.

Once Rose understood she'd be making the decisions, she pondered each choice as if her life depended on it. She insisted on seeing every option—every option—before finally deciding on the one she'd seen first. I don't know how I endured it, but after several hours, with my feet burning in my fashionable shoes, we'd reached our final stop, the drapers.

I paused outside the door as I felt what was becoming a familiar sensation of unease. Glancing to my left, I surveyed the shop-lined street. It took a moment to spot him, standing before a shop window two doors down, casually looking at the display. He was a middle-aged man with the appearance of an office clerk, in a wrinkled brown suit and felt hat. Ordinarily I wouldn't have noticed him but it was the same man I'd seen outside my house yesterday. And this was the third time I'd seen him on our excursion today.

If he was shopping, he was doing a very poor job of it as he carried no parcels or packages. Yet he appeared at every shop Rose and I had visited. Was he following us? This was a respectable center of commerce but I suppose thieves could be on the prowl anywhere. He didn't look like a thief though. He just looked threatening. Perhaps I should have hired a footman to accompany me through town.

I pulled open the door and ushered Rose inside, feeling safer once the door closed behind us, comforted by the familiar surroundings of the drapers. I loved this shop.

The front room was large and open, with bolts of fabric lining the walls, and ten square tables for displaying them. Customers gathered in groups around each of them, waiting for the thump and swish, as a new bolt hit the table, and the fabric unwound to reveal its beauty. It was intoxicating. I almost forgot about the strange man outside. Almost. Yes, I wanted to indulge my daughter but I'd feel safer once we were home.

By the time the clerk had shown us nine bolts of fabric suitable for bed curtains, my feet were screaming at me to sit, but the few chairs in the room were occupied. My gaze had drifted to the front window several times. Was he still out there? I had to push Rose along. "The fabrics are all the right weight, dear. Do you dislike these colors?"

She looked up at me, her round, blue eyes very serious. "They're all solid colors."

"I'm not sure a print would work in your room." Another glance at the window. "Perhaps we should come back another time."

"I like that one." Rose pointed to a bolt of fabric behind the clerk. Eager to end this transaction sometime before the shop closed, he brought it to the table before I could protest. Not that I had any objection to the fabric itself. The cloth was amazing, so heavily embroidered with a hunt scene, it was really more of a tapestry. But done up as bed curtains, her room would look like a gypsy camp.

Rose reached out, letting her fingers slide over the scene with reverence. "It's beautiful," she whispered.

"Unfortunately," the clerk said, "there isn't enough for bed curtains."

My instinct was to give thanks to whomever bought all the fabric. Then I turned to Rose, her shoulders slumped, as she gazed with admiring eyes at the hunt scene. Her disappointment reminded me that I had never been allowed to choose anything for myself, not even my husband. She deserved a choice.

"If you really love this fabric, we could buy a small length, and use it to trim one of these others." I pulled out a length of sky blue material and held it next to the embroidered scene. "Do you see how the scene repeats itself as you move up the length? We could cut it just here."

Her smile made my poor, aching feet seem trivial. "Can we do that?"

"If you think you can sleep with horses running around your bed all night."

Rose laughed and took hold of my hand. I nodded at the clerk to measure and cut our fabrics. "I'll dream about it," she said. "I can't wait until I'm old enough to ride in the hunt."

My stomach cramped at the thought. Riding to the hounds was a dangerous sport. But she wasn't nearly old enough yet. There'd be plenty of time for us to argue about that later. For now, I'd be happy to gain control of my nerves and get us home safely. Both my feet and the strange man made me decide against walking. I turned to the clerk. "Would you have someone hail a hackney for us?"

I didn't check the street upon our departure, but simply bundled Rose into the hackney. Of course we arrived home unmolested. I was behaving like a ninny. The man was probably unemployed and walking around the shops looking for work. I was jumping at shadows.

On our return to the house, Mrs. Thompson took custody of my coat and hat and told me I had a visitor waiting. I glanced at the card she handed me. Inspector Delaney of the Metropolitan Police. What could he possibly want from me?

"Rose," I said, "it appears I have some business to take care of. Why don't you go upstairs and see if Nanny is back from her half day?"

She dutifully took herself upstairs. I watched her turn at the top of the flight before I addressed Mrs. Thompson. "The Metropolitan Police? What does he want?"

The housekeeper spread her hands, clearly at a loss. "I'm afraid he wouldn't state his business, my lady. Only that he expected you home soon and he'd wait."

I frowned. He expected me home soon? "Have you put him in the drawing room?"

"No, ma'am. He's in the kitchen with a cup of tea where we can keep an eye on him. Should I bring him up?"

I nodded. "I suppose I'm curious enough to meet with him."

My curiosity was quickly relieved when Mrs. Thompson walked into the drawing room followed by the man I'd seen earlier on the street.

"You—"

"Inspector Delaney," he said, dragging his hat from his head, leaving clumps of gray-streaked hair standing on end. The style perfectly matched his eyebrows, which seemed to be growing in six directions at once. In my drawing room he seemed taller than I'd noted when I saw him on the street. And even more imposing.

Mrs. Thompson closed the door as she left. I stood facing him, my hands clasped to keep them still. "You were following me today."

"I needed to speak with you, my lady, and it turned out you were difficult to track down."

"Yet you managed to do so several times."

He narrowed one eye. "I didn't think you'd want to discuss this matter with the little girl in tow."

"I see. Instead you left me to believe you were stalking us."

"That wasn't my intention. You see, the only reason I became involved was because you fled Surrey."

"I did not flee Surrey." What was he implying? "I simply moved to Belgravia."

His gaze was steady. And rather unnerving. "I was told only that you were in town, so naturally I first called on you at Harleigh House. Ah, that reminds me." He reached into a coat pocket and pulled out a letter, pointedly studying the direction before handing it to me.

"Odd you haven't even told your mother you've moved."

I snatched the letter from his hand. It was indeed from my mother, sent to me at Harleigh House. The nerve of the man. I had been on the point of asking him to sit but now he could just stand there until he fell over. And I hoped he would. "Why are you in possession of my personal correspondence?" I narrowed my eyes. "And how did you know I'd be home soon?"

"The footman who provided me with the direction of your new residence asked me to deliver it, as I was coming here anyway. Yesterday, you seemed to be occupied. When I arrived today, I was told you were shopping, and I thought it might be better to have our conversation away from the house." His lips twitched. "Less talk among the servants that way." He shifted his weight and clasped his hands behind his back. "However, when I saw you with your daughter, I decided to return here and wait for you. I didn't think you'd be long as I could see your feet were giving you pain."

They still were, but I was not about to sit. "Since you've gone to so much trouble to speak to me, perhaps you'd like to state your business?"

"It seems there's been a development in the matter of your late husband's death."

"Oh, my heavens." I gaped at the man.

"Perhaps you should sit, ma'am."

My move to the sofa was slightly more graceful than a stumble, but not by much. His announcement had left me stunned. I took a moment to compose myself and waved him to a chair across from me. He sat and pulled a small notebook from his pocket.

"My husband died over a year ago, Inspector. What could possibly have developed?"

Delaney never took his eyes from my face. "There is a question about the cause of death."

"The cause of death? He had a heart attack. The doctor who attended him confirmed it."

"The police from the Guildford constabulary will be talking to him."

"The police from Guildford?" Heavens, it seemed all I could do was to repeat his words. Like a parrot. Or an idiot. "Inspector, would you please start from the beginning? Why are the police suddenly, and belatedly, interested in my husband's death?"

The inspector's gaze flicked toward his notebook, then back at me. "I'm afraid I don't have that information. This isn't my case, but since you were in town, I've been asked to obtain a statement from you, to the best of your recollection, about the activities of the household in the twenty-four hours before your husband's death."

I studied the man's face. This seemed so much like a bizarre joke, I expected him to burst into laughter at any moment. But he was clearly serious. "We were hosting a shooting party," I began haltingly, trying to bring the images of that day back to mind. I explained about the weather keeping everyone housebound. At his questioning, I detailed what was served for dinner and approximately how much food and alcohol Reggie had consumed. I concluded by telling him most of us had gone to bed early. That was not conclusion enough for the inspector.

"How was the body found?"

"How?" I looked into his face. His gaze was firm, but not unkind. He clearly realized how hard this was for me. I prayed he had no idea why it was hard. Hazelton, Alicia, and I had managed to maneuver Reggie back into his own bed somewhere around six that morning. As a servant would be in soon to build up the fire, and his valet would come shortly thereafter, we decided, rather callously I thought, to allow them to discover their master's body.

"The maid," I said. "She came to stoke the fire and found my husband lying half out of bed. She fetched Formsby, Reggie's valet, who confirmed Reggie's death and sent my maid to inform me."

I noticed my hands shaking and pressed them against my legs. I'd only had to tell that story once before and hoped I'd got it right.

"You said the doctor confirmed it was a heart attack?"

I nodded. "Yes, Reggie had a heart condition. He took digitalis to control his heartbeat. The doctor who attended his death was aware of it and had given him the medication."

Delaney closed his book around the pencil and returned it to his pocket. "I'm sorry to have troubled you with this, my lady.

I'll send my report back to the Guildford constabulary. I suspect they'll talk to the doctor and tie up whatever loose end they think they have."

"Is that what this is about? They have loose ends?"

"Most likely," he said, rising to his feet. "Unless they have some reason to suspect murder." With that he gave me a nod and showed himself out.

Chapter 4

My interview with Inspector Delaney caused me a sleepless night of worry. Did the police really suspect Reggie was murdered? The next morning I asked Jenny to bring a breakfast tray to the library where I wrote to Reggie's doctor to see what he might know about this business. After all, he was the one who determined how Reggie had died. If I'd known anyone at the Guildford constabulary, I'd have written directly to them. This would have to do for now.

With that done, I turned to the post. My mother's letter was on top. After speaking with Delaney, I'd forgotten all about it. At some point—soon—I'd have to tell her about my move. I had no illusions she'd receive the news with any pleasure. She'd worked so hard to marry me into that illustrious family, walking away from them would strike her as a sign of idiocy. Well, it was done now. She'd have to accept it.

Enclosed in her letter was a bank draft for a tidy sum. Interesting. I knew Mother was coming to England for the Season, as she insisted on bringing my younger sister out to London society. Apparently one disastrous marriage in the family wasn't enough to discourage her. I wondered why she'd sent money ahead, and scanned the letter.

Oh, dear. "*As the time approached for Lily's debut I found myself far too occupied to travel with her to England, yet Lily was so insistent upon having a London Season, I didn't have the heart to tell her no.*"

Odd, she'd never had any trouble telling me no.

I read further. "*It occurred to me since you should now be out of mourning, you could introduce your sister to society. We would have needed your sponsorship in any event, so I see no reason for my presence. Instead, I have enclosed a bank draft, which should cover a new wardrobe for Lily, and any expenses you should encounter, and I have sent Lily to you with your aunt Henrietta. I'm sure you'll be delighted to see them.*"

Aunt Hetty? She was sending Lily with Aunt Hetty? Not that I'd mind having her visit. Quite the opposite in fact. She was my father's sister, younger by ten years, and had lived with us since our Akron days, after her husband died of influenza. She'd still been young at the time, but rather than remarry she chose to live in our home. She even came with us when we moved to New York, and was one of the few things that made that city bearable. She was always friendly and outspoken, never giving up her small-town ways, which often embarrassed my mother as she tried to break into New York society.

Which was why I found it hard to believe she'd put Lily in Aunt Hetty's care for a trip across the Atlantic. Hetty would strike up a friendship with anyone. Heavens! Lily was as likely to spend the crossing playing cards with the stewards, as meeting what my mother would term, the "right" people. I mulled over the arrangement. Mother must be very busy indeed.

The letter went on to give the name of their ship and expected arrival date—in three days! She also professed all her love and that of my father. I stared at the signature for several minutes. Had this really been written by my mother? What had happened to her? In my season, the only time Mother ever left my side was when I was dancing. Yet here she was leaving me in charge of Lily's debut? And with no exacting instructions as to whom she was to marry? Was she leaving that for me to decide—or, heaven forbid, to Lily? Since there was no mention of these details, I'd have to wait and see what Lily could tell me.

On one point in the letter I had to agree; I'd be delighted to see both my sister and Aunt Hetty. Goodness, I'd better get busy. I should make some social calls immediately, and let it be known I was back in town, and would soon have my sister and aunt with me. And I should deposit that bank draft as soon as possible.

I buttered a slice of toast and opened the next letter, this one from my solicitor, requesting a meeting at my earliest convenience. Since Mr. Stone's office was near my bank, I penned a quick reply, stating I could be there in an hour's time, and had Jenny send it off with the kitchen boy. As that was the entirety of my correspondence, I settled in to enjoy my breakfast when I heard an imperious voice at the door.

"Of course she's at home. Where else would she be at this hour?"

Fiona?

I scrambled from the desk and rushed to the front hall. A tall, elegant woman with mounds of chestnut hair, topped with a plumed toque, was staring down her rather long, narrow nose at Mrs. Thompson.

"It's quite all right, Mrs. Thompson," I said, moving forward to greet my friend. "I'm delighted to see Lady Nash."

Fiona swung around at the sound of my voice, her green eyes sparkling. "There you are." I took her outstretched hands and guided her to the drawing room.

"Have you developed psychical abilities?" I asked, as we settled ourselves on the sofa. "How on earth did you know I was living here?"

"Well, I didn't until five minutes ago, when George told me you were his new neighbor. How could you let me hear of it second-hand?"

I instantly realized my faux pas. George is Fiona's brother. Fiona has long been my dearest friend. Oh, I'd written her letters while stuck at Harleigh, telling her how I longed to leave my in-laws. But once I leased the house everything happened so quickly I neglected to tell her I'd actually done it. Of course she felt slighted. "I'm so sorry, Fi. I should have sent round a note, but I've only been here a few days, and—did you just say five minutes ago?"

"Yes, I was having a spot of breakfast with George, when he mentioned you'd moved in here, so I rushed right over to see you."

"So you just left him at the table?"

She let out a snort of laughter, which completely contradicted her image as a perfectly polished lady. One of the things I loved about Fi was just how unladylike she could be in private moments. "Well, I suppose I did. Simply dropped my toast on my plate and ran out." She looked at me in wonder. "Do you know, I quite believe he expected that reaction? Probably gave me the news so he could rid himself of my presence and get back to his newspaper." She waved a gloved hand. "But forget George. Now that I'm here, tell me, when did you become so adventurous? You spoke of moving to town, but I can't believe you did it."

"Oh, Fi, it was well past time to be out on my own. I've been living as a guest, in what used to be my home, for far too long." Heaving an exaggerated sigh I lowered my voice several octaves. "I'm the elder countess now, you know."

Fiona wrinkled her nose in distaste. "That title only applies if you and Delia are in the same place." Her gaze darted around the room. "She isn't here, is she?"

I chuckled at her panic and shook my head.

"Whoever devised that term had no respect for women. It makes you sound so old."

"And useless. Delia managed the house. Graham managed the estate. I had no purpose, nothing to do. Even visiting was out of the question as I was in mourning. The very moment I could decently leave the house I came to town to meet with an estate agent. And here I am."

"Good girl." Fiona reached out and squeezed my hand. "And how clever of you to have your own money."

I chuckled. "The credit goes to my father. He set up this account although the Wynn family resented it at the time. They were rather offended at the idea of a wife having independent means—not the English way, you know."

"Well, I'm glad your father had such foresight, and that you can be independent."

"It's quite a heady feeling, but I will have to be careful. The account has to produce an income for Rose and me, and it will hardly allow for extravagant living. Although"—I couldn't help grinning here—"I did just receive a lovely check from my mother yesterday, which I was about to go and deposit when you arrived." I stood and smoothed the wrinkles from my skirt. "And I'm afraid I have an appointment with my solicitor. I hate to cut our time so short, dearest, but the only way I can get there on time is if I send for a hansom right now."

"You'll do nothing of the sort," Fiona said, rising to her feet. "My carriage is outside. I'll drop you at your solicitor's office. I must run an errand or two myself. They won't take long, but if you haven't completed your business by the time I return, I'll wait for you." She waved away my protests before I could even make them. "No, no. I haven't seen you for months, Frances. I'm not letting you get away from me so easily."

We left the house a few minutes later. I gave Fiona's driver the direction, and half an hour later, I was walking into Mr. Stone's office, still smiling at one of Fiona's jokes.

I'd always liked Mr. Stone. He was of my father's generation and worked with him on my marriage settlement. Once Reggie's parents had died, I preferred to work with him on any legal business pertaining to the estate, rather than use the family solicitors. A young clerk led me into Stone's lightly paneled and carpeted office, where he came around his desk to greet me, a warm smile on his round face.

"Good morning, my lady," he said, taking the hand I offered in a firm grip. "Thank you for responding so quickly to my message. Please take a seat." He directed me to one of two upholstered guest chairs facing the desk. "Would you care for tea?"

"Thank you, no," I said, as I seated myself. Surprisingly, he took the chair beside me rather than the one behind the desk. We passed a few pleasantries back and forth. Then he leaned forward, focused on the carpet a moment, and released a sigh. Oh, dear, this was not going to be good news.

His gaze returned to mine. "I have some unfortunate information to relate to you, my lady. Your brother-in-law seems to feel the funds your father set aside for you should belong to the Wynn family." He paused to let the words sink in.

"That doesn't surprise me, Mr. Stone, but how has this come to your attention?"

"He's filed a suit in court to claim the money."

"What?" This did come as a shock. "He can't be serious."

"I'm afraid he is, and before I say another word, I must assure you he has no hope of success in that claim. The documentation is clear, and states the account is for your personal use."

His assurance did ease my anxiety somewhat, but I was still confused, and appalled. "If that's true, why would he attempt such a thing? What can he hope to gain?"

"Such suits take time, and can also become public. He may hope to reach a settlement with you, so you may avoid inconvenience, or a scandal."

"I would think he would be even more eager than I to avoid

a scandal. As to inconvenience, what manner of inconvenience can this cause me?"

He sat back and sucked air in between his gritted teeth, then pressed his lips into a scowl. A knot tightened in my stomach. "Just tell me, Mr. Stone."

He released his breath. "Your bank account has been frozen until such time as the documentation can be reviewed by the court."

My astonishment must have shown on my face because he held up a cautioning hand before I could reply. "I will file a response immediately, asking the court to dismiss the case, due to lack of grounds, but it may not be successful. Your brother-in-law is a peer, and that does carry some weight."

My account frozen. And for how long? I had little money left at the house. How would I pay the staff? Or Mr. Stone for that matter? "How can I ask you to do anything about this, when it seems I have no money to pay you?"

"You will have, I assure you. Sooner or later your account will be back in your hands. Now, why don't I fetch that tea for you, and we'll discuss our options."

It didn't take long to discuss those options as they were few. I absolutely refused to consider paying Graham off to make him drop his claim. The account had been greatly diminished after negotiating the lease on my house—thank goodness that transaction had happened before it was frozen—but even if I had a fortune, I would never reward Graham for his behavior. So Mr. Stone would file his brief, and if that didn't work, I would somehow have to learn to live without money until the court made a ruling. A daunting prospect but after striking out on my own, I did not want to turn to my father for help.

Between the police looking into Reggie's death and Graham freezing my account, I'd had just about all the bad news I could take. My head was still spinning when I stepped out of the office building and walked to Fiona's carriage. She gave me a bright smile when her footman assisted me inside. "Perfect timing, my dear." The smile disappeared when she saw my face. "My heavens, Frances. What happened?"

Oh, dear. Perhaps it was the influence of Mr. Stone, but I should school my expression to be less transparent. Although it didn't matter at this point. I needed someone to confide in, and no one was a better confidante than Fiona. I revealed all while the coach took us through the busy streets to Fortnum's. Her astonishment grew with each word.

"The rotter! The absolute rotter! Well, thank goodness for your mother's check."

I clutched her hand as my stomach did a little flip. "I'd forgotten all about that check. Fiona, I'm saved. Well, I'm almost saved. The money is supposed to pay for my sister's wardrobe and our expenses."

"I remember your mother, dear. I suspect she was more than generous. It should stretch to pay your staff, and household expenses as well. At least for some little while."

"I didn't mention the check to Mr. Stone." I worried my lower lip between my teeth as I considered this problem. "How can I deposit it if I haven't an account?"

Fiona tapped on the little door in the roof, and when the coachman responded, she gave him a new direction. "We're going to your house?" I asked, confused.

"Robert should still be there," Fiona stated, referring to her husband. "As things stand, perhaps he should cash the check on your behalf. He can deposit it into our account, then withdraw the money for you. I think all your transactions should be in cash for the time being."

"That sounds rather like subterfuge," I said, searching for alternatives and finding none. "And I must say, I admire the workings of your mind."

Fiona's husband, Sir Robert Nash, was indeed still at home when we arrived, but on the point of departure as we met him in the hall. The smile lighting his pleasant face upon greeting me, changed to a look of surprise, as Fiona linked her arm in his and turned him back into the drawing room. I muffled a laugh at the sight of this slender woman steering the taller, much sturdier, figure of her husband. Once we explained my situation, he agreed with her assessment. "The man's a rotter," he growled. "You've already dug that family out of a hole once. If they're back in dun territory now, it's Graham's own fault."

In all fairness, I couldn't let that stand. "Well, actually it's Reggie's fault."

"But hardly your problem," Fiona pointed out, removing her hat from the artwork of her hair, and leaving it on a table near the door. "Come, let Robert take care of this business, and you and I will finally have that tea and gossip we spoke of this morning." Fiona guided me to a seat while Robert departed for his bank.

It didn't take long for the tea to provide the desired effect, and I began to see my situation more clearly. "I suppose I should wait to see if Mr. Stone is successful in having the case dismissed, before I tell my father what's happened. I'd rather not involve him if the matter can be resolved soon."

Fiona nodded. "You're afraid he'd become upset."

"No, I'm afraid he'd let Graham take the money, then tell me to give up the house and return to New York with Rose. He isn't aware I've moved out on my own yet."

"Would he really do that?" She wore a look of alarm. "I'd hate to see you leave England."

"I assure you I wouldn't like it either. Rose is British, and I want her to grow up here, and to be honest, I don't want either of us to live under my mother's influence. Rose would be polished and primed until she became so artificial, she wouldn't have a single thought that didn't come from my mother's head. And as for me"—I suppressed a shudder—"I'm not ready to have my mother select my second husband."

"Hmm, will there be a second husband, do you suppose?" Fiona took a bite of a biscuit and waggled her eyebrows in a wicked way. I had to laugh, but held up a restraining hand.

"Don't even think about it. Someone else has been controlling my life for as long as I can remember; first my mother, then my husband, then my husband's family. Now I finally have a chance to take control, and while it is a bit frightening, I quite like it."

"Point taken, but as a matter of reference only, you should be aware that with the right man, marriage can be quite wonderful." At my glare she held up her hands in surrender. "And that is all I'll say on the matter. Now about your sister. What do you have in mind for her?"

"Nothing yet, but since she'll be on my doorstep in a matter of days, I'd better make some plans." I rolled my cup between my hands as I tried to put my thoughts in order. "Of course I'll be paying calls to let everyone know I'm in town, and my sister will be joining me. I'm sure that will trigger some invitations." I looked up at my friend. "At least I think it will. Graham and Delia implied my living alone might raise a few eyebrows and cause me to be dropped from some guest lists. Would you agree?"

Fiona frowned as she considered my living situation. "I suppose that is possible with a few of the sticklers, but you are a widow so many people won't bat an eye at your living alone. However, once your aunt arrives, even the sticklers won't object. An older woman in your household should provide all the respectability you could want."

I couldn't help laughing. "You have never met my aunt."

"Your aunt could be completely mad and it wouldn't matter." She wagged a finger at me. "You know I'm right."

Indeed I did.

"Well, that's settled. When does your sister arrive?"

"The day after tomorrow. So I only have Thursday to make calls." I began ticking off items on my fingers. "I still need to get the house in order. I haven't arranged for a carriage. Now I have to take Lily to the modiste, and I should update my own wardrobe as well, if I'm not to embarrass her. Goodness, I do have a great deal of work ahead of me," I said, suddenly feeling overwhelmed.

"Nonsense. We can work this all out. Just make sure your reception room is presentable for callers and leave the rest of the house for later. I can stop by for you tomorrow, and we'll take my carriage to make calls and leave your cards. I can also take you both to the modiste later in the week."

This still seemed like a great deal to accomplish but with Fiona's help, and a systematic approach, it could be done.

"And don't forget you have George."

That pulled me up short. "George?"

"Of course. He has a carriage, and he lives right next door to you, and will probably be attending the same functions you wish to attend. And if he isn't, he should be." She gave me an emphatic nod. "I'll speak to him about it."

"Oh, no. Fiona, I don't wish to impose on your brother," I said, my stomach clenching as panic set in.

"Frances, he'd be delighted." She clutched dramatically at my hands. "I'd be delighted. Please, please drag my brother out for some fun and frivolity. He's finally settled in one place but all he does is work and go to his clubs. If we don't get him out, he'll soon become an old stick in the mud."

I was saved from having to answer by Robert's return. And I must say I felt much more secure with the large sum of money in my reticule. Well, I felt secure in having it, but anxious to get it home and locked up. Fiona sent me home in their carriage, promising to call on me the next day at noon.

If I had to be stuck in a series of drawing rooms, at least I was pleased with the group of ladies Fiona had chosen to call on. We were now at our fourth, and last, stop for the day—the home of Lady Caroline Fairmont. There were only six of us still here as the afternoon was getting on. Caroline sat on a sofa behind the teapot, with her mother and Fiona. I was seated across from her with two other ladies. One of them, a Mrs. Richardson, addressed Fiona. "Did you say you called on Anne Haverhill yesterday? Was there any progress on the robbery?"

"Sadly, no. They have not found the thief or the stolen items." This was news to me. "The Haverhills were robbed?"

"Yes, about a week ago," Mrs. Richardson explained. "They held a reception for a visiting dignitary, from some Eastern European country." She paused to release a weary sigh. "Haverhill's an MP you know. Always involved with foreigners though and constantly pursuing Home Rule for Ireland. I think our members of Parliament should be more concerned with the British."

"Well as Ireland doesn't have Home Rule, I don't believe it's fair to consider them foreigners," I said, certain Mrs. Richardson considered me a foreigner as well, though she wouldn't have the nerve to say as much.

Fiona called us back to the topic. "The day after the reception they realized five snuffboxes were missing from Mr. Haverhill's collection."

"Why, that's terrible."

"Indeed," she continued with an emphatic nod. "The missing pieces were quite notable, and worth a great deal, so after a thorough search of the house, they contacted the Metropolitan Police."

"But it's been a week, and they've had no success?"

I was addressing Fiona, but Mrs. Richardson, in her enthusiasm, responded before Fiona had a chance to form an answer. "Criminals these days are very skilled, and organized. I wouldn't be surprised if one or more of the servants was involved." Her eyes narrowed, and I could almost see her thoughts take a new turn. "You have recently set up your household, have you not, Lady Harleigh? I hope you were careful in hiring your staff."

I assured her I had taken meticulous care in interviewing candidates and verifying references. "Both my household, and my needs, are small," I said. "Although both are about to increase. My sister and aunt will be arriving this week and staying for the Season."

"Oh, so you'll be sponsoring your sister this spring," Caroline said. "How delightful for you."

"Delightful, you call it?" Mrs. Foster, Caroline's mother, wore an expression of pain. "I brought out four girls, and all I can say is I'm delighted there wasn't a fifth." We all chuckled as she'd expected. "I'm only half joshing you, my dear. Monitoring a young girl's behavior is no easy task. Not to mention a young man's."

"I suppose there are always some ne'er-do-wells to be avoided," Caroline agreed.

"I've been out of society for so long I'm not familiar with all the young men. I expect each of you to inform me if a particular gentleman should be avoided."

"Your sister must meet the new Viscount Ainsworthy," said Mrs. Richardson. A murmur of agreement followed.

"He would be this Season's great catch."

"Such a vulgar phrase, Caroline," her mother said.

"But true, nonetheless." She leaned in toward me. "The old viscount died just a few months ago, and I understand there was quite a bother trying to find his heir, a nephew who had been living in South Africa for years. The new viscount arrived in England about a month ago and has spent most of that time at the family estate in Kent. But he's been in London about a week now, and it's rumored he's looking for a wife."

"And is he the source of that rumor or its victim?"

"It is most difficult to know if this is idle speculation, or even wishful thinking," said Mrs. Richardson, oblivious to my joke. "But it would be a wise move on his part to marry well. He'll need a well-bred young lady, and her family, to guide him."

I thought the poor viscount had best make his choice quickly before the London mamas stepped in to make it for him. "Since Lily is an American, she's not a likely candidate. And as she's only eighteen, I won't encourage her to marry anyone this Season."

"Ah, but she may fall in love," suggested Mrs. Richardson, "and you never know where a young girl's heart may lead her."

A chill of dread rushed over me at the thought of my sister in love with a scoundrel, or a selfish philanderer like Reggie. Lily's life shattered. Her heart broken. All my protective instincts surged to the fore. "Should that happen, you may be sure I will be looking into that young man's background in great detail."

From across the table Mrs. Foster gave me a knowing look. "As I said, this is not an easy task."

Chapter 5

I was to think on Mrs. Foster's words frequently over the next few days. Returning home that afternoon I found another missive passed on from Harleigh House. This time from Aunt Hetty, telling me their ship had docked in Southampton, and their train should arrive at Victoria Station the following day. I engaged Mr. Hazelton's carriage, coachman, and a footman to collect them at the station, and expected them in time for a nice afternoon tea.

The carriage returned as scheduled, but brought only two servants, and a large pile of luggage. No sister. No aunt. No message for me. Their maids could only tell me the two ladies had decided to take the train. What train? To the best of my knowledge, there was no train service from Victoria Station to my door. Good heavens! What were they thinking? Were they now lost somewhere in the middle of London?

I sent the driver back to the station, with orders to look for a middle-aged woman and a young lady traveling together. As I hadn't seen them in years, that was all the description I could supply. I spent the next hour pacing my drawing room, worrying they'd been robbed, or kidnapped, or on a train to Scotland, with no servants and no clothing, when finally, Mrs. Thompson ushered in two disheveled women, whom I took to be Lily and Hetty.

The younger one ran forward and, with a squeal, threw her arms around me. My fears dissipated like vapor.

I held my sister close, hardly believing she was in my arms and all grown up—and smelling as if she'd just cleaned my chimneys. "What on earth happened to you two?"

Lily laughed as she backed away, and Aunt Hetty put her arm around my shoulders, giving me a peck on the cheek. "Greetings to you too, my dear niece."

Aunt Hetty had changed little over the last ten years. Her full cheeks had drooped a bit, and the delicate skin around her eyes was creased, but she was as tall and slender as I remembered, with my father's dark hair and eyes. Surprisingly, her hair was still untouched by gray.

Lily, on the other hand, had grown from a child into a lovely young woman. She was exactly as I would imagine our mother to have looked at her age—blond, blue-eyed, and petite. Tears stung my eyes as I realized how much I had missed of her life. And now, here she was, so grown up. And so . . . smoky.

"Where have you been?"

"We took a little detour once we arrived in London." Lily giggled, and Hetty was positively smirking, as if she had a great tale to tell. "We took a ride on the Metropolitan Railway—the one that runs underground."

"That's what I smell." I was appalled. "Why would you do such a thing? All manner of people ride those trains. You might have been robbed, or stabbed, or—"

"But as you see, we are fine," Hetty said, dismissing my concerns. "And it was quite an adventure."

"Not one I'd repeat," Lily added, although I believe it was only to appease my concerns. She shook out her skirt, and I'm not sure if I only imagined the ash floating down to the carpet. "And I would like to clean up if I may."

"Of course you would." I took them up to their rooms, still trying to regain my composure. They were safe. They were unharmed. And they would *never* do this again. I'd have to have a talk with Aunt Hetty to determine if she had any other adventures in mind for her stay here.

I slipped up to the nursery to bring Rose down for tea. By the time Lily and Hetty had changed their clothing, and freshened up, George Hazelton had joined us, wishing to assure himself that nothing had gone amiss in collecting my relations. Although I was eager to have them to myself, I encouraged him to stay, and performed the introductions. Both ladies greeted him warmly and turned to Rose.

"And who have we here?" Lily went down to one knee, putting herself at eye level for Rose. "This cannot be Rose. Rose is just a little baby."

"She was a baby when you and Mother last visited," I said. "But that was seven years ago. She's changed considerably since then. You both have."

"Well, I stand corrected," Lily said. "You are quite the young lady." She rose to her feet, her gaze darting between my daughter and me. "All that dark hair, and those lovely blue eyes, put me in mind of someone, but I simply can't think who."

Rose gave her aunt a smile. "Nanny says I look like my mother."

"How clever of you, my dear." Hetty leaned closer to Rose as if she were speaking to her in confidence. "Your grandmother came to see you when you were born, and her report was that you looked very much like your grandfather." She pulled a horrified face, making Rose giggle.

"Rose, why don't you invite everyone to the drawing room for tea?"

We moved into the newly, but still sparsely, decorated drawing room. I have to admit after living for ten years at Harleigh Manor, where every horizontal surface was littered with mementos from the earl's travels, or some unsightly heirloom, I just couldn't bring myself to fill my new house with bric-a-brac.

We all seated ourselves around the low tea table. Lily and I each took a chair, Hetty and George shared the sofa, and Rose moved among us, passing out plates of scones and biscuits, while I poured the tea.

While they chatted about London, my gaze landed on Mr. Hazelton. Heavens, should I tell him about my visit from the police? I couldn't recall if I mentioned his name to Delaney. Would the inspector pay a call on him? He should be warned.

When I realized the conversation had stopped, I looked up to see everyone staring at me. "Forgive me, I was lost in my plans for Lily's debut."

"Well, while you are seeking a lord for Lily," Hetty said, "I plan to do a little scouting for your father and Alonzo, as I do, you know."

I did know. My father was a shrewd investor, and Alonzo, my younger brother, followed in his footsteps. But nobody—*nobody*—could sniff out a potential gold mine like my aunt Hetty, and they never failed to take her advice. While this was profitable for all concerned, I always felt it was a shame Hetty couldn't transact the business herself. Unfortunately, business was a man's world.

"If it's the underground you're interested in, I can introduce you to some of the principals involved," George said.

"Mr. Hazelton, are you active in business yourself? Forgive my ignorance, but I didn't think men of your class worked for a living."

Hmm, Lily did need some polish. If she were asking anyone but Mr. Hazelton, I'd have been mortified by her question. But he merely smiled. "I may not report to an office every day, but since I didn't inherit the family title or fortune, I have to earn my living. I studied law, but I find business more interesting."

Lily still looked confused, so I explained further. "Mr. Hazelton is the son of an earl, but in England only the first son inherits. The heir usually provides for the other family members as best he can, but in general, they have to make their own way."

"But what exactly do you do for a living?" my aunt pressed. "Are you in some sort of business?"

George looked uncomfortable, as if this were too personal a question. I sought for a way to change the subject, when, to my surprise, he answered.

"I have invested in a few enterprises," he said in an offhand manner, "but as I mentioned, I was trained for the law, and occasionally I work on a case for the Crown."

Really? This was a surprise. I tried to picture George as a barrister, in robes and white wig, but the image wouldn't take hold. Perhaps it was a good thing my relations were outspoken, curious, Americans. I might actually learn something about my acquaintance.

Lily was still trying to grasp the concept of primogeniture. "So the reason you are *Mister* Hazelton, not *Lord* Something, is because you are a second son."

"It's worse than that," George replied, the twinkle returning to his eyes. "I'm a third son with two healthy, older brothers. Far removed from a title."

I rolled my eyes. "It's a wonder I allow him in my home."

"You are all condescension, Lady Harleigh." Although we laughed, Hetty and Lily seemed not to be in on the joke. Had I become too British for my own relatives?

"But Rose won't inherit a title either, yet isn't she called Lady Rose?"

"Yes, she is," I replied. "But it's all rather complicated. I'll go over it with you later if you like. I'm actually surprised Mother didn't drill you on all the titles and honorariums."

Lily struggled to hide a grin. "She tried, but I'm afraid I was a poor student."

"Well, that seems far too old a name for you, little one." Hetty gave Rose's braid a gentle tug. "I shall call you Lady Rosebud." Rose giggled and looked up at her with a shy smile. I could see she was on the verge of adoring her aunt Hetty. At Harleigh she'd never spent much time with adults, other than myself and her nurse. Perhaps we were both going to benefit from having my family here.

As if reading my mind, Mr. Hazelton placed his teacup on the table and rose to his feet. "Delighted to have met you both, but it's time I leave the four of you to catch up on family matters."

"I hope we'll be seeing more of you, Mr. Hazelton," Lily said.

"I've been given strict orders from my sister, whom I'm sure you will be meeting soon, to go out in society and enjoy myself. So consider me at your service as escort to all the balls, receptions, breakfasts, and picnics you wish to attend."

"Let me see you out, Mr. Hazelton." I walked him to the foyer and out of the hearing of my relatives. "I'm not quite sure how to bring this up but I must warn you of something."

He had one hand on the doorknob and a brow raised in question. There was no time to dither. "I had a visit from a police inspector," I said. "He came at the request of the Guildford police who had some questions about Reggie's death."

Both brows shot up. "What sort of questions?"

"Inspector Delaney asked me about the events of that day and how I learned of his death. He also suggested the Guildford police might suspect foul play."

"Good Lord. What did you tell him?"

"That's the problem. By the time he mentioned murder, I had already told him the story we had devised. I wanted to warn you in case he pays a call on you."

"Good to know." He darted a glance toward the drawing room. "We'll have to discuss this at another time. For now, try not to worry." He opened the door as if to leave, then turned back with a smile. "Thank you for the warning."

I stared at the closed door. Don't worry? That was not the reaction I'd expected. He seemed completely unconcerned about the business. I was beginning to find Mr. Hazelton quite the puzzle. And I had to admit, I found his confidence quite attractive.

When I returned to my guests, I saw that Lily was looking at me with one eyebrow raised in question.

"What is it?" I asked.

A sly smile spread across her lips. "Just that it looks like one gentleman of your acquaintance is pleased you are no longer in mourning."

Considering the direction my thoughts had just taken, I immediately became flustered, and felt my cheeks grow hot. Hetty misunderstood my reaction and gave me a sympathetic look. "Lily, that was unkind," she said. "Clearly Frances still feels the loss of her husband."

Lily was beside me in an instant, kneeling by my chair in an agony of remorse. "Frances, I'm so sorry. I must learn to think before I speak."

I placed a comforting hand on her shoulder. "It's quite all right, Lily. You just took me by surprise." What else could I say? Especially with Rose in the room. 'Don't concern yourself, it's been years since I mourned Reggie's loss'? Or perhaps the more impersonal 'Ours was not a love match'? Or even, 'How odd you should single out Mr. Hazelton, as he helped to move Reggie's body from his mistress's bed to his own.' I hated lying to her, but what choice did I have?

"Mother despaired of my ever carrying on a polite conversation."

"Speaking of Mother, I'm amazed she's not here with you. How did that come about?"

Hetty got to her feet and extended a hand to Rose. "While you two discuss your mother, perhaps Lady Rosebud will show me where she keeps her toys."

Rose jumped to her feet and placed her hand in Hetty's. "Have you any toy soldiers?" Hetty asked as they left the room.

Rose's giggles rang out as they climbed the stairs to the nursery. I looked at Lily. "We can't discuss Mother in front of Rose?"

"Aunt Hetty and I talked about this, and we decided we shouldn't discuss the family finances in front of Rose. One never knows what children will repeat."

"I take it Father's suffered a loss?"

Lily nodded. "A rather impressive one, I'm afraid. Both he and Alonzo consider it a temporary concern, but Father still didn't want to set Mother loose among the shops of London or Paris. And besides, Father did want Aunt Hetty to learn as much as possible about this underground transit business."

"Is that why he doesn't have the capital to invest in this project right now?"

Lily drew in a sharp breath and boggled her eyes. "Don't say that to Aunt Hetty or she'll say you know nothing about money."

"I'm afraid she'd be correct," I said with a rueful smile. "I'm only just learning."

"Well, it seems a project of this magnitude always requires a consortium of investors. That's what Father is trying to put together, but even with partners, he'll be hard-pressed to come up with his share."

"Then I don't understand why Mother didn't put off your Season until next year. You are only eighteen. One more year would make no difference."

Lily bristled. "Maybe not to you, but I could not possibly tolerate another year of Mother's How to be a Lady Academy."

I was beginning to see the true reason Mother bowed out of Lily's season. She didn't have as malleable a student in Lily. My sister had some fight in her.

"I assume, regardless of the financial setback, Father still plans to provide you with a sizable dowry?"

She nodded as she took a bite of scone.

"Then you should realize there will be men who are courting you for your fortune, so you must be careful. Don't be so eager for a match that you marry the wrong man." Lily twisted her lips into an exaggerated frown, but with a mouthful of scone, she couldn't speak. I took full advantage and became more insistent. "You're very young. You should take your time. If you don't make a match this year, so be it."

"But I can't go back home to Mother."

"Then stay with me. If Mother is as exasperated with you as you say, then she is unlikely to object." As soon as I'd said the words, I realized that might be a problem if I couldn't get access to my bank account. I wouldn't be able to support another person, especially if I couldn't ask my father for financial help.

Lily let out a whoop and threw her arms around my neck. Too late to take it back now. "You are the best sister, Frances. I do want to find a husband, but it's lovely to know I can stay here with you if I don't."

I laughed at her enthusiasm and pushed aside my concerns. "I'd be very surprised if you don't find several eligible candidates. I just want you to choose the right one."

Fiona joined us for breakfast the next morning. Mrs. Thompson led her in to the dining room, as she brought in the morning post. Lily, Hetty, and I had just filled our plates and were seated around one end of the large dining table, Hetty at the end and Lily and I on either side of her. Fiona declined anything but coffee. I made the introductions, and poured her a cup as she seated herself next to me. She was buzzing with excitement. I suspected she was filled to the brim with unspent gossip.

"You have news, Fiona. What is it?"

Her face took on a glow that put me in awe. This woman truly lived for gossip. Thank goodness she was loyal to me. "I do indeed have news." Her smile was pure glee. "There's been another theft."

"No! Who?"

"Mary Chesterton. You know she hosted a musicale two evenings ago?"

I shuddered involuntarily. "Yes. I received an invitation, but unfortunately I had to decline."

"As did we. She has two daughters out this year, and as they were the main performers, I'm sure it was a long evening, if you know what I mean. However, I do like to show support, so I visited Mary yesterday, and she confided that a necklace was missing."

"That's terrible," Hetty said. "They believe it was stolen?"

Fiona nodded. "It seems Mary couldn't decide between two necklaces." She threw me a sidelong look. "You know she can never make up her mind. Well, once she finally settled on one, guests had begun to arrive. Mary rushed down to greet them, and her maid ran off to help get the girls ready. The other necklace was left on the dressing table, but it wasn't there later when Mary retired for the night. By the time I visited today, they'd made a thorough search of the house, and the necklace is not to be found." Fiona signaled the end of her story with a flourish of her hand.

Lily, across from me, had set down her fork and was gazing at Fiona with wide eyes. "Was it very valuable?"

"Oh, yes. And quite lovely, too. Mary is beside herself at its loss."

"Have they contacted the police?" I asked, buttering a slice of toast.

Fiona shook her head. "They seem reluctant to do so. The police may attempt to question their guests."

"Well if the jewelry is insured, and they want to make a claim, they will have to get over their reluctance," Aunt Hetty put in. "The insurer will either want the police to investigate, or they will conduct their own investigation."

"Really?" Fiona and I spoke in unison, causing Aunt Hetty to roll her eyes and pick up the newspaper. I suppose that made sense. An insurer wouldn't make a payment on a missing item unless they made certain it was indeed missing. Hetty must think us complete fools.

"Regardless of any insurance issues," I said, topping off my coffee, "I think they should alert the police to the fact that there's been another theft. They need to put an end to this."

"I agree." Fiona, having delivered her news, was now fatigued with the topic. She eyed the stack of letters beside my plate. "What invitations have you received?"

I shuffled through the envelopes, pulled out three that were obviously invitations, and handed them to her. "We received two yesterday, but the events are not for another week, so Lily and I still have time to outfit ourselves." I glanced at the remaining letters. Nothing from the doctor yet, but one was from my solicitor.

"Oh, dear."

"Bad news, Frances?" Hetty asked.

Three pairs of eyes watched me break the seal on the envelope. "I'm not sure yet." I scanned the letter from Mr. Stone. "Oh, dear," I sighed again, handing the letter off to Hetty.

"The two of you may as well know." I massaged a spot above my left eye where a headache was beginning to throb. "Father isn't the only one dealing with a financial difficulty." I explained the situation to them as succinctly as possible, ending with Fiona's involvement. "If not for her, I'm not sure I would have been able to cash the draft from Mother. I'd hoped this would all be resolved quickly, but Mr. Stone says in his letter he was unable to have the case dismissed. Now I might find myself without funds for months, possibly a year, or even longer."

Lily placed a hand over mine. "But you do have the money from Mother."

"I could see using a small amount for my expenses, but she sent that for your wardrobe."

She stared at me as if I were dim. "Don't be ridiculous! I know how much she sent you. She expected you to take me to Paris, to see Worth, and I find no reason for such extravagance. I should think we could update both our wardrobes for half that amount. It's not as if I didn't bring clothing with me." She leaned forward over the table. "And by the way, she is asking you to do her an enormous service. Shouldn't you receive some compensation for that?"

"She's right," Fiona chimed in. "If you only spend half on clothing, the rest could be used to run your household, and cover your expenses, for four months or so."

I wondered how she knew that, then remembered her husband had cashed the bank draft for me. I suppressed a groan. My personal life was becoming an open book.

"Don't think twice about it," Hetty agreed. "After all, Lily and I are living here too, so you are not the only one to benefit."

While I felt warmed by my family's support, I could not shake my concern over having no income, and a finite amount of money in my possession.

"I do have one concern," Hetty said. "Do you trust this Mr. Stone? He's not the Wynn family solicitor, is he?"

"Actually, Father hired him. He's the one who set up the account for me, and I trust him to fight for my rights."

"All the same, I don't like the idea of putting all your eggs in one basket. You should at least have someone else look at the case and the earl's claims. Perhaps Mr. Hazelton?"

"I'm sure George would be delighted to help," Fiona added.

"Oh, no. I'd rather just keep this between ourselves. I don't want to cause even a whisper of scandal around Lily's Season."

Fiona looked affronted. "George is the soul of discretion."

"And he's studied law," Hetty added. "Even if he only confirms Stone is handling this properly, I'd be more comfortable with the whole matter. I could take it up with him today while you ladies are shopping."

"Aren't you going with us?"

"I stopped in Paris last fall, my dear. I suspect my wardrobe will be at the height of fashion."

"All right then," I agreed. It rankled, but I had no way of explaining to Hetty why I didn't want to involve George in any of my affairs. After all, I knew firsthand he was indeed the soul of discretion.

"Now that's settled, you two had better eat up," Fiona said. "We have an appointment with Madame Celeste, and we still need to go through your wardrobes first."

If anything was going to take my mind off my problems, it was a shopping trip, which, when I thought about it, was a bit daft, since I'd be spending money I ought to be hoarding. I couldn't remember a time when I was ever worried about money, or had even concerned myself with how much something cost. I don't believe I've ever been a spendthrift, but to be honest, how would I know? I've never gone without anything I wanted, and up until a year ago, Reggie paid all the bills. When I came to London on my house hunting trip, I bought five new gowns, and though they were rather simple, the bill, when I saw it, was quite a shock. I'd need at least a dozen more gowns to get through the Season, and at least some would have to be elaborate ball gowns.

So much for not worrying about my problems.

After several hours spent in Madame's shop, we set out in search of hats. Fiona told us of a clever milliner just down the street, and since the day had finally warmed a bit, we decided to walk. Our progress was slow, as the rare sight of the sun seemed to have enticed everyone out of their homes. Carriages rolled by slowly, as factions of the milling crowd crossed the shop-lined street, heedless of the traffic. Everyone nodded or stopped to speak to friends they hadn't seen all winter. For me it had been over a year since I'd been out in company, and it was lovely to find I hadn't been completely forgotten by my acquaintance. We had almost reached the milliner, when a gentleman backed out of a shop door, blocking our passage.

"Sir!" Fiona exclaimed, as we all pulled up short. The gentleman spun around in surprise, and I recognized him as one of Reggie's friends.

"Lord Kirkland," I said with a nod. By this time he was joined by another man exiting the shop. I'd never been much impressed by Oliver Kirkland, but he was one of Reggie's friends, so I must admit to some prejudging. He'd never done anything to offend me except to act like a young, single man on the town. Only he was forty, married, and a father.

The man standing with him was another story altogether. Younger, about thirty I'd say. Fine form; tall with broad shoulders, dark hair that waved away from his forehead, dark eyes, skin a little more sun-kissed than the typical London bon-vivant, and a rather dazzling smile, which he was exhibiting at this moment.

"Lady Harleigh." Kirkland's voice pulled my attention back to him in time to see him tip his hat. I nodded in return.

"You remember Lady Nash, I'm sure." The two exchanged polite greetings. "And allow me to present my sister, Lily Price, here from New York to enjoy the London Season."

Kirkland made some flowery comment as he bowed over

Lily's hand, and I almost choked when I saw her eyes roll. Oh, dear! I must take her in hand. One should never show impatience or derision in such a way.

"Allow me to introduce my companion," he said. "Viscount Ainsworthy, another recent arrival to London."

So this is the new viscount I'd been hearing about. No wonder the young ladies were all agog. Young, titled, and handsome. I wondered if he was also wealthy, but knew it wouldn't matter in the least. He was sure to be the catch of the Season. He bowed over each of our hands and expressed his pleasure in making our acquaintance. All very correct. I noticed Lily didn't roll her eyes this time. In fact, she was smiling rather brightly.

As we were blocking the walkway, other shoppers were required to step into the street to pass us, so we decided to move on, the gentlemen joining us. Lily and the viscount in front, Fiona, Kirkland, and I, a few steps behind. We had such a short walk to the milliner's shop, we moved at a snail's pace. "Have you been acquainted with Viscount Ainsworthy long, my lord? I understand he's lived in South Africa for many years."

"Not long at all. I met him at our club just a few days ago. He inquired about a decent tailor, so I've just introduced him to mine. As you say, he's only recently arrived in the country, so I doubt anyone can claim a long acquaintance with him."

I had no time to consider this as we'd reached the milliner's. "This is our stop, gentlemen. Thank you for escorting us." I walked up the steps, with Fiona and Lily following.

"I hope we will meet again soon," the viscount said. "Will you be attending the Stoke-Whitney ball, by any chance?"

When hell freezes over, I thought. I gave him a smile. "We've been in town such a short time, I'm afraid we haven't received an invitation to that affair."

"Ah, but that is only because I didn't know you *were* in town. Now that I do, I shall send an invitation immediately."

The words came from the shop door behind me. I recognized that voice. I turned, dreading the moment when I would actually look into her eyes. Yes, there she was, Alicia Stoke-Whitney. I believe I mentioned her earlier. She was my late husband's mistress.

Chapter 6

M_y reaction to meeting Alicia was intense, to say the least. Had I been alone I'd have given her the cut, but with an audience I hesitated to show my contempt. For the first time in my social life, I completely lost my composure. I hadn't seen the woman since Reggie's death, and every emotion from that horrible night flooded my mind. I was at a loss.

Fiona saved me. Taking my arm to steady me, she guided the conversation and performed the introductions. For her part, Alicia ignored my reaction, and acted as if we were any two ladies meeting on the street. I let the conversation flow around me for several minutes, until Fiona mercifully recalled some imagined appointment she must keep, and the three of us climbed into her carriage, which had followed us down the street.

I dropped into the far side of the forward facing seat and let my head loll back against the cushioned upholstery. After giving her driver our destination, Fiona seated herself next to me and patted my leg in a "buck up" gesture. Lily climbed in and took the opposite seat. Once the carriage began moving, her eyes darted between Fiona and myself, with an expression of bewilderment. "What just happened back there?"

Fiona looked to me for an answer. Coward that I am, I chose to ignore the question for the moment. "Did I really agree to attend the Stoke-Whitney ball? Have I lost my mind?"

"Yes, you did, and no, you haven't," Fiona said, with a firm nod. "You must attend. If for no other reason than to confuse the gossips."

"I know *I'm* confused." Lily's brow furrowed. "Is there something wrong with Mrs. Stoke-Whitney? You went so pale when you saw her, Frances."

There was a pause while I wondered how quickly I could invent a story she would believe. Fiona filled the silence. "You might as well tell her before someone else does."

I rolled my head to the side, locking my gaze with hers. "Tell her what? What do you know?" My heart pounded. Fiona couldn't possibly know what had happened between Alicia, George, and I at Reggie's death. Then, one beat after the panic had struck, I felt a wave of relief, as I realized she was referring to Reggie's infidelity. I'd never spoken to her about it, yet looking at the sympathy in her eyes, I had the sense she could tell *me* a few things about my late husband.

"Somebody tell me something. I'm ready to burst over here."

I released a sigh as I straightened to an upright position, my hands demurely folded in my lap. Lily was so young, and I didn't want to disillusion her, but perhaps a small dose of reality would keep her from being as foolish as I had been.

"Reggie and Alicia had a close relationship," I ventured.

Lily's face remained blank. Lovely. I'd have to say it right out. "They were lovers." I glanced at Fiona. "And apparently, everyone knew about it."

"No," Lily gasped. "How could he do that to you? Why, you are ten times prettier than she is. And years younger, too. What was he thinking?"

"Here, here!" Fiona said, giving my hand a squeeze. The small gesture, and Lily's outrage on my behalf, had me blinking back tears. Their attempt to comfort me touched my heart, but in truth, now that the words were out, I was surprised I felt no bitterness or pain.

"Thank you both for your support, but since Reggie was attempting to be discreet, he didn't choose to explain the attraction to me."

"Well, I have to agree with you," Lily said, her voice quivering in outrage. "We are not going to her ball. How dare she even ask you?"

"Oh, no. You must go," Fiona stated, as if she would brook no argument. "There were rumors about Reggie and Alicia, but no one ever knows that sort of thing for a fact. If you are notably absent from this event, gossip will flow again. People will say that of course you couldn't attend. After all she was your husband's paramour. On the other hand, if you are seen to be on friendly terms with Alicia, those same people will assume the old rumors were wrong all along." She sank back into the cushioned seat and gave me a firm nod. "You must go."

"I can't decide if that makes sense or not." Poor Lily. She still looked dumbfounded.

"I'm sorry, dearest, but Fiona is right. Gossip is like currency in this town, and it's best to manage it if one can. I should be seen to be on friendly terms with Alicia, and so should my family."

Lily huffed in exasperation. "I'm not worried about the gossip. I'm worried about you. How did you tolerate it?"

"For the most part, I didn't know. But I'm sure Alicia wasn't his only affair."

"Good heavens! Is that normal? And isn't Mrs. Stoke-Whitney also married?"

"I wouldn't say it's normal, my dear," Fiona said. "But it is hardly unusual either. I'm afraid the British aristocracy is still used to arranging marriages that are advantageous to their families. That often means the two parties don't suit. Society looks the other way if one of them, especially the gentleman, looks for romance outside the marriage."

Lily's gaze caught mine. "Did you and Reggie suit?"

"I'm afraid not. I was dazzled by him at first—fascinated really, and I thought myself in love. Mother, Reggie, and I all wanted the match." I frowned, staring down at my gloved hands, smoothing out a wrinkle, remembering how young and foolish I'd been at the time. "Reggie was part of a fast set. I assumed he'd settle down once we married. He may have assumed I'd join him in his lifestyle. But his primary goal was to have someone to fund that lifestyle. It didn't take long for us to form separate lives."

I looked across at my sister and gave her a halfhearted smile. "I'm sorry to disillusion you, dearest, but as you are about to enter society, and meet many eligible men, I think it's important for you to understand not everyone is what they appear."

"You should learn as much as possible about any men who are pursuing you," Fiona added. She turned to me. "And it should be done before Lily falls in love with one of them. Once that happens, you'll never be able to dissuade her, no matter what evil you hear of him."

"Is that what happened to you?" I asked with a smile. Fiona and Robert still adored one another.

Fiona returned my smile, then focused on Lily. "My mother was looking a little higher for me than a mere baronet, but she didn't try turning my head until I was completely besotted. I was fortunate Robert turned out to be everything I believed him to be."

Lily had regained her composure and looked somewhat relieved by Fiona's words. "So even with all the maneuvering and machinations there is the occasional happy ending?"

Fiona nodded, and we all sank into our own thoughts. For my part, I was still recovering from the panic that had seized me when I'd thought Fiona knew all.

The next day I'd planned to take Lily with me to pay some calls. Before we could leave the house, however, I received a caller of my own. Just before noon, Mrs. Thompson came to my room to present Inspector Delaney's card.

"Again?" I tried to infuse the word with disdain while in truth my first sensation was panic. It was highly unlikely the man was calling to inform me that all was well, so he either had bad news or more questions. I was seated at my dressing table as Bridget worked my hair into an appropriate style for the hat I wished to wear. I caught Mrs. Thompson's eye in the mirror. "Please show him to the drawing room and I'll be down directly."

"He's already there, my lady. Your aunt was coming down when he arrived. She's taken charge of him."

Oh, dear. What must Hetty think of a policeman calling?

I stopped at Lily's room to tell her our calls would be postponed while I met with a visitor, then headed downstairs. I took a steadying breath before pushing open the door.

"Ah, here is my niece now." Hetty was seated on the sofa facing the door. She stood as I entered and gestured me to her side. I hadn't planned on her staying for this interview. She introduced Delaney who stood on the opposite side of the tea table. He gave me a nod.

"The inspector and I have already met, Aunt. And I believe he wishes to speak to me alone."

"That is unfortunate as I have no intention of leaving you alone." With a determined air, she seated herself on the sofa, raising a hand against the protest she must have seen coming. "It has been my experience that a policeman—"

"Inspector," Delaney corrected.

Hetty gave him a rather chilling smile. "An inspector never calls to deliver good news." She patted the seat next to her and I obediently sank into it. "You may well need my support."

I considered arguing, but realized even if I insisted she leave, I'd only have to explain the purpose of his call to her later. "Very well." I turned to Delaney. "How can I help you, Inspector?"

Delaney took a seat and opened his notebook, flipping through a few pages before raising his eyes to mine. "The Guildford police have spoken to the doctor who attended your husband at his death."

Hetty gave my hand a painful squeeze. "Some questions have arisen regarding Reggie's death," I told her. "Although Inspector Delaney has been unable to tell me why." I glared at the man.

The inspector never took his eyes from my face. "I can tell you the doctor confirmed your husband had a heart condition which, without proper care and management, would naturally lead to heart failure."

I held tight to my emotions. As Hetty said, he was not likely here to deliver good news.

"Because death appeared to be of natural causes, the doctor did not call for an autopsy at the time."

A chill washed over me. "Surely you aren't saying he wishes to call for one now?"

"He will only do so if you request it."

"Absolutely not!" Hetty replied, before I could do more than gasp.

Delaney ignored her response and turned to me. "Lady Harleigh?"

"Are you saying this is my decision? The police cannot order an autopsy on their own?"

"If they had enough evidence, they could. So I suspect they don't have enough."

I stared at the man in astonishment. Exhume Reggie's body and cut into it? Religion had never played a large role in my life, but even to me this sounded like the worst sort of desecration. "The police want me to request an autopsy of my husband's body with no more explanation than a vague question about the cause of his death? If you cannot give me a more compelling reason, Inspector, my answer is no."

Delaney closed his notebook and came to his feet. "That is your prerogative, my lady."

"Come now, Inspector. This is not about any loose ends. They must suspect murder. Why won't you tell me what brought this about?"

"As I said before, they haven't given me that information. I'll deliver your answer and Guildford will have to decide if they have enough evidence to proceed without your permission." He gave us both a nod. "Thank you, ladies, for your time. Sorry to have disturbed your peace."

I let him leave the room and show himself out. I turned back to Hetty. "Who would want to murder Reggie?"

Hetty's gaze was full of wonder. "Well, I don't know how they came to this conclusion, but it sounds as though they think you did."

"Me? What would give them such an idea?"

"That's what I would dearly like to know." Hetty stood up and moved to a cabinet along the wall. To my surprise she opened a door in the front, removing a bottle of brandy and two glasses.

"Where did that come from?"

"I had Mrs. Thompson buy it yesterday." She poured a small amount into each glass, and brought them back to the sofa, handing one to me. "And it's a good thing I did. You had no spirits in the house at all, and they certainly come in handy at a time like this."

"When one has been accused of murder?" I looked from my glass to my aunt as she took a healthy sip. I'd had no idea Hetty was a tippler.

"When one has had a shock," she explained. "Go ahead. Brandy is an excellent restorative."

I took a drink and found she was right. After the liquor burned its way down my throat, I did feel somewhat restored.

"We'll find some nice decanters for you later," Hetty said, settling back into the sofa. "Now, what was the purpose of the inspector's previous visit?"

"He wanted to know everything that happened on the day Reggie died—who was there, what we did all day, what we ate and drank."

Hetty nodded. "That's good. You may not be their only suspect."

That did not give me any relief. "Why should any of us be a suspect? Reggie died of a heart attack. What else could have killed him in his sleep?"

"Poison, perhaps?"

Poison? The word gave me such a jolt, I took another sip of brandy. "Good heavens, do you think I should have let them exhume his body?"

Hetty's eyes widened as she gave a vehement shake of her head. "Definitely not. We have no idea if their suspicions have any basis in fact, so there is no reason to desecrate his grave."

"But what if someone did poison him?"

She placed a calming hand on my arm. "My dear, if they exhume his body and find some trace of poison, as his wife, you would be their first suspect."

"That's absurd. I was nowhere near Reggie when he died."

"With poison, I'm not sure you would have to be." Hetty finished off her brandy in a single swallow. "Let's just hope the police find no reason to pursue this further." She cast a pointed look at my glass. "Drink up, dear."

Lily and I still made our afternoon rounds. It was fortunate that paying social calls was such a habit with me. I could probably make small talk in my sleep. Between the shock and the second glass of brandy I'd had with Aunt Hetty, I was little more than an automaton, but no one seemed to notice. Lily was also unaware as I'd asked Hetty not to mention Delaney's call to her.

I was cognizant enough to see that Lily seemed to be enjoying herself. Especially in the drawing room of Lady Georgianna, Countess Grafton, our last call for the day. She'd been a young matron when I made my debut and had been very kind to me. She carried a lot of weight as a leader of society, and her approval would smooth the way for Lily. She also had a daughter making her debut this year, and as she and Lily took to one another quickly, I turned my attention to Georgianna.

"Amazing how time flies, is it not?" she observed. "It seems not long ago you were their age."

"And dazzled by my first London Season. I'm hoping Lily will be less so. I don't want her to be swept off her feet by some, some . . ." I let the sentence trail off, grasping for the right word.

"Fortune hunter?" Georgianna quirked a brow as she finished my thought.

I answered her with a grimace. "Yes, I remember. You warned me about Reggie. I just hope if Lily finds herself in the same situation, she will accept advice better than I did."

To her credit, Georgianna didn't gloat. Instead she placed her hand on my arm and changed the subject. "I saw your brother-in-law last night at the theater."

"Graham is in town?"

She nodded. "Just arrived yesterday for some committee meetings. And I have another word of warning for you. He is not happy you are living on your own. I can't imagine why he mentioned it to me, or what, if anything he plans to do about it, but I thought you should know he mentioned it."

Since I couldn't tell her what he was trying to do about it, I merely nodded and thanked her for the warning. With this new business of the police suspecting foul play in Reggie's death, I'd forgotten all about my problems with Graham. Is it possible only a week ago my worst complaint was boredom?

I watched Lily conversing with the group of ladies on the other side of the room. She seemed a little more reserved than her usual self, but not uncomfortable or awkward. I felt safe in leaving her to her own devices while pondering what was upper-

most in my mind. If Reggie really was murdered, had we de-
stroyed evidence by moving his body? In an effort to avoid
scandal, had someone gotten away with murder? Perhaps I
should allow the body to be exhumed. But would I then find
myself accused of murder?

The idea was ridiculous, but the police might not find it so.
And if he had been killed by poison, Hetty was right. It wouldn't
be necessary to be near him at the time of his death. But I could-
n't help remembering someone was near him at that time. Very
near indeed.

Chapter 7

"Mrs. Thompson said to tell you Mr. Hazelton has arrived, my lady." Bridget walked in from the dressing room with my gloves in hand. "He's waiting in the drawing room."

I nodded. Of course George would be on time. "Can you find out if Miss Lily is ready to go down?" As Bridget slipped out of the room, I turned to Rose, who was supposed to be acting as my assistant dresser, but now sat, cross-legged on the bed, chewing on the end of a pigtail. I gave her a warning frown, and she dropped the offending braid.

"Will I do?" I asked.

"You look beautiful, Mummy." Her smile warmed me. I was sure hers would be the most sincere compliment I'd receive tonight.

"When will I be old enough to dress up and go to balls?"

"About the same time you're old enough to ride in the hunt." I reached out and stroked her cheek. "So let's not make that too soon, shall we?"

I pulled on the gloves, then turned to the mirror for a final inspection. The dark circles under my eyes from another sleepless night had faded. I'd arisen this morning with new resolve. The police would act as they saw fit, regardless of how I worried the matter. Since I had no idea what had raised their suspicions in the first place, I had no way of responding to it. However they chose to act, I would find out in time. So I took a rare nap this afternoon, forcing myself to think of nothing but Lily's entrée to society.

I took a step back from the mirror. As for my dress, well, three days ago it had been a two-year-old riding habit. Madame Celeste was a genius. She'd narrowed the dark blue velvet skirt as the current fashion demanded, by cutting it into gores that flared out below my knees somewhat like a trumpet. A trail of silver bows and intricate knots wound around the skirt and served to trim the rather deep, wide neckline. Very décolleté.

"That dress is breathtaking!"

I turned to see Lily in the doorway—a vision in cream silk with blue trim. Rose bounced off the bed and threw her arms around her aunt. "You're so pretty!"

"I especially like the accessory attached to your hip," I said, carefully removing Rose's arm from Lily's dress, and moving back a few steps while Lily did a spin for us. I was relieved to see her neckline was quite a bit more demure than mine.

The longing in Rose's eyes was palpable. "Your turn will be here before you know it, dearest." I gave her a hug. "But right now it's time to go up to bed and dream about horses."

We kissed Rose good night and sent her up to Nanny. Then I linked my arm with Lily's as we headed downstairs. "That dress suits you perfectly, dear. I expect you'll be turning all the young men's heads."

Judging from our reception in the drawing room we were both quite presentable. "Well, aren't you two lovely?" Hetty remarked, as I eyed the deceptively simple creation she wore, showing she still had curves in all the right places. "The men of London will be swarming around you."

George, elegant as always, bowed over my hand. "I'm afraid all three of you will have your own swarms to deal with this evening. Before that happens, may I claim a dance from each of you?" I watched his eyes travel up my body before meeting my gaze with a smoldering look. Good heavens, I was feeling rather warm.

"Yes, thank you." Lily's enthusiasm brought me back to my senses. This was George Hazelton, I reminded myself. There would be no smoldering. Even if he did look devilishly attractive tonight. Even if his gaze did leave a trail of heat behind it. "Lady Caroline has arranged for me to dance the first with her brother," Lily continued. "But you could have my second."

"Excellent. And would you honor me with the opening dance, Lady Harleigh?"

"I'd be delighted, Mr. Hazelton," I replied, my voice a little husky. Good Lord, what was wrong with me? I'd been dancing and flirting with the opposite sex for years with no such uncomfortable reaction. But this didn't feel like flirting. It was much more intense. I wanted to reach out and touch him, but of course if I did, I'd have to strangle myself with my purse strings. George and I had an unpleasant past that precluded any kind of future. Although he was being kind to me, he'd never consider me in a romantic light. And just when did I start thinking of him as George? I gave myself a mental shake and picked up my reticule.

"If we're all ready, perhaps we should be off."

Alicia's ball was an unqualified success. We ascended the stairs to a magnificent view of the ballroom. Brilliant chandeliers hung from the coffered ceiling, casting a warm glow over the crowd below, some dancing, others mingling. The decorations, all done in white, allowed the ladies, in their colorful hues, to stand out. The music swelled over the din of two hundred voices, all chatting at once—a good turnout for so early in the Season. And to cap things off, even the Prince of Wales put in an appearance.

From a more personal perspective, I was delighted to see Lily enjoying herself. I doubt she sat down once. After dancing with Caroline's brother and George, Lady Georgianna found us, and introduced another young man, who then requested a dance. After that, as Hetty had predicted, the men swarmed.

To my surprise, I also had my share of dance partners, and Fiona graciously took over my responsibilities of vetting Lily's. About halfway through the first hour of dancing, it occurred to me that my dance partners might well consider me back on the market. The wink Hetty gave me, as she whirled past in the arms of Sir Robert, led me to believe she considered it so. At twenty-seven, I suppose I was still relatively young, and I'd had experience in running a household, something the land-owning gentlemen might consider an advantage. Of course the biggest advantage to any of them would be my father's fortune. No one here would know it was not quite what it used to be.

Neither would any of them suspect I might soon be accused of murdering my late husband. I imagined that would send them scattering. Regardless, I was not ready to be someone's potential bride. After all, I had only just gained my tenuous independence. Challenging myself to assert that independence, I rejected the next eligible bachelor, making my need to chaperone Lily my excuse. As a result, I found myself momentarily alone, scanning the crowd for a sight of her. I didn't notice my brother-in-law approach until hearing his voice from behind me.

"So, you've decided to rejoin society, I see."

The words were spoken in a pleasant tone, but the countenance I saw when I turned toward him was anything but. With his lips twisted in a sneer and his eyes glaring, he was a fearsome sight. I might have taken a step back if I hadn't been so angry myself. I was aghast that he would dare speak to me after attempting to lay claim to my bank account. I wanted to snub him completely, but as we were surrounded by the cream of society, many of whom brushed close enough to leave the scent of their cologne, I didn't wish to provide any fodder for gossip.

"Graham." I choked out his name and gave him a stiff nod.

"I understand you are sponsoring your sister this spring." He stepped beside me, hands linked behind his back, both of us gazing out at the dancers. "A costly prospect, I'm given to understand."

"That is hardly your concern," I replied, my lips frozen in a smile. "And rather a vulgar topic for polite conversation."

"Unfortunately, between us, money has become an important issue."

"Unfortunate, you call it?" I struggled to keep my voice down. "You are attempting to steal from me. I consider that more than just unfortunate. Your actions are reprehensible." I would have moved away at that, but Graham placed a staying hand on my arm.

"Any property you had upon your marriage belongs to the Wynn family and is therefore under my control. You have no right to draw on those funds without consulting me first."

Oh, if only I could slap the man. "Those funds are mine alone," I hissed. "As your solicitors will soon inform you. My father set that account up for me, as he didn't entirely trust the Wynn family, much to his credit. All you are doing with this suit is delaying the inevitable. You will not win, nor would it do you much good if you did. With the expenses of Harleigh you'd be lucky if it saw you through the year, but Rose and I could live comfortably on it for many years to come." I allowed myself one angry glare. "Withdraw your claim and leave us alone."

"Of course we won't leave you alone, my dear sister."

I turned my head at Graham's words and saw our hostess had joined us. A rush of heat reddened my cheeks. Regardless of his attempt to cover up our argument, Alicia had likely heard at least some of it. She was wearing her society face however as were we all: polite smile, and every other feature a mask. There was no reading the thoughts behind it.

"Such devotion to family does you great credit, Lord Harleigh." Her voice was smooth and sweet as cream, as she moved around Graham to my other side. "I hope you'll forgive the intrusion, but I hoped to steal Lady Harleigh away for a little chat."

"Of course," Graham replied. With a bow to each of us, he walked away, and was soon swallowed up in the crowd. If only the trouble he caused would disappear with him. I turned to Alicia.

She lifted her shoulder in a shrug. "Forgive my interference, but your brother-in-law appeared to be making a nuisance of himself. As hostess, I must make sure my guests are enjoying their evening."

"And you believed I was not?"

"Your claws were out, dear. Besides"—she gave me a charming smile—"if you wished to be in his company, I hardly think you would have changed your residence."

I was tempted to smile along with her, but I reminded myself that this was Alicia, not a friend. She was the only person who had been with Reggie at his death. Is it possible she'd done something to cause it? I frowned, bringing the emotions of that night to mind. Her grief and fear were so real, she couldn't have been playing a part.

Her smile faltered. "Something wrong?"

I forced a pleasant expression. "Only that I'm here to chaperone my sister, and I have been negligent in my duty. I should find her."

"Shall we take a stroll?" she suggested. "We are bound to see her."

I could hardly refuse. She nodded to our left, and we set off around the perimeter of the room. Uncomfortable though I was, at least I had the satisfaction of knowing Fiona would approve. I finally caught a glimpse of Lily on the dance floor and stopped short. Alicia let out a little squeak as someone bumped her from behind.

"Forgive me, dear lady." I turned to see Viscount Ainsworthy, holding Alicia's hand, and begging her forgiveness.

"The fault is mine, sir," I countered. "I drew up short, and you had no chance to move around us."

He graced us with a heart-stopping smile. Goodness, I nearly forgot to breathe for a moment. In evening dress, the man was a sight to behold. "As long as you are uninjured, ma'am?"

"Quite," Alicia replied, gazing up at him with hunger in her eyes.

With a bow, the viscount moved on, breaking the spell. I blew out a long breath. "I can't believe you didn't claim an injury," I said, watching him move through the crowd. "You might have kept him by your side for the rest of the evening."

She turned back to me, and on seeing my smile, burst into laughter, eyes crinkling, one gloved hand coming to her mouth, to smother the sound. It took all my determination not to follow suit. A few curious glances turned our way. "Stop it," I admonished in a whisper. "Or I shall not be able to control myself either."

Alicia was soon back to her senses. "He is devilishly handsome, is he not?"

"And as tempting as the devil himself," I agreed.

"I hope he will not prove to be that." She gave me a sidelong glance. "He has danced twice with your sister."

"Oh, dear. I have been neglecting her. If he's turned our heads, I can only imagine the impression he's made on her." I scanned the dancers once more, spotting Lily and her partner nearby. "Who is that she's dancing with now?"

Alicia turned to follow the line of my gaze. "Daniel Grayson," said a voice from beside me. "Lord Ballymore's son." I turned to smile at George Hazelton, then remembered who was standing on my other side. Oh, dear God! The three of us together again. What does one say under these circumstances? *Hello there. Moved any dead bodies lately?*

I glanced at Alicia, who was leaning around me to see who was speaking, then back at George. His look of shock was almost comical, but good breeding won out, and he soon recovered, schooling his face into a more bland expression. He gave Alicia a nod, clearly at a loss for anything to say.

Alicia put on a bright smile. "Well, this is rather awkward. I'm sure there's something else I should be doing." With that she hurried off, leaving George and me alone. "She's right. That was rather awkward," I said, without looking at him.

He moved closer until his shoulder touched mine, and I looked up into his face, seeing nothing but his usual inscrutable countenance. "The three of us shared a rather dark moment," he said. "It would be surprising if we could meet again with equanimity. Mrs. Stoke-Whitney has actually risen in my opinion, in that she hasn't been able to shake that moment off."

As we stood so close, I could speak without fear of being overheard. "I had another visit from Inspector Delaney. He asked permission to autopsy Reggie's body."

"Really? Rather a gruesome hobby for the man, but who am I to judge?"

I gave him a scowl. "Mr. Hazelton, you must take this seriously. The police certainly do. What if they come to question you?"

"As I had nothing to do with his death, I'm not overly concerned. But I do take this seriously. I'll see what I can learn about this investigation."

I shook my head. "Please don't involve yourself further, George. I should never have dragged you into my troubles. You were kind to help me, but now that the police are investigating, I've put you in a terrible situation."

"Your troubles were no fault of your own, Frances. You should be aware I am rarely kind, but I was pleased to be of service to you."

His words, the silkiness of his deep voice, and his use of my

Christian name all took me by surprise. He must have noticed it, for he raised a brow in question. "Did you not realize you just called me George?"

I hadn't. "Did I? You must forgive the familiarity, Mr. Hazelton."

"Oh, no. We are now Frances and George. There is no going back." With that he lifted my hand to his lips. "I'm glad we were able to clear the air."

As he turned away, I found myself rooted to the ground, staring at his back, wondering why I felt like purring. Perhaps the air was cleared for him, but my head seemed to be wrapped in a blanket of fog. I snapped my mouth shut, and glanced around, wondering if anyone had taken in that scene. I would have to think about it later as this was not the place for contemplation.

The music had stopped, and the dancers were moving off the floor. I made my way to where Fiona stood, at the opposite side of the room, and arrived just as Mr. Grayson returned with Lily. How they'd been able to dance at all was a mystery as the man towered over her. He was blond and quite handsome though, and I'm sure that was enough to turn her head.

"Frances, do you know Lord Grayson?" she asked, once we were all assembled.

I blushed, and was about to correct her, when Grayson stepped in. "Miss Price is too kind in her attempt to elevate me, but as it happens, I'm a mere 'mister.'" He gave me a nod and a winning smile. "I believe we met a few years ago at Lady Nash's country home."

"Ah, yes. You are a friend of Sir Robert's brother." And if I remembered correctly he caused some sort of incident during that visit, though I couldn't bring the details to mind.

He took Lily's error with good humor and that was a good sign. "Since we are Americans, a 'mister' is not a mere thing to us."

"Ah, I'm relieved to find you are not title-mad Americans."

I was surprised to find myself laughing at his quip since that was precisely the type of American I was nine years ago. "I'm equally relieved you don't hold my sister's confusion against her."

"A minor error and completely overshadowed by her charm."

He solicited another dance with Lily for later in the evening and left us soon after to find his next partner.

Lily turned to me as soon as Mr. Grayson moved on. "Are you all right?" She searched my face with concern. "I saw you speaking to Mrs. Stoke-Whitney. Was it horrible?"

I considered the conversation we'd had and was surprised to find it hadn't been horrible at all. "Not at all. In fact she rescued me from a heated conversation with my brother-in-law."

Fiona wrinkled her nose in distaste. "Is that fiend here tonight?"

"Yes, and making a pest of himself. He implied I was spending too much money if you can believe that."

"Bloody ass," Lily hissed.

Fiona's brows shot up, as my jaw dropped, and I whipped my head around to face Lily.

She took a defensive step backward. "Well, he is," she whispered.

"While I can't disagree with you, please never use that phrase again, dear. Where on earth did you hear it in the first place?"

Lily quirked her shoulder in a shrug. "Alonzo. He once said Reggie was a—well, that's what he called Reggie."

I tried to hide my smile. It was good to know I had my brother's loyalty. "Well, I can't argue with that either, but as a lady, you should not mimic Alonzo's vocabulary."

"Though it was appropriate," Fiona muttered.

I had to content myself with hoping Lily understood as just then her next partner came to claim his dance. I shared a look with Fiona as the couple took the floor. Her eyes sparkled with amusement. "Don't be so hard on your sister, Frances. She felt she could speak freely to us and I'm glad of that." She gave my arm a friendly squeeze. "I've spent much of the evening with her, and I find her openness and candor delightful. She may ultimately change her behavior as she mixes more in society; in fact, I'm sure she will, but I hope she never loses her spirit."

"Perhaps she will help me find mine."

"Ladies." We both turned to find Lady Georgianna behind us. "It appears," she said in a lowered voice, "the London jewel thief has struck again."

Fiona's eyes grew round. "Do you mean here? Tonight?"

"Indeed I do. Alicia Stoke-Whitney's bracelet has gone missing."

"But that doesn't mean it was stolen," I replied. "The clasp could have broken, or it slipped from her wrist. I don't believe the thief has even taken an object directly from someone's person."

Georgianna shook her head and continued in sotto voce. "She said the clasp on the bracelet was both new and quite strong. Even so, she's had a few servants searching for it, as inconspicuously as possible of course. She and I checked the ladies' retiring room ourselves to no avail. She has just gone now to consult with her husband, but I don't know what else she can do. She wouldn't wish to cause a commotion, not while the prince is still here. And what can she do that would not appear as though she were accusing one of her guests of being a thief?"

"If the bracelet *has* been stolen, then one of her guests *is* a thief," Fiona replied quite reasonably. "How can she do nothing and let someone walk out with it?"

Georgianna made a helpless gesture with her hands. "Would you call in the police to question your guests? After all, it could be one of the servants. She has hired some extra help for the evening, and I'm sure they will be questioned before they leave."

"I suppose that's possible," I conceded. Though I thought it unlikely, somehow it felt better than believing one's own friends and contemporaries would steal the very jewelry from one's wrist. Although how was that any different from what Graham, my own brother-in-law, was doing to me?

"Alicia wants to keep this quiet, so please let it go no further, or at least no further than your sister, Frances." I followed her gaze to where my sister was still dancing and wearing a lovely sapphire necklace. "I only wanted to warn the both of you in case the thief is still here."

The three of us shared an uneasy silence before Georgianna walked off to find her daughter. "Do you remember when a ball meant nothing but fun for us?" I mused. "Now we have to face our late husband's mistresses, our greedy relatives, and jewel thieves of all things. Rather takes the fun out of everything, doesn't it?"

Chapter 8

The rest of the evening flew by and was comparatively uneventful. Georgianna had been correct. Even after the prince left, not a word was mentioned about the missing bracelet. Other than a quick, whispered warning to Lily, I gave it no further thought. The supper dance began, and Fiona encouraged me to accept Viscount Ainsworthy's request for the honor. I didn't require much encouragement, I must admit. Ainsworthy was such a delight to the eyes, and, much to my surprise, he turned out to be quite amiable as well, without the calculated charm of a practiced flirt.

"I find it very interesting you chose me as your partner for the supper dance," I said as we executed a turn in the waltz.

He smiled, and I nearly forgot to move my feet. "You suppose I have a reason other than a simple desire to dance with you?"

"Oh, well said. But yes, I do believe you had another reason. I heard you have already danced twice with my sister, and therefore could not ask her for this dance, or take supper with her. But if you ask me to dance . . ." I let the sentence trail off. That he took my meaning was clear in his blush. I actually made a man blush! No, I made one of the most handsome men of my acquaintance blush. Of course his rosy cheeks had nothing to do with my charm, so I suppose it's of no real consequence. For a few seconds I was quite jealous of Lily.

"You give me more credit than I deserve, Countess. I admit to being quite taken with your sister, but I only thought to ask your permission to call on her."

The music ended and Ainsworthy guided me through the crowd, and down the stairs to supper, where another large crowd mingled. I caught a glimpse of Hetty in an animated conversation with a group of gentlemen. She was getting on well. I returned my attention to my companion.

"Has Lily agreed to receive you if you call?"

"I hadn't actually asked her." He gave me a wry smile. "It's been a long time since I've lived in England. I'm not familiar with every rule of etiquette, so I decided to err on the side of caution. I take it I should have asked her first?"

I nodded toward a table where Lily sat with Leo Kendrick, an acquaintance of Lady Georgianna. "It looks as though they have room at their table, so you'll have a chance to ask her now. If she agrees, you may be sure that I do."

His chance came quickly. As soon as we arrived, Mr. Kendrick slipped away to prepare a plate for Lily. I watched her blush as Ainsworthy spoke to her and felt I'd done Mr. Kendrick a disservice. I didn't know him well, but he seemed a pleasant man, and since he was clever enough to obtain the supper dance with Lily, he deserved to have her attention at supper, rather than to be pushed aside by a prettier face.

Not that there was anything wrong with Kendrick's face. His looks were chiseled where Ainsworthy's were painted with a fine brush. Ainsworthy was tall and broad, where Kendrick was a bit shorter, and lean. He didn't look as though he would crush Lily with a simple hug. Not that there would be any hugging. Good heavens, I was getting far too ahead of myself.

Kendrick returned with two full plates and a pointed glare for Ainsworthy. "Lady Harleigh must be famished, old man." He seated himself on Lily's other side and presented her with one of the plates. With obvious reluctance, Ainsworthy took the hint and left in search of sustenance while the three of us conversed.

"Is this your first ball of the Season, Miss Price?"

"Oh, yes. I've only been here a few days, so this is my first entertainment of any kind."

"If you have any thoughts of attending the theater, I hope you'll allow me to escort you." He glanced at me and added the word *both* as an afterthought.

Lily beamed. "I—we'd love to go to the theater."

"Excellent. If I may take the liberty of calling on you this week, perhaps we can settle on a date and venue."

Alarm bells sounded in my head. I'd just been doubting his chances with Lily, and now I needed to worry he was moving too fast. Settle on a date, indeed! Didn't he realize such a phrase would put ideas in her head?

Ainsworthy returned with not two, but three plates—one filled with a tempting assortment of cakes. "Just as I'd suspected, Kendrick," he said, dutifully seating himself next to me, but across the table from Lily, "you've forgotten the sweets. Miss Price, you must try some of this."

Lily, whose corset was every bit as tight as mine, wore a pained expression as Ainsworthy served her one of the sugary morsels. Kendrick opened his mouth to respond, when a gentleman bumped into our table, nearly sweeping my plate to the floor. I looked up to see Mr. Grayson.

"I beg your pardon, Lady Harleigh." He reached out to steady a wobbling glass. "The room is rather crowded." With a smile for Lily and a nod to the gentleman, he passed by. The incident had the happy result of causing a cessation of hostilities between the two men, and the topics of conversation became more general. Before long it was time to go back up to the ball-room. Ainsworthy and I had just reached the stairs when some-one called my name. I turned to see Mr. Kendrick holding my reticule.

"This was on the floor near our table," he said. "Does it be-long to you?"

"Oh, dear. I'm not normally so scatterbrained. Thank you for returning it, Mr. Kendrick."

In the cold light of day the following morning, watching Jenny arrange a third bouquet from one of Lily's admirers, I re-alized that Lily was viewed as another American heiress, and could be the target of any number of fortune hunters. I would have to make sure these men were more than just romantic fig-ures—that they were actually good husband material—before any of them engaged Lily's heart. I looked at the cards: two honorables and a title. That alone was enough to raise my sus-picions. Lily was a pretty girl, but she'd have to be much more than that for the average aristocratic mother to overlook her lack of blue blood. If the family were in need of funds, how-ever, Lily might be as welcome as a large bag of U.S. dollars.

I should start with a visit to Fiona. She might know if any of the three ought to be avoided.

That would have to wait until later though. It was going on noon, and I'd yet to eat breakfast. When I dragged myself out of bed an hour ago, my maid told me Lily was still sleeping, but she should be up by now. I'd forgotten how late into the night these society events lasted. We didn't arrive home until three in the morning.

I placed the cards back with Lily's flowers, and headed to the dining room, delighted to find both of my relations up and tak-ing nourishment. Well, Lily was anyway. Aunt Hetty was nurs-ing a cup of coffee and listening to Lily chatter between bites of egg.

She glanced up at me with sleepy eyes. "Ah, so you've finally decided to join us. I was beginning to wonder if you planned to sleep the day away."

"Me? Why I've been up for hours, supervising Lily's floral deliveries."

"Flowers?" Lily's head popped up. "For me? Where?"

"You'll find them in the drawing room." I barely got the words out before she scrambled from her chair and fled the room, tossing her napkin on the table.

"No flowers for us, Aunt Hetty. I'm afraid we made no conquests last night." I gave her shoulder a squeeze as I passed behind her.

"Goodness me, I gave up on conquests long ago, but I did speak with a number of intelligent gentlemen last night." She took a bite of toast and unfolded the newspaper beside her plate.

"Well, I hope you gave them good advice." I moved to the sideboard and examined the offerings. Hmm, a little egg, toast, coffee of course.

"I only give advice when asked," she replied, leafing through the pages, probably looking for the market reports. "However, I do believe the gentlemen were surprised to find themselves discussing business with a woman."

"Perhaps we should expect some callers for you this afternoon."

Hetty's look of derision told me she wouldn't rise to the bait. "Well, if you see me acting like your sister, please feel free to shoot me."

"She's still very young, Aunt," I said, seating myself beside her. "And this is all new to her. It's normal for a girl to be excited about her first Season, but I hope she's not quite ready to fall in love yet."

"I'm just glad she enjoyed the evening. Things didn't go as well for her at the affairs she attended in New York."

I glanced over at Hetty's face. She looked grim. "Why not?"

"She's young and enthusiastic. She and the Knickerbocker set just didn't mix. And you know your mother would never settle for anything less than an old, established family."

My heart went out to Lily. I knew how that felt, to be on the outside, looking in. Before I could inquire further, she floated back into the room, a bright smile on her face, and the three cards in her hand. I drew back as she fluttered them before my face. "Franny, look! Viscount Ainsworthy sent flowers. And that nice gentleman who took me to dinner, and Daniel Grayson." She frowned. "I heard Lord Ballymore is his father. Will he inherit the title?"

I tried to remember how many sons belonged to the Grayson family. "I'm not sure if he's the eldest son or not."

"Can we find out?"

"Is it important?" Now I was confused.

"Well, if there is a chance of marriage, I should learn as much about him as possible. You said so yourself."

I saw Aunt Hetty hiding her face behind the newspaper, struggling not to laugh. "I was referring to their characters, Lily, not their standing in society. But aside from that, you seem to be jumping from flowers to marriage much too quickly." I made a little flip- flop motion with my fork. "A London Season can be very exciting, but don't let it carry you away. There's no pressure on you to marry. Don't put that pressure on yourself, or the gentlemen you meet."

Lily looked aghast. "I know why Mother sent me here, Frances—to find a husband. And I must find one this spring or go back to New York as a failure."

"Lily, no." This was no longer amusing. Her attitude was far too much like mine had been at her age. "Mother's not here and I won't allow you to marry the first man who asks you, simply because that's her idea of success."

"But that's what you did."

"Exactly my point. I was on a quest to marry the most eligible man I could find, and once I did that, I thought I'd fulfilled my duty. But it doesn't end there. It's just the beginning of a new life, one in which you find yourself in the care of someone who is little more than a stranger."

Lily stared down at her plate, a sullen expression on her face. How was I to make her understand? "Don't rush into this. Once married, you belong to your husband, and you have no idea the misery your life can become when you are tied to the wrong man."

Her gaze softened as she looked up at me. "I'm so sorry, Franny. In my excitement I'd forgotten how awful Reggie was to you. But surely most men aren't that bad?"

Not that bad? "Dearest, Reggie was a wastrel, and he was unfaithful to me, but in some ways, considering how incautious I was in marrying him, I was lucky. He took my money then left me to my own devices. He was never cruel, or violent, or controlling." I searched my mind for the words that would make her understand this was a serious business she was undertaking. "A woman is completely under the power of the man she marries. Considering what brutes some men are, we must be fools to rush into marriage the way we do."

"Oh, come now." Hetty lowered her paper and glared at me. "They're not all bad."

"Of course not, Aunt Hetty," I was quick to agree, remembering how happy she'd been in her marriage. "But you must admit marriage is an enormous risk for a woman. I just want Lily to be sure she knows the man she says yes to—both his heart and character. And it takes time to learn if a man is like your husband, or like Father, or like Reggie, or worse."

I wasn't sure I was getting through to either of them. Hetty was frowning. Well, perhaps she'd had a wonderful marriage, but in my experience, those were few and far between. Meanwhile, Lily still looked bewildered. "None of the gentlemen I've met appeared to be brutes," she said.

"Anyone can be pleasant for the length of a dance," Hetty put in. "Frances is right. You need to spend time with a person, see them in a number of different settings, to find out if they have a temper, or some other character flaw you may not wish to live with. You might get lucky, but without taking time to develop a relationship with someone, you are taking a risk."

I silently thanked Hetty for her support. "And in this country, men have all the power in marriage, so a woman needs to be even more careful. Especially in cases like Lily's and mine, where the gentleman might be expecting a large marriage settlement."

"You mean they're only interested in me because of Father's money."

I felt as though I'd crushed her hopes. "I mean that's a possibility, and it would be wise to be suspicious."

She inhaled and heaved another dramatic sigh. At this rate there'd be no oxygen left in the room. "I suppose you are right, but is there no way to do this quickly? Find out their intentions, I mean. And their flaws, too."

I didn't have a good answer. "I know where we can find the gossip about them, or at least two of them. Ainsworthy has been here such a short time, few people will have more than a passing acquaintance with him. However, we should start with a visit to Fiona. She always knows the latest gossip, and may have some ideas about how we can learn more of Viscount Ainsworthy. She is rather devious."

"You could contact your solicitor," Hetty suggested, folding up the newspaper. "Through him you could hire a private inquiry agent."

I stared at her. "You mean someone who would follow them around? Spy on them? Are you serious?"

"Absolutely. If you think there are men who might romance our Lily, while having nefarious intentions, you need to find out everything you can. Your father and I have used inquiry agents before investing in certain companies in the past. It can be expensive, but the information they provide is well worth the cost."

"Excellent." Lily stood up with an air of impatience. "Send a letter to your solicitor, then we'll go visit Fiona. I want to get things rolling."

I dashed off a letter to my solicitor, intimating that I might be interested in hiring a private inquiry agent, to check up on the characters of the three gentlemen who might be courting my sister—that is if he thought the expense to be within my means. Although as an afterthought, I realized I could ask my father to cover that expense. I provided the names of the gentlemen and concluded with a request for any new information regarding my bank account. I sent the note off with the kitchen boy, and shortly after one o'clock, Lily and I were in the cozy intimacy of Fiona's boudoir, seated in tufted slipper chairs, sipping tea, and nibbling on sugary biscuits.

Fiona's eyes were alight with excitement. "So what do you think happened to Alicia's bracelet?"

"Her bracelet?" I was so wrapped up in Lily's suitors, I had all but forgotten about the stolen bracelet.

"Do you really think it was stolen?" Lily asked. "I assumed she just lost it. I'm sure it's turned up by now."

Fiona flashed her a look that implied Lily was spoiling her fun. "I suppose that's possible, but there have been quite a few thefts lately."

"Yes." I had to concede that. "But those were of objects taken from desks and shelves. I'm inclined to believe Alicia's bracelet was simply lost."

Fiona pursed her lips and sent a glare our way. "Fine, but I must say you are a couple of killjoys. Apparently you aren't here to speculate on the identity of the thief."

"No, not at all." I apprised her of Lily's potential suitors and asked for her thoughts. Fiona good-naturedly allowed the change in subject.

"Grayson wants watching," she pronounced. "You are wise to be suspicious. The family goes back for ages, and there is no reason to suspect any financial problems, but Daniel Grayson is the third son."

"Does that mean he won't inherit anything?" Lily sat on the edge of her seat, eager for information.

"That's part of the problem," Fiona agreed with a nod. "I believe he studied the law, but he has done nothing in that profession. That leads me to believe he has an allowance from his father, and it's not likely to be a large one. I wouldn't be surprised if he were looking for a wealthy bride. Not a bad thing in and of itself," she added, as if Lily or I were about to protest. "But it does call into question any feelings he may or may not have for said bride."

"So he might just be after my dowry."

"Too soon to tell. You should take care with him. However, you have two other lovely prospects." Fiona's face fairly glowed with excitement. The effect was to brighten Lily's countenance as well.

"I do?"

"Oh, my dear. Yes, indeed. Kendrick might be an uphill battle, but well worth the fight." She set down her cup and leaned forward in her chair. "The family's wealth came from mining, I'm told. The grandfather built the business himself, and his sons expanded it into other areas. Leo Kendrick's father married the Honorable Patricia Whiting, which was a huge coup for him, and now it's said the children are expected to marry into the peerage."

"Thus the battle," I added.

Fiona nodded. "But on the positive side, if he is attracted to you, my dear Lily, it is for your own sake."

Lily wrinkled her nose. "Well, that's reassuring. From everything I've seen and heard lately, it seems marriage is all about position and money."

"It is often a great deal about position and money," Fiona

said. "Which is why we need to find out how much influence Kendrick's family has on his decisions."

"Won't his actions tell us that?" I asked. "If he calls on Lily, and his manner is respectable, then it would appear he intends to make his own decision."

Fiona nodded. "Time will tell in his case. The family may not voice any objections unless he seems to be courting Lily in earnest. And they may not object at all, now I think about it, as Lily's dear sister is a countess."

I rolled my eyes, but realized Fiona was probably correct in this assessment. Still, we weren't hitting the points I was most interested in. "What about the characters of these gentlemen? There was an incident when both Grayson and I were staying at your home. I couldn't recall it last night, but now I remember he struck one of your grooms with a riding crop."

Fiona gasped. "Oh, yes. That's right. The groom hadn't tended to Grayson's horse after a hard ride. Grayson was furious when he returned to the stables and saw the beast standing outside still sweating."

"So he struck the groom?" Lily asked.

"Well, the groom had been terribly negligent and Grayson was concerned about his horse. I admit that was poor behavior on his part, but be assured the groom suffered much worse from the head groom afterward."

"I'm fond of animals too, Fiona, but I'd never strike a boy for neglecting one. Though I suppose in some cases I might be sorely tempted to do so. You must admit that shows Grayson has at least a bit of a temper."

Fiona sipped her tea as she considered this. "I suppose he does, but he was provoked." She gave Lily a nod. "You should be alert to any signs of that if he calls on you. Impatience or temper is so difficult to live with."

"Kendrick seems very upstanding," I said.

"And far too occupied with business to get into any trouble. I've heard nothing to his discredit but the fact that he's rolling in wealth means he can pay for discretion." She gave us a one-shoulder shrug. "He could be hiding a multitude of sins."

"But that's the type of thing our inquiry agent could discover."

"I didn't realize this would be so complicated," Lily said. "I'm beginning to consider all men as horrid and want nothing to do with them."

"There are many good men, Lily. Look at Lord Nash, or Alonzo. The problem is the bad ones are skilled at acting like good men, which is why we have to be so careful at choosing one. I still say the best method is to take your time, and let them court you, if they plan to do so. After spending time with them, you may decide you don't like any of them."

"But I do like all three of them," she said, forgetting her claim that all men were horrid. She brightened. "That's right. We haven't discussed Viscount Ainsworthy."

"There's not much to discuss there," Fiona said. "He's a bit of an unknown quantity, being so new in town. I spoke to Lady Bradley last night. She and her husband spent some time in the town of Kimberly, in South Africa. She said she would never have known him had someone not given her his name."

"If Lady Bradley would wear her spectacles she might see many more people she knows," I said.

"My thoughts exactly. But on further questioning, I learned she last saw the man some nine years ago and one does change considerably as one move from twenty to thirty. He owned a mining operation that occupied so much of his time, he didn't take part in the local society." She shrugged. "He was a rather distant heir, after all, with few expectations. Not really part of their circle. But he seems like a very good prospect now."

She looked up as her lady's maid slipped into the room. "Yes, Grace?"

"Begging your pardon, my lady, but you asked me to tell you when the children returned from their outing."

Grace curtsied, and was about to leave the room, when Fiona raised a hand to stop her. "Grace, do you happen to know anyone in service with Viscount Ainsworthy?" She gave the girl a winning smile, hoping to encourage gossip.

Grace frowned. "Well, I don't know him myself, but I met with a friend on my last half day who told me her cousin is the new butler there."

"Did she tell you anything about the viscount?" Lily blurted, before Fiona could form a more discreet question.

The girl looked down at her feet, uncomfortable with the conversation. "I wouldn't know, ma'am. If he did tell her about the gentleman, it wasn't passed on to me. But, if it's not speaking out of turn, my lady"—she turned to me—"he might have said something to your Bridget."

I blinked. "My Bridget?"

"Yes, my lady. Mr. Barnes, that's my friend's cousin, and your Bridget are . . . good friends."

I noticed her hesitation. She didn't want to say too much, but it appeared Bridget was stepping out with the viscount's butler. Disaster!

Fiona dismissed the maid and rose to her feet. Lily and I followed. "Thank you for your assistance, Fiona. Obviously you can see we must hurry home."

"Yes," Lily said with an excited squeak. "We must find out if Bridget knows anything about Viscount Ainsworthy."

"Yes, yes, that too, but more importantly, I may be about to lose my maid."

"Oh, no, my lady. You needn't worry about that. I like Mr. Barnes well enough, but I'm too young to think about marriage just now, and if ever I do marry, it wouldn't be to someone in service. Maybe someday I might want to tie myself down, but it will be to a man who wants some other kind of future, like an inn or something."

As soon as we'd arrived back home, I tracked Bridget down in my bedchamber and asked her about Ainsworthy's butler. Her words were music to my ears, but I knew if I let her continue, she'd go on long into the evening, regaling me with images of her glorious future. One I fully supported, of course, but not right this moment.

"I'm relieved to hear it, Bridget. Has Mr. Barnes told you anything about the viscount? He's called on my sister, you know." In fact two of Lily's three men had called while we were visiting Fiona, much to Lily's disappointment and my relief. I still didn't trust her ability to say no, should one of them suddenly pop the question.

Bridget was nodding. "He says Viscount Ainsworthy is an excellent man, my lady. A fair and kind master. He doesn't drink overmuch, or keep odd hours, like a lot of young men. He's a bit private, Barnes says, but he reckons that's just because he's not used to having servants around to do for him."

I could understand that. Servants ran the house, for goodness' sake. Privacy was out of the question. One was obliged to forget their presence and go about her business. If one wasn't used to that, it could be a bit overwhelming. "Thank you, Bridget. I was concerned for Lily's sake, as no one knows much about the viscount."

"I understand, my lady. If I hear anything to his disfavor, I'll be sure to tell you, but it sounds to me like he's a good man."

"Excellent," I said. "Now, we're dining out tonight, Bridget, then on to the Witherspoons, for what they are calling a musical evening." I prayed they would have actual musicians and not just somebody's debutante daughters.

"Very good, my lady. Perhaps you'd like to wear the blue gown?"

"Yes, that should be fine."

"And will you be wearing your new bracelet?"

I gave her a sharp look. "New bracelet?"

Bridget stepped into the dressing room for a moment and returned with something sparkling in her hand. My stomach did a flip.

"It was in the bag you used last night."

Oh, my heavens! I hadn't noticed it while it was on her wrist, but I'd wager my last pound I was looking at Alicia's stolen bracelet.

Chapter 9

After Bridget left me, I sat for a while at my dressing table, staring at Alicia's bracelet. It was heavy and studded with sapphires. How did it get into my reticule? I had spent some time with Alicia last night, but I had no idea if it was before or after she lost the bracelet. If before, might it have slipped off her hand and into my bag? One would be forced to wonder though, what her hand was doing in my bag. Could the clasp have given way?

I fastened the bracelet, and gave the two ends a tiny pull, terrified of damaging this most expensive piece of jewelry. The clasp held. I bit my lip and gave the ends a stiff tug. Again it held together. Of course it did. It was a foolish idea anyway. Even assuming the bracelet fell off her wrist, there was the question of how it had fallen into my bag, which had a drawstring closure. Someone, *some thief*, and a very good one at that, had deliberately removed the bracelet from Alicia's wrist and, just as deliberately, placed it in my bag. But why?

Well, whatever the reason, I had to get this bracelet back to Alicia as soon as possible. It was only five o'clock. I still had time to pay her a call, give her the bracelet, along with my explanations, vague though they were, then return home to change for the evening.

Just as I'd made this decision, Bridget knocked, and entered my room. "My lady, Lord and Lady Harleigh have called for you."

Lovely. A visit from Graham and Delia. I wondered at the audacity of Graham showing his face here after our conversation last night and briefly considered saying I was out. It would be unkind to slight Delia, as she'd done nothing to offend me, but it would take every bit of the good manners my mother drummed into me, to sit through half an hour with him. To ensure this visit wouldn't develop into another argument about money, I gave Bridget instructions to bring Rose down to greet her aunt and uncle.

I swept into the drawing room, all false confidence. "Delia. Graham. How kind of you to call." Both rose on my entrance, and I stepped to Delia's side. She was dressed for town in a tailored walking suit in a deep burgundy, with a leghorn style hat, sporting silk flowers of the same hue. She gave me an affectionate peck on the cheek.

"I didn't realize you'd come to town with Graham," I remarked, as we all seated ourselves. Delia and I shared the sofa, with Graham opposite in a chair. It was a little late for tea, and since I didn't know what they were about, I decided to bide my time for now.

"Oh, I only arrived today for a brief visit to my mother, just a few days, then I'll return. She has a charity event on Thursday, at the Savoy Hotel, so I decided to come and lend my support. Will you be attending?"

Hmm. Apparently we were going to pretend all was well between us. Perhaps Delia didn't know about Graham's lawsuit. That actually made a certain sense. If he won, he wouldn't have to share. I filed that possibility away for later consideration. "I shall check our schedule," I said. "If we're available, we shall certainly attend."

"We?" She looked surprised. "Oh, that's right. Graham tells me your aunt and sister are with you at present."

"Yes, my mother wanted Lily to experience a London Season, and our aunt Henrietta accompanied her. It's been lovely having them with me."

"And it helps to make your situation here more acceptable, now that you're not living alone."

I gave her a tight smile.

"And how is Rose?"

"She is very well, but you may see for yourself in a moment. I've asked to have her brought down to greet you."

Delia's face took on a wistful expression. One would think she hadn't seen Rose for years. "We miss her so, her cousins and I. I wondered if you might like me to take her back to the country when I leave. With Parliament in session, Graham is staying in town. I'd so enjoy her company in his absence. I'm sure she found the city exciting at first, but by now she might be longing for home."

I knew Delia meant well—at least I gave her the benefit of doubt—but the comment stung. "This is Rose's home now," I replied.

"Yes," Graham added, "but you must be so occupied with your sister's social activities that there can't be much time for your daughter."

I did not give Graham the benefit of doubt. How dare he imply I'd been neglecting my daughter? But as I drew breath to speak, Delia took him to task.

"Graham, it's so obvious you have only sons. Rose is likely reveling in the attention of her two aunts and fascinated with all the dressing up. I'm certain she's having a lovely time." She turned her sympathetic gaze back to me. "But the Season is so hectic, it might be best for Rose to return to her routine. She so enjoyed taking lessons with the boys. And to be honest, the air in town is not altogether healthful for a child's young lungs."

Rose entered the room at that moment, escorted by her nanny. I had a little time to consider Delia's suggestion as Rose skipped straight to her aunt, regaling her with the wonders of shopping. "We had such a good time, Aunt Delia!"

I suspected Delia was trying to manipulate me somehow, though for what purpose I had no idea.

"Then we went to the drapers, and I picked out my own fabric."

Unless this was a first step in luring me back to the old pile. But manipulation or not, I had to admit her words rang true.

"It's embroidered with horses, and riders, and hounds."

Perhaps it was wrong to interrupt her studies for the whole spring, and thanks to Graham, I couldn't afford to hire a governess for her just now. Her attention span might extend to another week, but soon she'd become restless. And while we took a daily walk together, Delia was right: no one would call the London air fresh or invigorating.

"Then we went to Fortnum's, where they have the prettiest tea cakes."

Oh, dear. Delia's face reflected her amusement of Rose's account—hardly the typical activities of a seven-year-old. Was I a terrible mother?

I found myself twisting the ribbon on the front of my blouse and forced my fingers to drop it. "Rose," I said, "your aunt Delia suggested you might want to join her when she returns to Harleigh in a few days. Would you like that?"

I fought the urge to cry at the way my little girl's face lit up. "I'll be able to ride Pierre," she squealed.

Damn! Replaced by a pony. I consoled myself with the fact that she didn't mention her cousins either. At her age, perhaps no human could compete with a pony. After some consultation,

I agreed it might be beneficial for Rose to return with Delia at the end of the week. She wouldn't be so far away, I reminded myself. Harleigh was near Guildford, just a short train ride away. I could travel there whenever I needed to see her. And it wouldn't be forever either. As soon as the Season ended, I'd bring Rose back home, and if Graham and I were still battling over my bank account, perhaps I'd ask Aunt Hetty to pay for a governess.

I gave in at that point and rang for Mrs. Thompson to bring tea.

"Yes, my lady. And Mr. Kendrick has just arrived to call on Miss Lily. As this room was occupied, I put him in your library while I came to check with you."

My library? I suppose I couldn't fault Mrs. Thompson for her actions as I had no spare rooms for visitors to wait. But the library was my private space and Kendrick was little more than a stranger. "I'm sure Miss Lily will be happy to come down. If you'll let her know she has a caller, then see to the tea. I'll fetch Mr. Kendrick myself."

I excused myself from Graham and Delia and headed to the library, pausing at the doorway when I caught sight of Kendrick at my desk. In the palm of his hand he held one of my prized possessions, a crystal wave that seemed almost to be in motion. A tiny inkwell, in the shape of a shell, rested at the base of the wave, empty as I thought the piece too beautiful and valuable to stain with ink, and far too small to bother filling. He gazed at it with the eye of a connoisseur. Or maybe a thief. I felt a tingle of suspicion.

"My father found that in Paris when he last visited," I said, stepping into the room.

His head snapped around in surprise. A smile transformed his expression to one of pure delight. "The workmanship is amazing. Is it Baccarat?"

I nodded, removing the inkwell from his grip and returning

it to the desk. I know he'd been left here to his own devices, but it bothered me to see him handling my things. After all, there was a thief about. "You have a good eye."

"I appreciate objects such as this, both useful and lovely to gaze upon." He turned his own gaze from the inkwell to me, his eyes still glowing with pleasure. "If one must make inkwells for a living, why not make them works of art?"

"I suspect the craftsman who made this saw himself as making a work of art in the form of an inkwell."

His smile did not quite ease my suspicions. "Did you happen to attend the Chesterton musicale earlier this week?" Heavens, did I really ask him that?

"I did, or rather I put in an appearance. Unfortunately I couldn't stay for the entertainment. I understand the Chesterton girls were to sing. Why do you ask?"

Why? Because the man had handled something valuable of mine should I assume him to be a thief? What was wrong with me? Still, I was burning to know if he'd also been at the Haverhill reception but could think of no way to ask without looking ridiculous.

The stolen bracelet upstairs was making me overly suspicious. Kendrick's fortune gave him no reason to resort to theft. I gave him a smile. "I simply wondered if your taste in music matched your taste in art."

Taking his arm, I guided him toward the door. "I'm afraid you must endure a family gathering if you wish to see Lily. Lord and Lady Harleigh have paid me a visit and we are just about to have tea. Lily should be down momentarily."

I led Kendrick to the drawing room. Amid introductions, Lily arrived, followed by Jenny with the tea service. The two young people seated themselves at one end of the sofa and fell into private conversation, while I poured tea and made small talk with Graham and Delia. This left Rose at a loose end.

Never a shy child, she stepped right over to Lily and Kendrick and insinuated herself into their conversation by whispering something into his ear.

Kendrick responded with an exaggerated expression of shock. "Are you seriously considering leaving town already? Why, you've only just arrived."

Rose shrugged. "I like the country."

"But what have you for comparison? Tell me, what sights have you seen in London? The Tower perhaps, or Madame Tussaud's?"

"Gore and horror stories," Delia said, brushing the suggestion aside with a flick of her fingers. "Hardly of interest to a young girl."

I hid my smile behind my cup, noting the growing interest in Rose's eyes. Had Delia forgotten she'd spent the last year with her two male cousins? Rose had as much fascination with gore and horror as the boys.

"Then there's the Crown Jewels," Kendrick added suggestively.

"Remember how you miss Pierre, dear."

I gaped at the two adults. Were they fighting over my daughter?

"I do miss Pierre," Rose confided to Kendrick. "He's my pony."

"Ah, then the wonders of London can't compete." He raised his hands in a gesture of surrender. "I understand."

Our guests lingered another three-quarters of an hour. By that time it was too late to pay a call on Alicia. In fact, Bridget barely had time to get me dressed for dinner, after which we left, with Fiona, to attend the musicale.

The hostess had coaxed a talented soprano to perform for us, but the music flowed by without my notice—as did much of the conversation. With my mind on returning Alicia's bracelet, I became as dull as the beige-painted walls. Even Fiona stopped trying to engage my interest.

I was tempted more than once to confide in her and enlist her aid in my mission. But temptation battled with pride, and pride was the victor. I would not use my friend as a buffer or a crutch. I'd faced Alicia twice now and survived. In fact, our last interaction had been quite cordial. I could do this myself.

As we drove home, I allowed Fiona to berate me for my lack of attention all evening. Since I had no ready excuse, I pulled myself from my fugue long enough to correct Lily when she referred to Mr. Kendrick as "Kenny," and rejoice with her about a proposed outing with Ainsworthy. He was to take her driving tomorrow. Lucky girl! I made a mental note to ensure Aunt Hetty would be home when he called, as she would need a chaperone, and I had to return that bracelet.

I had two choices in paying my call to Alicia. I could wait until early afternoon, the acceptable time for a morning call, hope she had no other callers, and if she did, I had to outlast them. The thought of doing so set my head pounding. The alternative would be to call on her at an unacceptable time, which was any time in the morning, and hope Alicia would make herself available to me.

I decided to take the second option and hedged my bet by sending a note in advance of my call. I told her I had information about her bracelet and asked if she would receive me this morning. The reply came just as I was ready to leave.

Please come at once.

Bridget attended me on the short walk to Alicia's home on Belgrave Square. I had the bracelet in the same reticule she'd found it in and held it clutched in my hand. Thankfully we arrived without incident. The butler led me to a sitting room near the back of the house and announced me. I was so anxious by this time, I didn't even wait to hear my name before walking around him and straight to Alicia. She stood and smiled a greeting.

"Thank you for seeing me, Alicia," I said. "I'm relieved to find you at home."

"Imagine my relief when I read your note. You said you had news of my bracelet?"

"I have more than news," I replied, pulling open the strings of my bag. "This is your bracelet I presume?" Alicia's eyes rounded as I produced it from the bag and held it out to her.

"How?" she breathed, gently pulling the bracelet from my hand.

"An excellent question,"

I spun around as I heard the voice behind me and found myself facing none other than Inspector Delaney. What on earth was he doing here? He wore the same rumpled brown suit and looked completely out of place in Alicia's feminine sitting room, filled with delicate pieces of furniture and an excess of fringe. He glared at me through lowered eyes. I wasn't sure if they held suspicion, but there was no doubting the recognition.

"Frances, this is Inspector Delaney from the Metropolitan Police. I called him to report the missing bracelet. He was here when your note arrived, so I asked him to stay." She turned to face Delaney. "Inspector, this is my friend, Frances Wynn, the Countess of Harleigh."

To my great relief, he didn't let on that we had already met. His bow was only slightly more than a nod. "My lady."

"Inspector." I needed a moment to recover, but as they both watched me, eager for an explanation, I had to proceed. Once we'd seated ourselves, I took a deep breath. "I agree with the inspector. How I came to be in possession of your bracelet is an excellent question, but I've been unable to do more than speculate on the answer."

"I was under the impression the bracelet was stolen." His voice held a note of accusation.

"Indeed, that was the impression we were all under, Inspector," Alicia replied. "But I don't imagine Lady Harleigh stole it."

He raised a brow. "Yet it was in her possession."

"And I do believe it was stolen," I added. They both turned to me in surprise. Delaney recovered first.

"Are you admitting to the theft, Lady Harleigh?"

I scowled at the man. "Of course not." I explained how Bridget had found the bracelet in my reticule, and my surprise when she showed it to me the day before.

"I had no chance to return it to you yesterday or I certainly would have done so. It distracted me all evening, and in my ponderings, I've come to the conclusion that it was no accident." I turned toward Alicia. "The clasp on the bracelet is sturdy, and in perfect condition. It's inconceivable to think it fell off your wrist and into my bag, which was drawn closed. Somebody must have opened the clasp and removed it from your arm. A practiced thief—someone who just appeared to be brushing against you as he passed by. After that"—I gave them both a helpless shrug—"the picture is not as clear. Perhaps he realized you discovered the bracelet was missing and disposed of it in the nearest hiding place."

"But in your bag? How could someone open your bag without your knowing?"

"I was part of several groups that evening. One does get jostled from time to time. The bag was also lying on the table at supper, and our table was quite crowded. Again, if the thief was skilled, it would be a small matter to hide the bracelet."

I turned back to Delaney. "So, Inspector, I do think the bracelet was stolen, and I think it was stolen by the same person responsible for the other recent thefts. Furthermore, it's my opinion the thief is a gentleman."

The inspector released a weary sigh. "What leads you to that conclusion, my lady?"

I could see he was losing patience with me. Understandable, I suppose. I was so shaken by seeing him again, I was really making a mess of this. I just couldn't escape the fact that this man considered me capable of murdering my husband. Thank goodness he seemed to have no intention of mentioning his suspicion.

I took a breath and collected my thoughts. "It's the way the crimes have been happening. The owner notices an expensive object missing the morning after an entertainment has taken place. More than one household has been affected, so that tends to rule out the servants."

Delaney raised a brow. "Don't hostesses bring in extra servants when they entertain?"

"If necessary, but from what I understand the Chestertons lost an heirloom necklace, taken from Mrs. Chesterton's dressing table, during a musicale. They wouldn't have had to bring in any extra servants for such a small entertainment. And the Haverhills wouldn't need to hire extra hands for any event, and they were also victims of the thief after their reception. That was just about a week before the Chesterton event."

Alicia nodded as if she were following my logic. "We did bring in outside help, but you are right, it isn't always necessary. However, to say the thief is a gentleman means it could be any one of a hundred or more gentlemen in London."

"Wouldn't each of the hostesses have prepared a guest list?" the inspector asked.

"Of course, but everyone invites the same people to every affair. That would hardly reduce the possibilities."

"But we can reduce the possibilities because the thief must have been close to each of you at Mrs. Stoke-Whitney's ball."

Alicia and I glanced at each other. "I suppose that might bring the number down, if each of us can remember whom we were near during the course of the evening," I said.

"Not all evening," Alicia said, brightening. "At least an hour before supper, I was speaking to Lady Marsden, and she admired my bracelet. By supper it was gone. So I need to remember which gentlemen I was near between the hours of ten-thirty and perhaps midnight."

"Actually, I heard the bracelet was missing before the supper dance, perhaps around eleven-thirty, so I need to concentrate on those gentlemen I saw between then and the time I left, which was around two."

"Ahem."

We both turned to the inspector. "Yes," Alicia prompted. "Is there something we missed?"

His face held a pained expression as if he were suffering from a headache. "No, I wouldn't say you missed anything, but I am wondering why you both ruled out the ladies."

"The ladies?" Alicia shook her head. "I don't see this as something a lady would do. If the thief is a member of the aristocracy, then I would imagine he's just doing it for some type of thrill."

"Or to prove he can," I added. "Even if he's caught, he'd simply pass it off as a prank or a wager."

"And there's bound to be an old school chum who would back up his claim." Alicia let out a *tsk* and raised her eyes to heaven. "I find men will say anything for the sake of old school ties."

"Hmm," I agreed. "But if caught, a lady would find herself absolutely ruined. Nobody would stand by her. I can't imagine any lady of my acquaintance taking such a risk. And I do know most of the ladies who were present."

Delaney's brows came together in one bushy line as he gave us a look that reminded me he was the one in charge here. In our enthusiasm, we may have overstepped our bounds.

Alicia seemed to be thinking along the same lines. "Perhaps we should have some refreshment while we consider the possibilities." She crossed the room to the bell pull by the wall. A young footman entered immediately. At Alicia's request for tea he bowed out to do her bidding.

Once Alicia regained her seat, we both turned to the inspector, waiting for his pronouncement. After a few moments he satisfied us. "It's been my experience that if someone is desperate enough, man or woman, they will do whatever is necessary to achieve their end. In other words, let's not rule out the women just yet." He glanced at me in a way that told me his last comment was for my benefit. I was still a suspect. "We have no firm leads in the case of these robberies, so I'm not ready to exclude anyone at this time. And while you have offered one theory, I can think of two others."

"You have our attention," I prompted.

"The thief may not have been looking for a safe place to hide the bracelet, he may have wanted it to be found—in your possession." He turned an inquiring look my way. "Do you have any enemies, Lady Harleigh?"

I heard Alicia gasp, but I couldn't tear my gaze from Delaney's penetrating stare. Good Lord in Heaven! The man possessed an endless supply of shocking pronouncements. First, my husband's death might actually have been murder; now someone is trying to make me look like a criminal? My thoughts flew to Graham, but that was absurd. Fighting over money was one thing, but this went beyond the pale.

Delaney watched me, noting my hesitation. "No, Inspector. I may not be loved by all, but there's no one who would wish to see me branded a thief. You mentioned another theory?"

He turned his gaze from me to his notebook. I felt certain he didn't believe me, but at least he seemed willing to let this pass for now. If we must speak privately later, and I suspected we would, then so be it, but I was not willing to discuss my family matters in front of Alicia. He turned to a fresh page in the notebook and glanced back at us.

"I need to ponder that one a bit more," he said evasively. "For now, let's assume your theory is correct, Lady Harleigh. So if you ladies are ready, I'd like to prepare a list of everyone you can remember having encountered during the hours we discussed."

Over the next half hour Alicia and I racked our brains, trying to remember every exchange we had with the other guests that evening, and whether it happened during the relevant time. Inspector Delaney took notes, while devouring several delicate sandwiches, and three cups of tea. When we'd exhausted our memories, he cross-referenced Alicia's list with mine, and came up with ten names, of both men and women, who could have stolen the bracelet from Alicia, and later disposed of it in my bag.

While the footman removed the tea service, Delaney perused the list. "So we have Mr. Hazelton, Viscount Ainsworthy, Lady Marsden, the Earl of Harleigh, Lord and Lady Nash, Mr. Kendrick, Lady Grafton, Mr. Grayson, and Mr. Forester. Does that sound about right?"

It sounded absurd. Most of these people were my friends. I took the list from Delaney. "Well, George Hazelton's name should be removed. Wouldn't you agree, Alicia? I can't imagine him doing anything dishonest. And Lady Nash is my close friend." My eyes widened as I read further. "Goodness, all three of Lily's suitors are on this list. Ainsworthy, Kendrick, Grayson—all respectable young men."

"Lady Harleigh." Delaney's voice was weary. "You suspected a gentleman of this crime. You must have assumed he'd be respectable."

"That's true." And two of Lily's suitors did take supper with me that night. Both had the opportunity to slip the bracelet into my bag. Considering how quickly Delaney had accused me of the theft, I hesitated to mention it. But he should be informed. I provided that information and added, "I also happen to know Mr. Kendrick attended the Chesterton musicale."

Delaney made a note in his book.

"I'm sure it's just a coincidence," I said. "But I'm rather relieved I decided to have them investigated."

From the way their heads snapped in my direction, I could tell I'd surprised them. Even the footman gave me a curious glance before returning to his work. "Well, she is rather an heiress, you know," I said by way of defense. "I wanted to make sure they were courting her rather than her money."

"An excellent notion," said Alicia. "Whatever gave you the idea, and how on earth did you find an investigator?"

"My aunt brought to my attention that my father has used an inquiry agent, before entering into certain business transactions with gentlemen he didn't know well. Since I don't know these men, I asked my solicitor to find someone for the task." I turned to Inspector Delaney as another thought struck me. "I suppose it wouldn't be improper to share with you any information he turns up, Inspector, as you would be looking for a financial motive for this crime."

"Actually, Lady Harleigh, that won't be necessary." He paused. "Your solicitor hired me to do your investigation of those gentlemen. I wasn't aware you were the client."

"Really?" Good heavens, it seemed Inspector Delaney would be invading every aspect of my life. I squirmed in discomfort at the thought of employing the man who might be investigating me for murder. I should speak to Mr. Stone about hiring someone else for this assignment.

My expression must have urged Delaney to provide an explanation. "My wife is expecting our third child," he said with a shrug. "I take the odd job now and then, when we need a little extra."

"Well, I know you've had little time, but have you learned anything that would make you suspect one of them in this crime?"

"Nothing as yet, my lady, but as you said, I'm just getting started."

We decided nothing more could be done at this point, but a good start had been made. I was a little annoyed the inspector wouldn't let me vouch for the characters of George or Fiona, but that was hardly surprising considering what he thought of mine. However, I was still satisfied with our morning's work. The bracelet was back with its rightful owner, I was sure the inspector was on the trail of the thief, and he'd said nothing to Alicia about our previous meeting. It was half past noon as we made our way home under a heavy, gray sky. Bridget handed me a note.

"Mrs. Stoke-Whitney's footman asked me to give this to you, ma'am."

"A note from the footman?" I took the stiff paper from her and unfolded it as we walked.

> *Lady Harleigh, I have some information about one of the gentlemen on your list. Something no one else is likely to turn up. I assure you this is important to your investigation. Tomorrow is my free afternoon, so I can come to your home. It would be best if I go to your servants' entrance, so please let your housekeeper know if you wish to see me.*

It was signed *James Capshaw.* I glanced at Bridget. "Have you read this?"

Her eyes looked in every direction but mine. Finally she bobbed her head in the affirmative. "It wasn't sealed, my lady."

"I suppose he overheard my conversation with the inspector, and wants to profit from his knowledge, don't you think?"

"Well, you know yourself, ma'am, servants know a lot about their employers. Maybe he used to work for one of the gentlemen."

"That would be my guess as well. Perhaps I didn't need to hire an investigator after all. Odd though, that he didn't approach the inspector instead of me."

Bridget shrugged. "As you said, he probably wants payment for his information. Maybe he assumed you'd be a softer touch."

I nodded. That was very likely true. As we turned onto Chester Street, I caught sight of Mr. Grayson heading toward us. Bridget noticed him as well and fell a few steps behind. I smiled as he approached and removed his hat.

"Good afternoon, Mr. Grayson."

"And the same to you, Lady Harleigh. I stopped by to call on Miss Price, but I find she's away from home yet again." His voice held a note of irritation.

"Were you expected?"

"Well, no. I'd simply hoped to catch her at home."

Waiting breathlessly for you to call, I thought. I gave him a smile. "Well, she is bound to return home in any event. Perhaps you should call earlier next time."

"Perhaps I shall."

We said our good-byes and Bridget and I moved on. I wondered what the footman might know about someone like Grayson and recalled he had stopped by our table at supper. Was that when my bag fell to the floor? I was still pondering the possibilities, when we walked up my front steps, and were met at the door by Mrs. Thompson, who, though normally unflappable, looked completely—well—flapped.

"Whatever has happened, Mrs. Thompson?"

"An outrage, my lady, just an outrage! Someone broke into the house while you were gone."

"What? Was anyone hurt?" I nearly stumbled over the threshold. "How could someone break in in broad daylight?"

Mrs. Thompson took my wrap and hat as she told me the news. "Whoever it was, was gone before any of us knew what happened. Jenny took some linens up to the closet and noticed the mess when she passed by the door to your room."

"My room? Someone broke into my room?"

"Yes, ma'am."

I rushed up the stairs to see the damage, stopping as I flung open the door. "Oh, my goodness."

This was the result of an intruder? The room looked more like some force of nature had swept through, rather than a single person.

Chapter 10

"Bit of a mess here."

I threw Inspector Delaney a glare that, had he been looking, would have told him I didn't appreciate his sarcasm. Instead, he was surveying the shambles of my bedchamber. I hadn't allowed anyone to touch a thing until he'd arrived.

"I'd say that's something of an understatement, Inspector. A bit of a mess might be the gowns strewn across the room, or the shards of glass over there from the broken window. Perhaps even the contents of my dressing table emptied onto the floor might be considered a bit of a mess, or when every article of clothing has been pulled from the drawers of my dressing room, and dumped out here." My arms flailed as I pointed out each bit of destruction. I noticed my voice rising in both pitch and volume and took a deep breath. "But when all of this has happened in one room, a 'bit of a mess' doesn't begin to describe it."

"On the positive side, this does give some credence to your theory about the bracelet theft, in that he only intended to leave it with you temporarily."

I had to agree. In fact, that was why I'd sent a message to Inspector Delaney as soon as I'd seen the room. "I hope that means I'm now free from suspicion."

He snapped around to face me, brows raised in question.

"That was your second theory, wasn't it? I stole the bracelet?"

I watched his expression turn from surprise, to assessment, to amusement. My face grew hot. I didn't see anything amusing. Finally he gave me an ironic smile. "Let's just say, that's no longer a strong theory."

"I would hope not. Obviously the thief was here, searching for the bracelet." I raised my brows in question. "Or do you think I staged this scene for your benefit?"

Delaney shook his head as he looked around at the mess. "A possibility, I suppose, but I can't imagine you creating this much damage, no." He moved over to the broken window, stepping carefully over randomly discarded combs, gloves, and articles of clothing. The window opened out to a small balcony on the back side of the house, facing the garden. "Looks like a sturdy trellis out here. You might want to have that removed."

"I suppose that's how he came in," I said, watching him examine the door. "This is all very confusing. Why would he assume I'd still have the bracelet? If I hadn't been so busy yesterday, Bridget would have brought it to my attention sooner, and I would have returned it then. I had believed the thief was a gentleman, but this makes me wonder. Any gentleman would expect my maid to find the bracelet, realize it wasn't mine, and ask me about it."

Delaney was now looking over the balcony. "Perhaps he expected you to keep it. Despite the fact that several of you had learned the bracelet was stolen, it wasn't exactly bandied about the ballroom at the time, was it? Mrs. Stoke-Whitney kept that quiet."

"Yes, I suppose she did." I tried to follow his line of reasoning. "So when I found the bracelet in my reticule, I might not have known to whom it belonged, or how to return it. Even so, I would hardly leave it in my bedroom. It would be locked in my safe."

Delaney poked his head back through the door. "Did you check the safe?"

"But the bracelet isn't in the safe."

"We know that. But the thief doesn't."

Oh! I called for Bridget, gave her the key, and instructed her to check the contents of the safe, although I told myself it would be a remote possibility anything would be gone. When I turned back to the room, Delaney had left the balcony, and was shaking out one of my gowns.

I rolled my eyes from impatience. "I employ servants who can do that."

He didn't stop, or even look up. Instead he seemed to be fluffing up some trim on the neckline of the dress. "No need to worry, Lady Harleigh, I'm not trying to replace your lady's maid."

Then it hit me. "I see, something belonging to the thief might have caught on one of the gowns—a ring, or button, or something else that might identify him."

"Only a possibility, but it would be foolish to dismiss it."

I agreed, and reached for a gown myself, giving it a good shake. "I feel the same about the safe, you know. Breaking in here to search for the bracelet is one thing, but proceeding through the rest of the house in the hope of finding a safe would be far too risky."

Nothing had fallen from the gown so I draped it over a chair and moved on to the next one. "Surely he wouldn't be that desperate, would he? He's been rather successful thus far. Why not give this item up as lost and go on to steal something else?"

Delaney answered with a grunt, or maybe it was a growl. In any event it was no language I was familiar with. "Well?" I prompted.

He turned with a sigh and gave me a look I hadn't seen in quite some time. It was Reggie's look, and he used it whenever I asked too many questions. It was usually followed by Reggie rising from his seat and leaving the room. How unfortunate for the inspector that he couldn't leave. I returned The Look with my brightest smile. "Is it so difficult to discuss this with me, Inspector? I told you all about my theories this morning. What are yours?"

"Too many to mention, ma'am. Is he desperate enough to search your home? I don't know. He broke in here in the first place. That seems desperate to me. I can't say until I understand his motive."

"Wouldn't it be money?"

"Ah, but you believe the thief is a gentleman."

I shrugged. "Gentlemen need money, too."

Delaney let a short blast of breath escape his pursed lips. He turned toward me and placed a hand on his hip, a gown still clutched in his fist. A sense of dread rushed through me. Had I done something wrong?

"I believe you were rather coy with me this morning," he said. "When I asked if you had any enemies. Is there something I should know?"

He righted the chair to the dressing table and placed it in front of me. I took a deep breath and seated myself. Delaney stood before me, his hands clasped.

"Perhaps," I said. "But I don't see how it could have anything to do with this crime." I looked up to meet his eyes. "My late husband's brother has been making my life difficult lately. My father gifted me with some funds that were meant to be for my sole use, but the earl claims the money belongs to the family. He's filed a suit in court, so the account has been frozen."

His brows rose in question. "So you have no money?"

I let out a groan as I imagined his mind moving back to theory number two, and my guilt. "Actually, my mother has recently provided me with some funds, so I expect to remain solvent until our disagreement is resolved. Even if that were not the case, the account was frozen only a few days ago, so I had no motive for the first two thefts."

I paused, wondering if I needed to provide an alibi, then realized I had one. "I wasn't even in town until a week ago, so I couldn't have robbed the Haverhills."

"But this latest crime was different. It's quite possible the bracelet wasn't stolen by the original thief."

That took the wind out of my sails. "How was it different?"

He spread his hands wide as if the answer were obvious. "It was unsuccessful. The thief didn't get caught, but neither does he have the bracelet. Either the same criminal made a mistake, or someone else had the brilliant idea of copying him."

"What is this, Inspector? Some cat-and-mouse game? Are we back to the theory that I am the guilty party?"

"No, my lady. Not you. But what of the earl? Is it impossible to think he might wish to ruin your reputation, to improve his chance of winning his lawsuit?"

Graham? *Impossible* was the perfect word. "No," I said. "I cannot believe that of him. Nor can I believe he dislikes me to such an extent. He may want what is mine, but he could never want to hurt me in such a way."

Delaney did not appear convinced. His eyes held a touch of pity as if I were fooling myself. I found that sentiment rather annoying. "You should trust my judgment on this point, Inspector. Even if I considered the earl capable of plotting such a scheme against me, the idea of causing a scandal would stop him. I am still a member of the Wynn family. Any scandal he brings down on me, he brings down on his own head."

"The reward might be worth the risk," he said, his voice calm and sure.

I gave him a withering look. "If the reward is my bank account, it is not that great, I assure you. And if Graham wanted me to be found with the bracelet, why break in here to get it back?"

The detective's lips compressed into a thin line, as he considered my words. His eyes seemed rather kindly as he gazed back at me.

He gave me a quick nod. "You could be right."

I'm not sure why, but I was overwhelmed with relief at his pathetic vote of confidence.

"I'm sure you're curious," he began casually, "as to what sparked the sudden interest in your husband's death."

The change of subject threw me off balance. "If I remember correctly, you said you didn't know."

"A slight prevarication. In truth, I hadn't the authority to share that information with you. I was there only to ask my questions and of course observe your reaction."

I leaned forward in anticipation. "I assume my reaction must have been appropriate because I sense you are about to share that information with me now."

Delaney gave me a grim smile. "It isn't your reaction, but the events that are happening now, that have me wondering if you are not as much a victim as your husband."

I gasped. "Then Reggie really was murdered?"

"Forgive me, ma'am." He held up a hand to calm me. "We don't know that yet." Turning aside, he ran a hand through his hair, leaving a few strands standing straight up. When he faced me again, it seemed he'd made a decision.

"Let me start at the beginning. Police often receive anonymous letters. People may have information about a crime, you see. But they don't want to involve themselves." He raised a fuzzy brow. "Do you follow me?"

I nodded. "I suppose I can understand that."

"The Guildford police received one just this week about the late earl. The writer implied your husband did not die by natural causes, and that they suspected you as the murderess."

There was a sudden ringing in my ears as the blood rushed to my head. I barely heard Delaney say, "Might your brother-in-law have sent that letter?" Foolishly I tried to stand. I must have looked a little wobbly, because Delaney reached out and caught me just as my knees gave way and I pitched toward the floor.

I don't think I actually fainted since I could see and hear everything that was happening. That is, I could hear anything louder than the high-pitched ringing inside my head. Delaney called for assistance, then hoisted me in his arms, and carried me over to the bed. By this time the room had come back into focus, and I saw his intent. "Not on the gowns," I cried, but just then Bridget came rushing into the room, sweeping them aside a moment before Delaney set me down.

Aunt Hetty peeked through the doorway. "What on earth is going on here?"

"The countess was overcome, but she's recovered now," Delaney responded.

"Yes," I said, rolling into an upright position. "Just let me catch my breath, Aunt Hetty." Bridget was staring into my face as she helped me swing my legs over the side of the bed. "Perhaps a cup of tea, my lady?"

"Excellent idea, Bridget." Then I remembered her earlier task and caught her arm before she moved away. "Did you check the safe?"

"Oh, yes." She pulled the key from her pocket and handed it to me. "Everything was as it should be."

As Bridget left for the tea, Hetty stepped over and took my hand. "If you're feeling better now, let's move you over to the chair by the table. It will be much easier for you to have your tea."

I looked up at Delaney who was standing some distance from the bed, looking a bit shame-faced. "I apologize for shocking you, my lady. Clumsy of me."

"What's happened to this room?" Hetty helped me to the

chair and turned to glare at Delaney. "And why are you back here?"

"I sent for him," I said, and gave Hetty the few details I knew about the break-in. She'd been visiting with Mr. Hazelton for the past hour, and Lily was out riding with Ainsworthy.

"Alone? You were supposed to be with her. Why do you think I made sure you'd be here when he called?"

"She's not alone," Hetty explained with exaggerated patience. "I sent Jenny with her. The viscount was waiting with his carriage when Lily and I returned from the library. We were a little late, and it looked as though his horses were eager to be off. Jenny had just opened the door for us, so I sent her on with Lily, while I took our books inside. Then I went next door to see Hazelton." She placed her fisted hands on her hips and leaned over me. "Now stop trying to distract me and tell me why you fainted."

Oh, yes, that. "Inspector Delaney has just informed me why they are looking into Reggie's death again. Someone wrote to the police, implying I may have murdered him."

"A poisoned pen letter." Her voice held a hefty amount of venom.

"We were just discussing that possibility." I turned to Delaney, who appeared to be trying to hide a smile. "What do you do when you receive such a letter?"

"Just what we have done, attempt to determine its veracity. As I told you on my last visit, the doctor won't call for an autopsy without your permission. Unless the Guildford police have enough evidence to request an autopsy through the court, there's little more they can do. It takes more than one anonymous letter to exhume the body of an earl. More important to me now, is who wrote that letter."

"And you suspect my brother-in-law?"

Hetty gasped.

"Someone is trying very hard to make you look guilty of something, whether it be jewel theft or murder."

"I thought the fact of the break-in ruled out the chance that someone wanted me to be found with the bracelet."

Delaney shrugged. "You ruled it out. I didn't. Think of it. The thief breaks in here and makes a mess. You call me and in my search, I find the bracelet. You still look guilty."

I considered his words while Bridget brought in the tea service. "That seems like a great deal of trouble to go through."

"But effective, if you hadn't already returned the bracelet."

Delaney declined the offer of tea, and returned to shaking out my gowns, this time with Hetty's help. Although with all the questions she asked she was more of a hindrance. Over the next twenty minutes, I gave her the details about the stolen bracelet, and advised her that the inspector was also the inquiry agent who would be looking into the background of Lily's young men.

"Goodness," she said, staring at Delaney. "Are you the only member of the Metropolitan Police?"

"Please don't burden Lily with any of this, Aunt Hetty. I suppose we should tell her about the break-in, but I don't want word getting around about the bracelet being here."

"Is she aware you're investigating her suitors?" Delaney asked.

I chewed on my lip. "Yes, but she doesn't know you'll be investigating them in relation to the thefts. And that reminds me, Inspector, a footman in Mrs. Stoke-Whitney's employ claims to have information about one of the gentlemen on our list. He delivered a note through my maid, saying he'd like to meet with me tomorrow."

I pulled the note from my reticule and handed it over to him. His brow furrowed as he read it. "I'd like to be here when you meet him."

I frowned, disliking the idea. "He may not be as forthcoming if you're here. In fact I'm quite sure he won't be, else he would have spoken to you about it while you were at the Stoke-Whitney home this morning."

"He probably chose to speak to you, Frances, because he expects some type of payment," Hetty said, still shaking gowns.

"And I'll gladly pay for any pertinent information he may be able to provide."

"Consider also, Lady Harleigh, he may have information he may *not* want you to know. Perhaps he wants this investigation stopped and is coming here with the intention of threatening or harming you."

Well! I hadn't considered that.

"With all that's happened to you lately, you would be foolish to put your trust in this footman. You'd be taking a dangerous risk in meeting him alone."

"I appreciate your caution, Inspector, but from a practical view, can you afford to give up an entire afternoon waiting for him? He doesn't say at what time he'll call. I'll have my aunt with me, and my staff nearby. What harm could come to me? And I promise to share with you anything he tells me. Will that set your mind at ease?"

"With all due respect to you, ma'am"—he nodded at Hetty—"a footman is usually tall and strong. You would not provide adequate protection. And while I can't forfeit an entire afternoon, I can post a constable here for that time. In fact, I was planning to post one on the street anyway because of the burglary."

I was already shaking my head, but Aunt Hetty spoke up before I had a chance to respond.

"George Hazelton," she said. "He can give up an afternoon, and I'm sure he'd be happy to do so. He can be here as a deterrent, should the footman pose a problem, but he should not keep the man from speaking freely."

My protest of this plan went unheeded, while Delaney and Hetty discussed it, as if I weren't even there. Poor Mr. Hazelton was about to be dragged into yet another of my problems.

Chapter 11

~

"Ah, here you are." I was surprised to see my sister ensconced in the window seat of the small library I used as an office. A few weak rays of morning sun cast a glow on Lily's blond head, making her seem somewhat ethereal, but the glow in her eyes, and her smile, had been there for the past two days. I wondered if she was simply enjoying herself, or if young love was blooming. Was that possible in so few days?

Lily's pencil was sweeping across her sketch pad. "Have you been drawing all morning?" I asked.

"No, actually, I just finished a letter to one of my friends back home, telling her how wonderful you've been to me and how much fun I'm having." She looked up long enough to send a beaming smile my way.

Now that I was sitting at my desk, I did indeed see the evidence of Lily's work here. I opened a drawer in search of something I could use to wipe up a small puddle of ink from the blotter before I managed to run my sleeve through it. "That's lovely, dearest. I'm happy to see you enjoying yourself." I settled on a sheet of paper, folded it in half, and pressed it into the puddle.

"In fact," she continued, "while I was writing to her, I had a wonderful idea." Lily scrambled from the window seat and pulled up a chair to the opposite side of the desk. "Until Father's fortunes turn for the better, why don't you make your own fortune, bringing New York girls out in London society?"

This was a wonderful idea? "Are you suggesting I become some sort of matchmaker?"

"Of course not. Just sponsor other young ladies like me. Look how well you've done so far. Already, three gentlemen are courting me, you're making sure they're eligible, and I'm sure one of them will propose soon."

"You sound very confident."

Lily blushed. "Not exactly confident, but I'm sure they aren't courting me because they lack anything better to do. It shouldn't be long before one of them asks me to marry him. So I hope your investigator is working hard."

I hated to tell her my investigator was working on another case altogether. Of course there was my meeting today. "I might receive some information this afternoon in fact. But I still advise you not to be in such a hurry. Don't say yes to any proposal of marriage unless you love the man."

Lily pulled a face. "They're all very nice men."

"But you don't feel more for one than the others?" She hesitated, and I reached across the desk to squeeze her hand. "Give it time, Lily. Who took you riding yesterday?"

"Viscount Ainsworthy. We drove through Hyde Park in his carriage." She flipped through her sketchbook. "I did a sketch of him yesterday." She turned the drawing toward me, then flipped forward another page. "I did this one of Mr. Kendrick just now, but I'll have to see him again to make sure I've got him right."

I turned back to the first sketch. "You did this while in a moving carriage?"

"Well, no. We stopped, and walked a bit, and—"

"Found a secluded spot somewhere in the park?"

Lily put on an innocent face. "It wasn't very secluded."

"Lily, you must take better care of your reputation. Thank goodness Aunt Hetty is your chaperone today. Jenny must have felt it wasn't her place to advise you."

"Aunt Hetty is coming with me today? How am I to get to know these gentlemen with her at my side?"

"By talking with them. And with Aunt Hetty drawing them out, you're likely to learn more, not less."

"I'd much rather Jenny chaperone me."

I held up my hand to stop her. "You cannot coax me out of this decision. I have an appointment this afternoon, and Jenny has work to do. It isn't as though I have a surplus of servants in this house. When Jenny spends two or three hours with you, someone else has to do her work. So it's Aunt Hetty, or you stay home."

"Well, if you put it that way, I suppose it's Aunt Hetty."

I patted her cheek. "And no pouting."

"I'm not pouting. And I like Aunt Hetty, really. She's just so, so—"

"American?" I supplied.

"Oh, worse than that."

I gasped theatrically. "Worse than American?"

Lily pinned me with a glare. "You must admit she's more outspoken than even most Americans."

"When a woman reaches a certain age, she's earned the right to speak her mind. Many British ladies of my acquaintance behave in the same manner. As I said, she'll draw the gentleman out. You'll enjoy it, you'll see. Who is taking you out today?"

"Mr. Kendrick. He is a little quiet so you may be right. Aunt Hetty might be just the thing."

As I recalled, Mr. Kendrick was also very proper, so Aunt Hetty might be a little too much for him, but he should know in advance the family he might be marrying into.

Lily left to change her gown for the outing, and I took up the business that brought me to my office in the first place. Mr. Hazelton would arrive shortly and I wanted to be ready. I hadn't told him about the footman calling. I'd just sent a note asking if he were free this afternoon to lend his assistance. Now, as I posted a few receipts to my account book, I realized I was nervous about spending this time with him. I'd had nothing but kindness from him since we'd met up again in London, but still he made me anxious. Probably because he knows my secrets, or *secret* actually. There is just the one, large though it may be.

It was quite an ironic twist of fate. As much as I'd give to forget that moment in my life, I seemed constantly to be thrown together with the two people who'd shared it with me.

I was saved from further contemplation by Mrs. Thompson, who informed me Mr. Hazelton had arrived, and she'd put him in the drawing room. He was studying a framed photograph of Rose when I walked in. "Believe it or not, Graham made that photograph," I said.

He gave me a smile as I stepped beside him and took the picture, admiring my darling little girl. "It was about three years ago. We were all at Harleigh Manor, and Graham had one of Mr. Eastman's cameras. He'd only recently learned how to use it and was photographing anything that stood still. In fact, it was rather amazing one didn't have to stand still longer." I turned to look up at George. "Do you remember what it used to be like? Have you been photographed before?"

He laughed. "Yes, and I do remember. My school cricket team, if you can imagine that. All those young boys forced to remain still while the image developed."

"And yet this image of Rose was formed between the blinks of her eyes."

"It's rather breathtaking when you consider all the new inventions that have happened just in our lifetimes."

I set the picture down and led him over to a seat on the sofa.

"And here we are, standing on the brink of a new century. Can you imagine what's ahead?"

George shook his head. "Some things, yes, but I expect there will be many surprises. In fact, I'm surprised by your interest in mechanization and invention."

"Oh, come now. Americans are always interested in the next idea, the next invention. I'm surprised by your surprise."

"I see your point," he conceded with a grin. "I must try to get to know you better, in order to avoid further surprises."

And as quickly as that, our easy camaraderie vanished. Is he flirting with me, or is this just his friendly nature? I couldn't tell. My mind was scrambling for a new subject when Mrs. Thompson tapped on the door.

"Mr. Kendrick has called for you, my lady."

"Me? I'm sure there's some mistake. He's here to take my sister and aunt to the park."

"I'll be sure to let them know he's arrived, but he specifically asked to see you." She paused. "I believe he has something to show you."

I gave Mrs. Thompson a nod. "Please show him in."

George and I exchanged a look while the housekeeper backed out and was replaced by a smiling Mr. Kendrick. As we bid one another good day, I couldn't help noticing the basket he carried. I first assumed it was a picnic luncheon. Then it moved.

"Mr. Kendrick, what on earth is in your basket?"

"Just a small token for Lady Rose." He pulled aside the cloth, tucked into the basket, and a small, furry head popped out.

"A kitten!" In fact it was the sweetest, most lovely kitten I'd ever seen. White with patches of black, or perhaps the reverse, but whatever its color, it climbed into my arms when I reached for it, then snuggled into my neck.

"Oh, heavens," I said, cradling the dear little thing. "You brought this for Rose?"

"It seemed wise to make sure she met with your approval first."

George's lips tightened as he turned toward the other man. "I assume you have your answer."

"Of course I approve." The little creature was now purring against my ear. "Rose will be delighted. Whatever gave you the idea?"

Kendrick wore a gratified expression, but before he could answer, Lily and Hetty strolled into the room. "Someone has an idea?" Lily's eyes rounded. "Frances, what is that wrapped around your neck?"

The kitten had indeed become a bit too clingy. George peeled her gently away from my throat and handed her into Lily's willing arms.

"I thought Lady Rose might enjoy life in town better if she had the company of a pet," Kendrick said, giving the kitten a little scratch. "She seems to have a fondness for animals."

"How thoughtful." Lily gave him a smile. "Shall we take her up to Rose before we leave?"

"Yes, please do. You don't mind going with them do you, Aunt Hetty?" I was fairly certain she did mind, but I needed the room to ourselves, so I could provide some explanation to George before the footman showed up.

"Oh, what fun," Hetty muttered, ushering the young people out of the room.

"Thank you again, Mr. Kendrick, for the lovely gift," I said as they left. I was still smiling when I turned back to George. "What a good-natured young man."

"Exactly what he wants you to think."

My smile faded as we returned to our seats on the sofa. "Do you mean you don't like him?"

"I mean I recognize the gambit. You are acting as Lily's guardian. If he makes you happy, you may encourage his suit."

I tutted. "How cynical of you. Are you speaking from experience?"

George struggled to keep from smiling. "I've taken the occasional calculated risk."

"How was this a risk?"

"You may not have liked cats."

He didn't attempt to hide his smile at this, and I grinned right back. "You can be assured he won't win my favor that easily." I used those words to remind myself that Kendrick was on the list of suspects. Of course, so was George. How confusing.

"Now, I suppose you're wondering why I asked you to call."

"I'm prepared for any duties you see fit to lay before me."

"Oh, excellent! I almost wish I had some dangerous feat to test that claim, but the truth is, I'm simply in need of your presence this afternoon."

His brows rose. "I had no idea my presence was so desirable."

I was quite sure he had some idea, but I chose to ignore the comment. "I'm expecting another caller, a young man, employed as a footman with the Stoke-Whitneys. He proposed this meeting as he wants to impart some information about one of Lily's suitors. The police inspector didn't consider it wise for me to meet with him alone and—what's wrong?"

George was gaping at me as if I were speaking in a foreign language. "However did you meet a footman from the Stoke-Whitney household? And why are you being advised by the police?"

"Right. Clearly, I need to bring you up to date." I started to explain how I met the footman, then realized I needed to back up to the stolen bracelet, in order to explain my meeting with Alicia and Delaney, and that I'd mentioned investigating Lily's suitors at that meeting. Showing him the note I received from the footman, I explained about the break-in, and concluded with Delaney's hesitation about my meeting the man alone.

I couldn't quite read George's expression as I imparted all of this. He was paying rapt attention, his brows lowered, with two lines puckering up between them. He might have felt concern, horror, disbelief, or some combination of all three. "Please, say something," I finally urged.

He pursed his lips and blew out a breath. "I wasn't sure you'd finished," he said.

"Isn't that enough?"

"Beyond enough! Why didn't you call on me sooner? This Delaney chap is right. You might well be in danger."

Ah, concern it is. Well, perhaps a touch of horror and disbelief too, but at least concern was uppermost. "Well, I didn't actually recognize any danger until Delaney brought it to my attention." I gave him a helpless shrug. "I appreciate your willingness to help, but what would I have asked you to do? Stand guard at my house? I had no idea anyone would be breaking in."

I had to increase the volume on my last few words as George, in an agitated state, rose to his feet and strode across the room. I found myself speaking to his back. What on earth?

"George?"

He turned, and ambled back toward me, his brow still furrowed in thought. "Who knew you were investigating your sister's suitors? Something, by the way, with which I could have helped you."

"You could? How? Do you even know which gentlemen they are?"

He swept a casual hand through the air as if that point were immaterial. "There are a dozen or so popular clubs in London, and most gentlemen belong to two or three. I'm sure I have at least one club in common with any gentleman in town." He lifted his shoulders in a shrug. "You strike up a conversation, ask a few innocent questions over a drink or two and"—he snapped his fingers—"you can find out almost anything."

Hmm, as easy as that, is it? "Well, I'll be sure to keep your investigative skills in mind the next time I need that service."

That surprised a smile out of him. "You think there will be more?"

"Lily's just been launched into society and she is considered an heiress."

"Considered?"

Heavens, the man missed nothing.

"My father has had a bit of a financial setback, but Lily's dowry is still intact, so yes, this might be just the beginning. Besides"—I smiled at the thought—"she's urging me to sponsor other young ladies from New York, so I may be making a habit of this."

"It seems like a rather dangerous occupation to me."

"You think one of Lily's gentlemen might be involved in the theft? I've been wondering about that myself." I shook my head. "That's right. You asked me who they were."

"And who was aware you were investigating them?"

"No one who could have informed them. The gentlemen were Viscount Ainsworthy, Daniel Grayson, and Leo Kendrick. Only my aunt, Lily, my solicitor, and Delaney knew about the investigation." I paused as I realized this wasn't exactly correct. "Well, Alicia and her footman found out when I spoke of it yesterday. But that was after the bracelet was stolen, and probably while my house was being ransacked, so I don't see how they could have had anything to do with it."

"Has your sister seen any of these men alone? Is it possible she told one of them?"

"Yes, she has, but I don't think she would risk offending them by telling them I hired a private inquiry agent to spy on them."

George's brows rose as he pressed the matter. "But she might have let it slip?"

Here I hesitated. "I have to concede it's possible, but I doubt it. Where are you going with this?"

"Whoever did this must have had some grudge against you by the evening of the ball, or why plant the bracelet on you?"

"Goodness, George," I sighed. "Now you sound like Delaney. *Why you, Countess? Why did the thief choose you?* Well, I must ask why *not* me? Honestly, isn't it possible my reticule just happened to be nearby, when the thief needed to hide his stolen goods?"

George held out a hand to placate me, which had the effect of infuriating me instead, especially while he stood, looming over me. "No, George, I'm willing to concede the thief could be one of Lily's suitors, although I find that rather far-fetched. I'll even go so far as to admit they each had access to my reticule at supper. But the theory that one of them stole the bracelet, then placed it in my bag for the sole purpose of making me look guilty, is beyond credulity. If one of them is interested in Lily, why instigate a scandal in her family? Why have her sister branded a thief? And why come to my house looking for the bracelet the next day?" I ticked the questions off on my fingers. "It makes less sense than Delaney's theory about Graham."

All the while I was talking, I could see George working himself up for a big argument, until he heard that last point.

His brows shot up. "Graham? Your brother-in-law? What has he to do with this?"

I groaned. Why did I have to say that? I looked up at George.

His eyes narrowed.

"All right, Inspector Delaney agrees with you that I was a deliberate target, but he suspects Graham as the villain in this affair."

George's face softened as he sat down on the sofa next to me. "Why would Graham do such a thing to you?"

"He wouldn't. I'm certain he wouldn't. However, since we are in a legal battle for the money my father gave me—" I bit my lip, cutting myself off. "Hetty did tell you about this, didn't she?"

"Yes, and he's wasting his time. But please continue."

"Delaney suggested Graham might instigate a scandal to discredit me and win the case."

"That seems a bit of a stretch for Graham."

"There's more." I winced at the thought of what I had to tell him. "Do you recall my telling you the police are looking into Reggie's death?"

"Of course."

"Well, Delaney told me the police received an unsigned letter urging them to do so."

"Ah, so that's what sparked their interest."

"Yes, and it further suggests I killed him."

He shook his head in wonder. "You really are having a bad week. Let's see if I have all this straight. In the past two days, someone has left stolen goods in your bag, broken in to your house, and accused you of murder." He stopped to give me a penetrating look. "Have I left anything out? Any further trials you haven't told me?"

"No, I'd say that sums it up," I replied, my hackles rising. I wasn't sure I liked his tone. Was he simply speaking emphatically, or taking me to task? "It's not as though I've done anything to bring these troubles on."

"Of course not," he said, resuming his pacing. "You're simply an easy target. A woman, alone and unprotected. This would not have happened if you were married. You should be married."

What on earth? "That's absurd! I was no less vulnerable when I was married. You know the man Reggie was, and the amount of protection he afforded me. If nothing like this happened to me then, it's only because I was stuck in the country, running an estate, while my husband spent my father's money, enjoying himself in the city. Good Lord, I've only just shed myself of that family. I'd have to be insane to repeat such a mistake."

George had moved to the window overlooking my small garden, and there was little satisfaction in arguing with his back. I stepped over to his side and placed a hand on his shoulder, turning him to face me. "And because someone has broken into my house? Isn't that a ridiculous reason to marry? If I find myself in need of security, I'd do better to get a dog."

George's eyes sparkled with amusement. His lips quirked up in a smile as he held up his hands in surrender. "I concede your point. If you are completely against the idea of marriage, you must at least allow me to offer my protection."

"You? Heavens, George, you were not suggesting that you and I should marry?"

George was biting down on his lips in an effort to hold back his laughter. How dare he?

"Are you laughing at me?"

He held up a hand while trying to regain his composure.

What on earth was wrong with him? "At least it's good to know I haven't broken your heart."

"My heart?" The words came out rather like a squeak. He drew a steadying breath. "Frances, you would have completely unmanned me if I weren't such an arrogant sot!"

I felt my jaw sag as I gave in to complete and utter confusion. "Did you, or did you not, just ask me to marry you?"

"As long as you are wearing that look of horror, I'll admit to no such thing. Though I don't quite understand why you'd object so strongly. You're a single woman. I'm a single man." He drew his fingers lightly down my arm as he spoke, stirring some rather delightful sensations, "It seems a logical solution." Then he raised my hand to his lips and pressed a kiss against my pulse. My eyes drooped closed. Holy mother of God!

"However," he murmured, his lips tickling my wrist, "since you're against the idea, I've just devised a better one. But first you must excuse me for a few minutes."

My arm fell to my side, as he dropped my hand, brushed past me, and left the room. After another few seconds, I heard the front door close.

Chapter 12

A better idea? I sank back onto the sofa, trying to compre-
hend what had just happened, when Jenny poked her head
around the door.

"I was about to bring in the tea, my lady, when I heard the
door. Has the gentleman left?"

I stared at her blankly before coming to my senses. Yes, tea
would be good about now. "It appears he has, Jenny, but I'd
like the tea anyway." She slipped out for a moment, returning
with a heavily laden tray. "I shall have to work hard to do justice to such a feast!"

"I expect Mrs. Thompson was thinking men have heartier
appetites." Jenny set the tea things out on the low table in front
of the sofa.

"As it stands, one has left, and I've seen neither hide nor hair
of the other." It was possible Jenny knew nothing about the im-
pending visit from James Capshaw, but much more likely that
she was in full possession of every detail. Her next words confirmed it.

"If Mr. Hazelton has left, my lady, would you like someone
to sit with you when you interview Mr. Capshaw?"

I must admit, my brain hadn't been functioning at full strength while George was taking his leave, but it seemed to me he said he would return. Still, I didn't know how long he'd be gone. "Yes. Why don't you send Bridget in? She's working on some mending in my dressing room."

I was just taking my first sip of tea when Bridget arrived, sewing in hand, and made as if to take herself off to a seat in the corner of the room. I called her over to a chair near me instead. "Since part of your job at the moment is to keep me company, please take a break from your sewing, and share my tea."

With any other maid this would be an outlandish request, but Bridget had been with me for years, and was used to my oddities, one of which was calling her by her first name. Due to her station, I ought to call her McCardle, her surname. But I explained to her some time ago that it just felt too impersonal to call her anything but Bridget. I recall her blushing as she agreed to my request, so I doubt she minded. Taking tea together wasn't common for us, but neither was it unheard of— nor was my confiding in her.

"Bridget," I said, staring at the detailed molding around the ceiling. "I'm not certain, but I may have received a proposal of marriage."

"From Mr. Hazelton, my lady?" she said, completely nonplussed. She added a bit of sugar to her cup and took a sip. "Did you give him an answer?"

I nodded and brought my gaze to meet hers. "I told him it was a ridiculous idea. That I would be a fool to marry again." I paused for a moment, recalling my tirade. "That I'd be better off buying a dog."

Bridget winced. "Sounds like an awkward conversation, my lady."

"To say the least. But before you feel too badly for Mr. Hazelton, he claimed he had a better idea." I checked her expression to see if she looked as confused as I felt. "Then he fled."

"He fled?"

"Out of the room like a shot."

Her gaze drifted off. "How interesting."

"How infuriating."

I took a long drink of tea, hoping to clear my head. If he hadn't meant to propose, why the seductive caress? As if he wanted me to know what I'd be missing. It was all so strange. "Whether he proposed or not," I mused aloud, "doesn't really matter. His reasons for marriage were all wrong. He wanted to rescue me from all my travails. He thought I needed protection."

Bridget shook her head in sympathy. "Men do like to protect a lady, don't they?"

"When they're not doing the reverse. After all, isn't it men they want to protect us from?"

"Mr. Hazelton isn't the type to do the reverse. He's a good man, I think."

There was a certain earnestness in her words that surprised me. Not that I didn't consider George a good man, of course, but it sounded as though she'd already given this some consideration. "I think you're right. I wonder why he hasn't married."

"Probably his work for the Home Secretary kept him too busy." I stared in surprise while Bridget sipped her tea. "All that coming and going between Ireland and France," she added.

"Kept? Past tense?" I straightened in my chair. "How do you even know this?"

Bridget shrugged. "His valet's been with him for some time. Likes to talk about their travels and important meetings. The new government's not so keen on Irish Home Rule though, so he left that work. Leastwise Blakely thinks that's why he left."

It was an endless source of amazement how much servants knew about everyone in this town. If George had been involved in the security of the country, protecting one small woman would be a small task. Perhaps I would enjoy his protection.

My thoughts drifted back to that sensual caress and the seductive look in George's eyes. A warm glow wrapped around me.

I was wrenched back to reality when Mrs. Thompson knocked, then opened the drawing room door. "Mr. Hazelton, my lady. Again."

As George strode back into the room, my face grew hot. I stood and extended my hand in greeting, and I must admit, a certain amount of apprehension. Mrs. Thompson had backed through the door, and Bridget had set down her teacup and plate, looking as if she were about to beat a hasty retreat. The surprise of George's return, right in the middle of my musings, seemed to bring the workings of my brain to a halt. Did I want her to stay or leave?

Too late. She'd already bobbed a curtsy and exited the room before I had a chance to decide. But I was being an idiot. I didn't need a third person in the room in order to control myself.

"Please sit down." I gestured to the chair Bridget, the traitor, had vacated.

He stood his ground, his expression serious. "Before I do, are we still friends?"

Friends? Aggravating man! I bit back my disappointment. Apparently there would be no need to control myself as there was to be no temptation. Fine.

"Of course we're friends, George. Please forgive my outburst. It was an insensitive response to a gallant gesture. I suppose you can see I am far from ready to marry again."

He gave me a rueful smile. "I did receive that message, yes."

"Then if you can forgive me for being so rude, I hope we can continue as we were. I truly value your friendship."

"And you will have it, but I do have a different proposal to suggest."

Seating myself, I gestured for him to do the same. "What type of proposal?"

"A partnership of sorts. Like you, I have an interest in finding the thief."

He paused, noting my look of surprise. "As I mentioned before, I do some work for the Crown."

"Is that a reference to your work with the Home Secretary?"

His gaze sharpened. "How do you know about that?"

"Your valet is very proud of you. He spoke of it to Bridget."

"Ah, well that is in the past. Now I'm only called on an 'as needed' basis, and at the moment I'm charged with retrieving some stolen items."

"You think the jewel thief took them? What are they?"

"I'd rather not say what I'm looking for, but they went missing at the same time the snuffboxes were stolen from Haverhill."

"But Mr. Haverhill reported the robbery to the police."

George shook his head. "Anne Haverhill called in the police. And as far as she knew, only the snuffboxes were stolen. Haverhill was frantic when he learned of it. If the police find the—other items, it could cause a great deal of trouble."

"This sounds rather dodgy." I studied him with narrowed eyes. "Something was stolen from Haverhill and he wants it back, but he doesn't want anyone to know about it." I thought of Mrs. Robinson complaining about Haverhill's dealings with foreigners. "What are you involving yourself in?"

George smiled. "Nothing criminal, I assure you. Haverhill's an old colleague and friend. He's doing good work for his district and the country and this could put an end to it. So I'd like to ask this footman a few questions when he arrives. In return, I may be able to assist with the issue of Reggie's death. I have an associate who owes me a favor, so I went home to telephone him."

There was nothing else he could have said to more rapidly redirect my thoughts. "You have a telephone? In your home?"

George shrugged, as if everyone had a telephone in their home. "It does prove to be convenient at times."

I made a mental note to see this device someday and turned my questions to the matter at hand. "Who is your associate? And what could he do?"

George shook his head. "I'd rather not give you his name."

I huffed. "It seems you'd rather not tell me anything. Can you at least tell me what you asked him to do?" I wasn't sure I liked the idea of some stranger knowing I'd been accused of murder, even if it was by an anonymous source.

"Only to look at the letter the police received and find out how they intend to proceed. If they plan to open an investigation, he and I will do some investigating of our own." He reached out and took my hand. "I can vouch for his discretion. No word of this will become public."

"I'm amazed at what I'm learning about you this afternoon. And while I don't know how you can conceive of this as a partnership, as I seem to be doing nothing, I won't turn down your offer of assistance. Inspector Delaney said the doctor won't call for an autopsy but the police may look for evidence that will allow them to do so themselves. For his part, I think Delaney is beginning to see the letter writer as someone simply making mischief for me."

"And he suspects that someone is Graham?"

I tried to remember exactly what Delaney had said. "No. He asked me if I considered Graham capable of doing such a thing. He didn't actually accuse him."

George stared off into the distance. "Interesting," he murmured.

"I must admit I can't imagine anyone else sending such a letter either. Do you think it possible someone may have murdered Reggie? He was with Alicia when he died, but might someone have given him some sort of poison earlier?"

George seemed far away, but I could see he was listening, as he raised one brow and murmured, "Poison? I doubt that."

I gave him a moment to continue, but he simply stared past me. Why do people leave comments half spoken? "George," I said in an attempt to gain his attention. His gaze darted to mine as if he'd just snapped out of a trance. "Why do you doubt poison?"

"The doctor was convinced Reggie died of natural causes. He would have noted signs of poisoning."

I blinked in surprise. "How do you know that?"

"When you first mentioned the police had contacted you, I went to Guildford and spoke to the doctor myself."

"He never even answered my letter, yet he spoke to you?"

George gave me a sheepish grin. "I told him I'd pass the information on to you. Since you said the police would be speaking to him, I wanted to get to him first."

"Did you convince him not to call for the autopsy?"

George shook his head. "It wasn't necessary. His decision was based on the fact that Reggie had a heart condition. He was lax in taking his medication, drank heavily, and took little exercise. In short, he felt Reggie was an excellent candidate for a heart attack."

"If that's the case, perhaps the letter was written by someone making mischief for me."

"Between the letter, the bracelet, and the break-in, someone is trying to make a great deal of mischief for you. Perhaps we'll learn something from the footman."

"I can't believe anyone would go to so much trouble simply to make me miserable."

A knock at the door was followed by Jenny rushing into the room.

"My lady," she said in a breathless voice. "If you could come at once. Mrs. Thompson's not well at all."

"Goodness, what's happened?" I rose to my feet and moved to the door, where Jenny stood shaking. I wrapped an arm around her shoulder.

"Mrs. Thompson went out to the kitchen garden and there was a man out there. She came running back in, shaking and crying."

"Heavens, I must see to her."

George followed as Jenny and I rushed through the baize doors and down the stairs to the kitchen. "If someone has accosted Mrs. Thompson, I should come, too."

"No one accosted her, sir. Mrs. Thompson said he was dead."

Chapter 13

I settled poor Mrs. Thompson in her room with a tot of Aunt Hetty's brandy and called Jenny in to sit with her. Then I made sure Nanny kept Rose occupied in the nursery. Good heavens, I'd be lucky to hang on to any of my staff after this. First a break-in, then a body in the garden! They likely all rued the day they first set foot in this house.

Fortunately George took it upon himself to check on the body. He confirmed the poor man was indeed dead. Grim-faced, he rushed home to place a call to the police.

So, once again I found myself in conference with Inspector Delaney. He'd actually arrived half an hour ago, along with the coroner, and instructed us to wait in the house, while they examined the body and surrounding area. I poured some of Aunt Hetty's brandy for George, and after a moment's consideration, I poured another glass for myself, but the waiting still had us on pins and needles.

Delaney removed his hat, and dipped his head in greeting as he ambled into the drawing room, where we both waited for him. I introduced the two men and waved Delaney to a chair. George and I sat on the sofa, facing him, anxious for his report.

"Can you tell us what happened?" I asked, as soon as the inspector was seated.

"His throat was slashed, my lady."

"Oh, good heavens!" I'm not sure what I'd expected, but the image of someone slicing into that poor man's neck, spilling his life's blood into the dirt, made the bile rise to the back of my throat. It took a few seconds to gain control of myself. George squeezed my shoulder and turned to Delaney.

"How did it happen?" he asked. "Was he followed here, then attacked?"

Delaney shook his head and pulled out his little notebook. "Either that or someone waited for him at your garden gate. I'd say he was approaching your house from the mews along the side, rather than from the street out front. That way, he had to walk past the gate before turning the corner and arriving at the servants' entrance. We could see from the dirt and gravel outside the gate that there was a bit of a scuffle. It looks like he was pulled inside the garden and, well, you know the rest."

Delaney had a habit of speaking slowly, measuring his words. In this case he was definitely trying to instill a sense of calm. I appreciated his discreet summary, which I'm sure was for the benefit of my sensibilities. Under normal circumstances, I assume he would be more descriptive. I was seeing much more of the man than I cared to, but each time I gained more respect for his abilities.

"I spoke to the servants before you arrived, Inspector. Only two of them had been in the kitchen, and they say they heard nothing out of the ordinary."

"I suspect it happened very quickly." He looked down at his notes. "Mr. Capshaw likely didn't have a chance to call out. The coroner is with him still. He'll make a thorough examination, but it doesn't appear he's been dead long, under an hour, so it's a good thing your housekeeper didn't step outside any sooner."

I clutched at George's hand. "This situation, whatever it is, has gotten completely out of control." I turned to Delaney, hoping he had the answer. "Mrs. Thompson is my employee. She's under my protection and has every right to expect a safe place to live. But first someone breaks into my house, then someone else is gutted in my back garden."

"Someone was gutted in the back garden?"

I turned to see Aunt Hetty and Lily standing in the doorway, just returned from their ride in the park.

"No one was gutted in the back garden," George said firmly.

"No, a man's throat was slashed." It was time to stop hiding everything from Lily.

She paled at my pronouncement, then slipped into a chair next to Delaney as if her legs might not hold her up. "Are you a policeman?" she asked.

Delaney had risen from his seat when the two women entered the room. He now took Lily's proffered hand in his large paw and gave her a nod. "Inspector Delaney," I said, "this is my sister, Lily Price. And I'm sure you remember Mrs. Chesney, my aunt." Honestly, one would think this were a society event.

"So now there's been a murder?" Aunt Hetty entered the room in a more sedate manner, removing her hat and gloves, and leaving them on the table near the door. "Who?"

"Mr. Capshaw, the footman we were waiting for this afternoon."

"You were waiting for a footman to visit?" Lily's expression revealed her confusion.

"It's a long story, dear, and I doubt the inspector has time for it." I turned to Delaney. "Do you mind their being here? I'm sure you have questions for the two of us." I motioned to George and myself.

"I do have questions, Lady Harleigh." He stood, eager to get on with it. "I would prefer to speak with you one at a time. If there's somewhere Mr. Hazelton and I can go, I'll speak with him first."

I escorted them to my library, then returned to the drawing

room to bring Aunt Hetty and Lily up to date. Since I'd been shielding Lily from some of the incidents of the last few days, I had to provide details of the stolen bracelet and the house-breaker.

"Holy cats!" she said when I'd finally finished. "Nothing like this ever happens at home!"

"Nothing like this ever happened here before either," I was quick to assure her. "And please don't use that phrase again. I don't know exactly what's at the bottom of this, but I must assume it's associated with one of your gentlemen."

"I have to concur, Frances," Aunt Hetty said. "None of this happened until those men started calling on Lily."

Was that true? I reached for my forgotten glass of brandy, swirling the contents in an attempt to slow my thoughts. Somehow this felt like we were jumping to conclusions. "Lily had only just met them when the bracelet was stolen at Alicia's party. The question is, are any of these events related to each other?"

"The stolen bracelet and the break-in are related, don't you think?"

I nodded at Hetty's observation. "Yes, I firmly believe the thief came back to retrieve his stolen goods. And I'm quite certain the footman was coming here to reveal something about one of Lily's gentlemen. So it is conceivable his information, and his death, are related to one of those three men."

"You don't know that, Franny, and I can't believe any of those gentlemen is a murderer. Are you sure he wasn't coming here to tell you something about the thief? Maybe he knew who it is."

I pondered that possibility for a moment, but it just didn't feel right.

"Mr. Capshaw worked for the woman whose bracelet was stolen." Hetty was quicker to voice her thoughts. "If he knew who took it, it would make more sense for him to tell Mrs. Stoke-Whitney."

But Lily wasn't prepared to give up without a fight. "Then the footman must have overheard something else you were discussing."

Hetty gave me a searching look. "Did you discuss anything else that might have prompted him to seek you out?"

I struggled to bring the scene back to my mind. "The footman brought the tea tray when we were discussing the names on the list of suspects. That's when I noted that all three of your suitors were on the list. I also mentioned hiring the investigator. He left the room at that point and never returned."

My gaze drifted across the tea table to see Lily watching me. I recalled how headstrong she'd been as a child and saw a hint of that stubborn streak in her expression now. "Lily, I'm sorry, but until we know who murdered that poor man, I don't want you to see any of those three gentlemen."

Lily leapt to her feet. "Franny, you can't be serious."

My patience was wearing thin. There was headstrong, and there was plain foolish. "Lily, a man's throat was slashed! Do I need to take you out to the back garden so you can see for yourself just how serious this is?"

Her resistance crumbled at the mention of the murdered man.

"I agree with you, dear. The very idea is almost incredible, but one of those men may be a ruthless killer."

"But even if that's true, then two of them are kind, respectable gentlemen."

"I'll grant you that, but which two?"

Lily appeared taken aback by that thought, but as I watched her chewing on her lip, her hands on her hips, I could tell she was trying to come up with a way around this prohibition. "Well, it couldn't be Mr. Kendrick," she said. "He was with Aunt Hetty and me when the murder happened."

My fingers rubbed at a spot between my eyes that was beginning to throb. I now knew why my mother chose to stay at home and leave Lily's coming out to me. I was never this stubborn. Fortunately Hetty came to my rescue.

"I have to agree with Frances on this. But we need to come up with some subterfuge in order to avoid the gentlemen."

"What do you mean?" I asked as Lily pulled a face and dropped into the chair.

"All three gentlemen will find it strange, possibly insulting, if we refuse them entry to the house. And one of them may become suspicious. If the killer is one of these men, we don't want him to think we know who he is, do we? Especially since we don't."

"That's sound logic, Mrs. Chesney."

We all turned to see Delaney in the doorway, with George right behind him. The two men entered the room. George ambled over to the sofa and seated himself beside me. Delaney remained standing, his gaze traveling from Lily, to Hetty, to me. "Is it possible for you ladies to remove to the country? Until we discover who murdered Mr. Capshaw and why, you may not be safe staying in this house."

My thoughts flew to my daughter. "Then I definitely want Rose moved to safety. And you as well, Lily." But Hetty's words from a moment ago, not Lily's defiant glare, made me second-guess this decision.

"On the other hand, it would look odd for Lily to leave at this time." Seeing Delaney's expression of doubt, I explained. "Lily was just introduced to society, and the Season is rather a short period of time. To leave London so soon would raise everyone's eyebrows, and might send a signal to the killer that we suspect him."

"Perhaps if we put it about that Lily became ill, and needed some fresh country air for her recovery," George suggested.

"That's a thought." I played around with an idea forming in my head. "Delia, my sister-in-law," I added for Delaney's benefit, "has offered to take Rose back to Harleigh when she returns there in two days. I could ask her to take Lily as well, for a week or so. We could concoct the story that Lily has found London society a bit overwhelming, and longs for the solitude of the country."

Lily's gaze shot daggers at me from across the room. "I'm hardly overwhelmed, and I don't want people to think I can't hold my own in London society."

"No one else will hear that story, dear, only Delia." I spoke in a most sympathetic tone. I truly felt her disappointment, but I needed to hold firm on this point. "To everyone else, we'll say you've been taken ill, and that's why you've gone away. Don't we have some soiree or other tonight? You could actually start acting as if you were unwell there. Mention a headache or something vague."

"But I don't want to be ill, or act ill, or go away. I want to stay here."

Hetty pinned her with a look. "The only other option is to turn the gentlemen away at the door, and not only is that unkind, it might put the entire household in danger."

Bravo, Hetty, I thought. Fight drama with drama.

"I suppose I have no choice then," Lily grumbled, as if she were being sent to prison rather than a lovely English manor house. "But it's only for a week?"

"Until it's safe to come back," I amended.

"What about you and Mrs. Chesney?" Delaney asked.

"I'm not leaving. If you recall, I'm still in a legal battle with my brother-in-law and I want to stay in town where I can keep an eye on him. And I'd like to be on hand to see this case resolved." I could see Delaney didn't like it, but he could hardly force me to leave. "Aunt Hetty, what say you? We should be safe from Lily's beaux as long as she's in the country, but you're welcome to go with her if you like. You are her chaperone after all."

Hetty's eyes glistened with mischief. "I think Lily will be adequately looked after at Harleigh, and my services might be better utilized here." She gave me a firm nod. "I'm staying."

"This feels very unfair." Lily's face was the picture of outrage.

"Lily, my dear, those men have no interest in Frances or me. It's you they're pursuing. So while you may be in danger if you stayed here, I will be perfectly safe. The men will simply cease to call."

No one but Hetty and I seemed pleased with this decision. Lily was sullen and silent. George seemed on the verge of protest. Delaney grumbled something unintelligible, then said, "Well, if this is settled, perhaps we could have our conversation now, Lady Harleigh?"

"Of course." I rose to lead him from the room. "Aunt Hetty, you might want to ring for a fresh pot of tea for Mr. Hazelton." Instead, as I left the room, she headed over to the brandy cabinet.

Delaney followed me to the library. Rather than use the desk, we seated ourselves in two chairs near the window. At his request, I relayed the events of the afternoon, from the time Lily and Hetty left, to the point when Delaney himself arrived. Although I didn't mention the details of my conversation with George.

Delaney scribbled notes in his book until I'd finished, then flipped back a few pages. He released a sigh. "So you and Mr. Hazelton were together when the body was found. Were you together the entire afternoon?"

I was about to answer in the affirmative, when I remembered George had actually left for a time. Good heavens! Did I have to go over that with Delaney? I lifted my gaze to see his brows raised in question.

"Mr. Hazelton returned to his home for a short time. I'm not sure how long. Perhaps fifteen or twenty minutes."

"I see." He scribbled something in his book. "Glad I pressed you. It seems you weren't going to mention that detail." He looked up and pinned me with a hard look. "Had you forgotten?"

I shrugged. "I suppose I must have, with all the excitement that came afterward. It can hardly surprise you."

Delaney shook his head as he wrote down a few more words in his book. "Poor man," he muttered.

"I beg your pardon? Are you referring to Mr. Capshaw?"

"Hazelton. I'd hate to think that if I proposed marriage to a woman, she'd forget about it in less than an hour."

My face grew hot. I wasn't sure if it was anger or embarrassment as I felt a large portion of both. "It wasn't a proposal. It was more of a misunderstanding."

Delaney's brows slanted upward. "Really? He called it a proposal."

"Did he?" The inspector chuckled at my eagerness. Damn the man and his impudence! "Inspector, if you already knew Mr. Hazelton had gone home, why did you even ask me?"

"I needed to hear your answer." He leaned toward me. "Did you forget, Lady Harleigh, or were you trying to provide an alibi for Mr. Hazelton? Did you think he was planning to use you as an alibi?"

"An alibi? Certainly not." I fairly spat the words. "Yes, I did forget that Mr. Hazelton had left. No, I did not forget his proposal, if that is any of your concern." I sat back in my seat, crossing my arms. "I can't believe he gave you such personal information."

Delaney cocked his head. "I asked why he left you alone, when the plan was for him to be here when you spoke to the footman. It's never my intention to intrude on anyone's personal lives when I investigate a murder, but it always happens. No need to worry though. I don't talk to the papers."

I glared at the top of his head, listening to his pencil scratch across the page. "Now, what did you do while Mr. Hazelton was gone?"

I was surprised by the sudden turn in the conversation. "Oh, well, I had ordered tea earlier, and Jenny brought it in right after Mr. Hazelton left. He indicated he was coming back, but since I didn't know how soon, I asked Jenny to send my maid, Bridget, to me. She stayed with me until Mr. Hazelton returned."

"I'd like to speak to them before I leave, if I may?"

"Of course." I couldn't stop myself from rolling my eyes.

"So you say Mr. Hazelton returned to his home."

Lovely. Once again I had no idea what George had said. I didn't want Delaney to know I'd told George about the anonymous letter, but what if George had already done so? I decided to reveal as little as possible. "He didn't tell me where he was going at the time. He left through the front door, and returned about twenty minutes later, when he told me he had placed a telephone call. I asked if he had a telephone at his home. He said he did, so I assume he went home. If so, I'm sure you can confirm that with his staff."

"Do you know whom he telephoned?"

"I do not," I said, pleased I could answer honestly.

Delaney nodded as he continued writing.

"You don't actually suspect him of murdering Mr. Capshaw, do you?"

He looked up at that. "He's on the list of suspects for the stolen bracelet."

I bristled at the suggestion. "He shouldn't be."

"But he is. And if you recall, his name came up when we were at Mrs. Stoke-Whitney's home preparing that list, so the footman may have heard it." He set the notebook in his lap and pointed the stubby pencil at me. "You believe Capshaw wanted to give you some information about one of your sister's gentlemen, but what if it was Hazelton he was coming here to talk to you about? Someone stopped that footman from talking to you. Mr. Hazelton knew Capshaw was coming here this afternoon.

And he conveniently went missing for approximately twenty minutes."

"But his staff—"

"You can be sure I'll talk with them. Chances are they'll completely exonerate him. With any luck, they may even be able to provide his whereabouts at the time your house was broken into."

"My aunt was with him that afternoon." I was becoming heartily sick of Delaney's attitude about George.

"We don't know what time that crime took place."

"You cannot seriously suspect him of breaking into my house!"

"I suspect each and every one of the ten people on that list until I have evidence to the contrary." He must have noticed my stricken face as he glanced up at me. He closed his notebook around his pencil and blew out his breath in a puff. "I'm investigating a crime, Lady Harleigh," he said in a softer voice. "And I must follow where the evidence leads me. I can't take someone off my list because you think he's a nice man."

"Oh, come now, Inspector."

"Isn't that what this boils down to? You want to defend him because he's been a friend to you. But how well do you really know him? After all, you refused his offer of marriage."

"He is my dearest friend's brother, and his offer of marriage was an act of gallantry. He was trying to protect me. Shouldn't that speak to his character?"

Delaney shook his head. "Then I hope you're correct in your assessment of him. I hope the evidence leads me in another direction, but I still have to investigate each name on that list, including Hazelton. If he's innocent, nothing will come of it." He stood as if to leave, thought better of it, and sat back down.

"There's one more thing, Lady Harleigh," he said. "These crimes keep circling around you, and while you're afraid for your daughter and sister, I fear you're not concerned enough about yourself. You should take the advice you gave your sister and go to the country."

I shook my head. "You're mistaken, Inspector. I'm quite aware I'm in the eye of this storm, at least for the moment. I don't want to jeopardize their safety by going with them."

He nodded. "I see. Then please take care, and perhaps keep some distance from Mr. Hazelton. At least until I can clear him of suspicion. At the risk of earning your anger, there's one more thing I'd like you to remember in regard to him. He was at your home when your husband died."

I felt a cold chill at his words. "You can't have it both ways, Inspector. If you believe the anonymous letter, then I am the accused. If you don't believe it, then Reggie died of a heart attack. Or are you suggesting Mr. Hazelton gave my husband a heart attack?" I spoke with as casual an air as I could muster.

Delaney cocked his head, reminding me of a terrier. "Interesting you should use those words. Heart attacks can be induced by certain drugs." Again he rose to his feet. "Your staff is waiting for me belowstairs. I'll speak to them now, then go next door to interview Hazelton's servants."

I let Delaney take himself downstairs to the kitchen, where the staff were waiting. The man had left me with more questions than answers. So there were drugs that could induce a heart attack? Why hadn't the doctor mentioned that? But where would one find such drugs, and who on earth wanted Reggie dead? He and I had lived such separate lives that I barely knew his friends, much less his enemies, if there were any. Had he dallied with someone's wife?

Stupid question! Of course he had. Alicia for one. But I couldn't see Arthur Stoke-Whitney whipping up enough anger to kill the man who bedded his wife. As long as they were discreet, that is. But perhaps Reggie had cuckolded some other man. Someone not quite so understanding as Arthur. I gave myself a shake.

This was getting me nowhere, and my head was spinning. Did Reggie's death have anything to do with the current crimes?

I leaned back in my chair and considered that possibility. Only if he really was murdered, and even then, it was just a possibility. And I still couldn't bring myself to believe George had anything to do with these crimes. Delaney had told me to take the advice I gave to my sister and leave town. I thought of another piece of advice I had given her. Any man can act like a nice man. One must take the time to find out if he really was.

Chapter 14

The next morning I was heading upstairs to change for the fashion show when I heard Mrs. Thompson at the door with Graham. I instinctively clenched my teeth. Could I continue my ascent unseen? When I glanced over my shoulder, he was waiting in the foyer, looking up at me. Too late.

"Good morning, Graham." I stepped down to the foyer. "To what do I owe the pleasure?"

"Frances. You're looking well under the circumstances." He nodded toward the drawing room. Since I saw no point in refusing to speak to him, I led him inside.

"What circumstances are you considering?" I took a chair by the tea table.

Graham held up a newspaper, folded to a story titled GRUE-SOME MURDER IN BELGRAVIA!

"Oh, I haven't seen that one."

"Well, I suppose that explains why you aren't packing."

I gave him a hard stare. "Packing?"

He tossed the paper on the table and seated himself on the edge of the chair next to mine, resting his forearms on his knees as the leaned toward me. "A brutal murder took place right in this very neighborhood. Surely you don't contemplate staying here? You can return to Harleigh tomorrow with Rose and Delia." He sat back in the chair as if that settled the matter.

It was far from settled. If Graham thought he could sweep in here and tell me what to do under the guise of ensuring my safety, he had better think again. If he knew the murder had occurred in my own garden, I could understand his concern, but under these circumstances, his behavior was simply too highhanded.

"I thank you for your concern, but I have every intention of remaining right here."

He examined my face as if he wasn't quite sure I was serious. "What a foolish notion. Do you not recognize the danger?"

"I don't see my neighbors fleeing their homes. Are they all fools, too?"

"They are not women living alone."

"Neither am I, which reminds me, what would I do with my aunt and sister if I returned to Harleigh?"

He waved aside my protest. "They are welcome to come as well."

"And what of the house?"

His expression brightened. "I've spoken to an estate agent and the house can be sub-leased and provide you a steady income until such a time as you wish to sell. I can take care of that for you."

My mouth had fallen open as he spoke. I snapped it shut. Graham had read the story this morning. How had he managed to contact an agent, obtain a meeting with him, and learn the details of my lease before noon? Impossible. He must have been working on this scheme for days. Heavens, he really did think I was a fool.

"This has nothing to do with my safety at all. You simply want me back at Harleigh so you can control the income from leasing this house." I rose to my feet, fists clenched at my sides. "You should leave now."

Graham stood as well. "I'm astonished by your lack of gratitude to this family. You have no sense of duty."

"If familial duty means I must fund the Wynns forever, I am glad to be rid of that sense."

As he headed to the door, he paused and turned back, his face contorted in anger. "You are the most unnatural female I have ever come across. You have not heard the end of this."

I glared at the door as it slammed shut behind him. This clumsy maneuver convinced me Graham was working alone to gain control of my money. Delia would never have been so obvious. And the only reason he'd take these measures without her knowledge was if he didn't plan to share. Considering each of them coveted my money for their own purposes, perhaps it was time to tell Graham's wife what he was up to.

Fashionable London between Easter and Whitsuntide, while not the height of the Season, could still drive one to distraction. The flood of people coming to town, and the constant whirl of activity, left one with barely time to breathe, much less think. And thinking, or better yet, planning was exactly what I needed to do. Instead, here I was, with Hetty and Lily, at the Savoy Hotel, for tea, and Mrs. Worthington's charity fashion show. But Mrs. Worthington was Delia's mother, and I needed to speak to Delia, so my presence here was a necessity.

I sipped my tea as yet another young debutante glided down the serpentine runway in a rather daring evening gown. I'd say the charity was doing quite well today. The young ladies had to pay a fee to walk the runway. Those attending, and it was quite a crush, had to pay an entrance fee, and I understood there would be an auction for a few of the more noteworthy gowns— all proceeds going to the charity.

Meanwhile, we squeezed ourselves behind small tables, too

many of which were stuffed into an overly warm room, made smaller by the addition of a runway. We drank tepid tea and ate delightful cakes. Yes, the delightful cakes spoiled my tirade, but they did make the afternoon bearable—just. I'm sure everyone here wished they'd just sent a donation and stayed home, but that wasn't the point. One must come to be seen, and to mix with society.

My point in coming was to speak to Delia, who persisted in eluding me. I couldn't see her anywhere in the crowd. I'd sent my card backstage to let her know I was here so I assumed she'd join us after the show.

"Why do you suppose Mrs. Worthington didn't invite me to model the clothes?" Lily asked. "This is my first Season, too. And we are related, in a way."

"Mrs. Worthington is on the committee but she isn't in charge of the production." If she were allowed any power on these charitable committees, much of the proceeds would find their way into her pocket. Further, I knew Mrs. Worthington to be an implacable snob. In her mind, Lily didn't have the pedigree to participate in her show.

While galling, perhaps it was for the best. I wanted Lily in the background for now, and completely out of the picture as soon as possible. Her safety was more of a concern than her popularity. I had just drawn that conclusion when Hetty applied a sharp elbow to my side. I looked up to see Viscount Ainsworthy bowing over Lily's hand, her face in full blush.

He turned and nodded to my aunt and me. It was impossible for him to maneuver around the table to our side. "Good day to you, Countess. Mrs. Chesney. Have you seen anything you simply must add to your wardrobe?"

I gave him my most brilliant smile. "Not yet, my lord, though I believe one is expected to purchase something."

He glanced around the room. "That explains why all the other gentlemen here are with their wives. I'm afraid your sister-in-law will be disappointed in me, but I was actually about to slip out the back door. When I saw you ladies, I had to come by and ask if you'll be attending the Roswell ball this evening."

"Yes, indeed, we'll all be there. Mrs. Roswell is an excellent hostess, and her events are always entertaining. May I assume you will be there as well?"

"I will," he said with a nod. Then he turned his dazzling smile on Lily. "If you're not already engaged, will you honor me with the first dance, Miss Price?"

Lily beamed, and accepted, while Hetty and I ogled. He left us a few minutes later, and Hetty sighed. "Lily, if you don't marry Viscount Swoonworthy, I swear I will!" Our laughter caused an older woman at a nearby table to cast a curious glance in our direction, but it definitely lightened my mood.

The show ended before long, and soon Delia squeezed over to our table. After showering her with accolades for a wonderful event, I brought up her return to Harleigh. She was delighted at the prospect of taking Rose with her while clearly confused at the addition of my sister to her party. After much debate with Hetty and Lily, we had concocted a new tale for her withdrawal from town, which I relayed to Delia, sotto voce. In this story Lily had attracted an undesirable admirer. She was infatuated, but I was certain he only wanted her fortune, and I considered him in desperate enough financial straits that a week's absence would cause him to seek a new heiress.

"Of course we'll put it about that Lily was taken ill and returned with you to recover in the country air. I wanted you to know the truth, however," I added, crossing my fingers at the fib.

"How clever of you, my dear. We certainly don't need anyone grasping at your sister's fortune," she added with a firm nod.

As she said this with a complete lack of irony, the only polite thing to do was agree. Delia's eyes were alight with curiosity, but she was far too proper to ask the name of the gentleman. I was content to leave her wondering. Let her try to wheedle the name of the non-existent suitor out of Lily.

Now for the difficult part. I leaned closer to Delia. "I wish I could provide something for your mother's charity, dear, but that lawsuit of Graham's has frozen my account."

Delia cocked her head, giving me a look of confusion.

"Didn't you know? Graham's filed a claim for the funds my father gave me." I shrugged. "He can't win, of course, but he's temporarily made me a pauper."

Delia was no fool and the horror on her face showed me her train of thought. Graham did this without telling her, which means he wouldn't have given her a shilling. Nor would she be able to come to me for her pin money.

She placed a hand over mine. "I'm so sorry, Frances. But don't you worry. I'll speak to him before I leave tomorrow and put an end to this nonsense."

"That would be such a relief, Delia."

We made the arrangements for their departure in the morning, and while I felt a little misty about losing the company of my daughter and sister for the next week—if not longer—I was satisfied they would be safe now. As we headed back home, I felt a welling of gratitude for Aunt Hetty in staying with me, as well as a desire to spend more time with my daughter before she left me in the morning.

"What do you say to collecting Rose from home and taking her on an outing to Hyde Park?" We had just pulled up to the front of my house as the idea struck me. "It's a lovely day, and I daresay George can spare his carriage for another hour."

"You should see if he has an hour of his time to spare as well," Hetty said, her expression turning grave.

Lily took the decision of inviting George out of my hands, as she climbed down from the carriage, before the driver could come around to assist her. "That's an excellent idea. The two of you can get Rose ready, and I'll collect Mr. Hazelton."

Hetty and I descended in a more decorous fashion. "I understand you want to spend time with the girls," she said, stepping down to the sidewalk, and turning toward me, "but you do need to be cautious."

"I doubt we'll be overset by marauders at Hyde Park, Aunt Hetty."

"No, but a band of Lily's suitors is not out of the question. And if one of them is a murderer . . ."

"I see your point, but considering Delaney's suspicions of George, is it being cautious to include him in the outing, or is it throwing caution to the wind?"

As we climbed the steps to the front door, Hetty turned sharply toward me. "You don't imagine he had anything to do with these strange goings-on, do you?"

I smiled at her outraged expression. "Actually I don't, but I wasn't aware you were Mr. Hazelton's staunch supporter. How did this come about?"

Hetty let out a bark of laughter. "I'd like to think that at my age I've become a good judge of character. Although I do make my share of mistakes, I find it best to follow my instincts in assessing people, until there is evidence to prove me wrong, of course." She gave me a pointed look. "That's what you should be doing, my dear. Follow the evidence. Perhaps it will lead you out of this mess."

"Me? Isn't that what we trust the police to do?"

"Well, you trust them if you think that's best, dear. It's your life after all. By the way, I have several letters to write, so I'll let you young people enjoy your outing while I get to work."

I watched her walk up the stairs with my mouth half open. Her parting comment hardly rang with approval. But did she honestly think I should take this investigation on myself? I had no skills or resources for such a task. Still, as I climbed the stairs, heading to the nursery for Rose, I felt oddly disappointed in myself.

* * *

It was the perfect afternoon. The sun peeked out from behind a thin layer of clouds to remind us of its presence. There was a gentle breeze, but no real chill. And our attempts to amuse Rose had the three of us feeling like children ourselves. We'd left the carriage with George's driver and took to our feet soon after entering the park. Rose squealed as the riders pounded down Rotten Row. She told George, in great detail, about the pony she'd left behind at Harleigh, and how eager she was to see him again. Delia was right; there was much more for a child to do in the country, and I'd been far too busy, since we'd come to London, for many outings such as this.

After eating ices from a vendor's cart, we wandered over to the Serpentine to watch two young men rowing their ladies across the smooth water. George promised to take Rose out in one the next time she came to London. This time, she'd have to be content to walk across the bridge. As we headed in that direction, Rose took Lily's hand, so I walked with George. The arrangement pleased me, as I'd been wanting to ask him a question since talking with Hetty this morning.

"Do you think the police will get anywhere with this investigation?"

He gave me a surprised glance. "Do you mean will they find Capshaw's murderer?"

I considered the question for a moment. "No, I mean all of it. Will they find the murderer? And since we weren't able to talk to Capshaw, will we find the jewel thief or the housebreaker? Will I find out, once and for all, if Reggie died of natural causes? Will my life ever get back to normal again?"

"I'm sure everything will be resolved, Frances." He drew my hand through his arm and gave it a little pat. I wanted to cringe. Did he just pat me on the hand? Really? Oh, this was worse than Hetty's disdain. Did I give everyone the impression of some fragile flower, needing to be cosseted and protected? Is that who I was?

I had to ponder that a bit. So I bought myself a house and struck out on my own in a display of independence. But at the first sign of adversity, I let others take care of me. Granted, it was a great deal of adversity, enough to knock anyone off their feet. But wasn't it time I stood back up?

I gave George a warning look from the corner of my eye. "Don't patronize me, George. I'm your partner now. I want your honest opinion—good, bad, or indifferent."

He turned to look me full in the face, one brow arched in surprise. "All right, then, Honesty it is. They have a good chance of finding Capshaw's murderer. He may have told someone he was coming to your home yesterday, and the police will be able to talk to his friends and associates. The fact that they're investigating a murder, means they'll likely get more cooperation, and Delaney may be given some help.

"Regarding the other matters, the thefts and your house-breaker—and I suspect those crimes were committed by the same person—I don't have much hope."

"Why not?" I said.

George had been looking at me as he spoke. Now he turned and gazed ahead at the path we were taking, leaving me with a view of his profile. "The problem is that while no one ever wants to talk to the police, the aristocracy can actually get away with not doing so. If no one cooperates with them, the police can't do much unless they catch the criminal in the act. They may place a few more constables in the area for a time, in the hope of catching a man running down the street with a Ming vase, but if that doesn't work, those constables will be moved to other, more pressing assignments."

I sighed. "I suppose that's all we can expect. After all, they don't have unlimited resources and there are more serious crimes for them to solve."

"They've probably already closed the file for Mrs. Stoke-Whitney since her bracelet has been returned. And in your case, nothing was stolen, no one was harmed." His brow creased in a frown. "I don't mean to diminish the crime, but from the perspective of the police, you see—"

"So that means it's up to us to find him."

He slanted his gaze my way. "Us?"

"Yes, *partner*. You still have your items to recover and how else will I ever learn if one of Lily's suitors is a thief, or possibly a murderer?"

"I see. What do you propose?"

"We can start by finding out if any of the three attended the other events where we know there was a theft. I already know Mr. Kendrick attended the Chesterton musicale."

That earned me a look of approval. "Good work, Frances. How did you learn that?"

"I asked him, but it was rather clumsy. I suggest we check with the hostesses instead. After all, the gentlemen could simply lie."

"I suspect Delaney has already done that. If you can be patient, I'll check with him."

Patience was not my strongest attribute.

We'd caught up to Lily and Rose on the bridge. Rose was standing too close to the railing. I leaned over to place a restraining arm around her, starting a chain reaction that happened in the blink of an eye.

I stepped in the path of a passerby who bumped against me rather roughly, spinning me around. Lily shrieked, and jumped between me and the railing, in an attempt to keep me from sailing over the side. I was still reaching for Rose so my arm was out as I stumbled around and, to my horror, I knocked Lily rather neatly over the railing.

"No!" I shouted, as George's arm snaked out to grasp her wrist. I steadied myself and turned back to the water, only to see Lily, swinging in the air, one hand clinging to the stone railing, the other clasped in George's hands. Good heavens!

It was the work of a moment to haul her back up onto the bridge—George was strong, I was capable, and Lily was so slight—but staring into her frightened eyes made me feel as though time had stopped, and we would never get her up. Once she gained her feet, she slumped against me, gasping, and weak with relief. Rose threw her arms around Lily's waist and cried. And I noticed we'd drawn quite a crowd. I shot a glance at George. "Let's get her home."

Between us, George and I peeled Rose away from my sister, and transferred Lily to his arm. The two of them made their way to the carriage. I took Rose's hand and followed, answering inquiries along the way, and assuring everyone Lily was unharmed, but she'd had quite a fright. Finally we reached the carriage and headed for home, and I was able to determine if I'd been speaking the truth. Lily did appear fit, all things considered. Her dress was torn where it had scraped against the stone wall, and she would likely have bruises, but nothing was broken, and that look of terror had left her eyes. Once we arrived at home, I put her to bed like the baby sister she was, and had Mrs. Thompson prepare a hot toddy to help her sleep. I stayed with her until she dozed off.

"It's still not too late to go back home if you aren't up to this." I glanced behind me for Lily's reaction, and instead saw Aunt Hetty shake her head, while George scowled in exasperation. Well! Perhaps this was the third or fourth time I'd said something like this to Lily in the past two hours, but she'd steadfastly insisted she wanted to come to the ball. Now, as we were climbing the stairs of the Roswell mansion in Mayfair, I had to admit it actually was rather too late to turn back.

"Franny, I assure you I am completely fine, and since this is my last night before I'm banished to the country, I intend to enjoy myself. Now stop fussing."

Easy for her to say, I thought. She'd only fallen over a wall and dangled by her fingertips above a large body of water. I had to *watch* that happen to my only sister! Still, I bit back my arguments. The plan for this evening had been to convince the general public that Lily was feeling unwell and needed to go to the country. In my opinion, the accident this afternoon, which everyone would have heard about by now, provided ample excuse to absent herself from town, making this charade unnecessary. At least it seemed unnecessary to everyone but Lily.

We left our wraps with a footman, greeted our host and hostess, and melted into the crowd. I could hardly fault Lily for wanting some fun, or wanting to make use of her moment of fame. And while I was here, I might as well start gathering information.

Ainsworthy arrived to lead Lily out to the dance floor, George immersed himself in a group nearby, and I asked Aunt Hetty if she'd mind playing chaperone, while I looked for a friend. "Go ahead," she urged. "I'll guard Lily's virtue as if it were my own."

I tried not to imagine what she might mean by that as I scanned the room for Alicia. I finally spotted her in a dark corner dazzling a tall, well-built man who was young enough to be—well—far too young for her. As I approached, he ran a finger around the edge of her ear. Goodness, they were behaving far too intimately for such a public place. If I could see them, so could anyone else.

Alicia caught sight of me and glowered, backing up a pace or two from the young man.

"Please forgive the interruption," I said, then took a step back myself as the young man turned around. Grayson!

"Mr. Grayson." My voice was chilling, but the anger burning in my veins was white hot. How dare he?

Grayson's jaw sagged open for a moment, before he visibly collected himself. "Lady Harleigh, what a surprise to see you here."

"Clearly."

Alicia hid a smirk behind a gloved hand, amused at his discomfort. "Mrs. Stoke-Whitney had something in her eye," he said smoothly. "I was simply removing it."

"How very kind of you." I turned to Alicia. "How is your eye now, dear?"

She fluttered her lashes. "All better."

"Good. I'd like to borrow you for a moment." I placed my hand on the lady's arm and drew her away from the sputtering Grayson.

"This had better be important," she said. "I had that man quite captivated."

"Yes, I noticed," I said through gritted teeth. "You'll have to excuse my poor humor. He was one of Lily's suitors, and I'm very disappointed in his behavior."

"What do you mean, 'was'? For heaven's sake, a suitor is not the same as a husband. I'm sure he'll behave admirably once he's married."

I gave her a quelling glare.

"In the man's defense, I was using all my powers of seduction."

I couldn't stop the chuckle that burst forth. "You are incorrigible, Alicia. But you must realize if you continue down this road, you're bound to come to a bad end. In fact, the way Grayson was stroking your ear, you just might have been about to lose another piece of jewelry."

Her fingers flew to the earrings. Finding them still in place, she pursed her lips and gave me a sidelong glare. "He is on the list," I reminded her.

"But you don't really believe he's the thief, do you?"

"I wouldn't have believed he was a philanderer either, until a few moments ago." At her *tut* I relented. "But you must be more careful. If someone else had seen the two of you, your reputation would be in tatters."

She linked her arm through mine, and slowed my pace, guiding me around the perimeter of the ballroom. "It's my only enjoyment in life," she said, her voice bordering on a whine. "Now, did you really need to speak to me, or were you just out to ruin Grayson's fun?"

"I do need to speak to you. Ruining his fun was just a boon. I wanted to inquire about your footman."

"Oh, yes. Poor James." She paused and gave me a sharp look. "How did you hear about him?"

"He was murdered in my garden. Didn't you know?"

"No!" A couple nearby turned and gave us a curious look.

I gave her arm a little pinch as I smiled and nodded at them. "Compose yourself," I hissed.

"Yes, of course, but this is rather a shock. Delaney didn't tell me about that, and the papers only said James' body was found in Belgravia. What was he doing at your house?"

"He overheard our conversation with Inspector Delaney the other day and gave my maid a note for me. He asked to meet with me, saying he had some information to provide. I believe it was about one of Lily's suitors, but he was killed before he could speak to me. Now I'm worried one of those three men could be his killer."

Alicia was staring at me with an expression of amazement mixed with horror. "Your face, Alicia! For goodness' sake, smile."

In an instant she was composed, and we nodded at some acquaintance as we brushed past them, both of us looking as if we were sharing recipes, or speaking of our children. Much better.

"So are you telling me James, *my footman,* knew who stole my bracelet, and decided to tell you, rather than me or the police?"

"No. I'm sure if he knew who stole your bracelet, he would have come to you, probably before you even called in the police. So I had to remember what else we discussed that he might have overhead, and the only thing that made sense was my comment that three of the names on the list were Lily's suitors.

There was nothing else we discussed that would send him to me, rather than you."

Alicia's brow furrowed. "I wonder what he wanted to tell you."

"So do I, but I'm afraid we'll never know. Unless, of course, you care to help me?"

Her eyes widened. "How can I help?"

"Did the police come and interview your servants today?"

"Yes, Delaney came, along with a constable."

"Good. I suspect he was trying to determine where Capshaw went before coming to me. Somehow the killer found out he would be at my house, and I've begun to wonder if Capshaw might have tried to blackmail the killer, you see? Pay me off, and I won't tell the lady what I know."

"I do see. So you think James mentioned where he was going to a friend in my household yesterday?"

"Exactly." We had reached the opposite end of the room and turned, pausing for a moment in the pretense of watching the dancers, flowing to the strains of a Strauss waltz. "Do you know which servants Delaney spoke to, and what their answers were?"

Alicia shook her head. "I can try to find out, but why don't you ask Delaney?"

"I intend to, but I'm not sure he'll tell me. He won't want me interfering in his investigation. If you can provide me with that information, then he won't have to know."

"Whether he knows or not, it does appear you're interfering with his investigation. May one ask why?"

I gave her my most chilling glare. "Need I point out that three of the suspects in James' murder are courting my sister?"

"Ah, yes, including Grayson. It seems we do need to keep an eye on that boy. Well, point taken. You have every right to that information."

"I'm pleased you see it that way, because there's one other

thing. Did Capshaw provide references when he came to you for employment?"

"Of course. Do you need those, too?"

"If possible. I can't think how he could have any association with one of Lily's suitors except through his employment, so I'd like to find out where he's worked before."

Alicia gazed at me with something like wonder in her expression. "Frances Wynn, I am developing a whole new respect for you. You have quite a knack for ferreting out information. Even Delaney didn't ask to look into James' former employers."

"Why, thank you, Alicia, how kind of you to say so." Goodness, was I blushing? I couldn't remember the last time someone told me I had a talent for something. Let's see, it must have been—never! I had to revel in this sensation for a moment. With an effort, I brought my thoughts back to the matter at hand. "Delaney may still request this information, so it might be best if I copy what you have, and leave the original documents with you."

"Of course. May I assume you'll come by tomorrow?"

"If that's convenient?"

"Perfectly. I'll have a talk with my butler in the morning. He sat in on all the interviews with Delaney, so if anyone mentioned where James was going he'll know. This is rather exciting." She gave me a conspiratorial smile. "If there's anything else I can help you with, feel free to ask."

I hesitated a moment. She was being awfully cooperative. Dare I trust her? "There is one more thing, just your opinion actually."

Her brows rose expectantly. "Yes?"

"I'm not quite sure how to phrase this. It's a rather ticklish question." I gave myself a mental shove. Just do it. "Have you ever wondered if Reggie did not die of natural causes? If, in fact, you know of someone who might have wanted him dead?"

"But Reggie died of a heart attack."

"Yes, well, I have recently been informed there are drugs that can induce a heart attack."

Alicia's eyes grew wide. "Really?"

"So I'm told. I can't vouch for the accuracy of that information, but assuming it's true, I wondered if you know of anyone who might have wanted to—well—kill him?"

To my surprise, she remained calm and considered the question. "Well, I admit when it happened, and just for a moment you understand, I wondered if Reggie had been murdered." She lifted a shoulder in a casual shrug. "But naturally I thought you had done it."

"Me?"

"That was before I realized you didn't know about our relationship of course."

Lovely. Perhaps the wife was always the first suspect. "I don't suppose you wrote a letter to the police to that effect, did you? Alicia! For goodness' sake, close your mouth."

She recovered immediately. "Then you must stop shocking me. Are you saying someone, and you don't even know who, wrote a letter to the police, accusing you of drugging your husband into a heart attack?"

I instantly regretted discussing this with her. "Not exactly that, but close enough. Please, Alicia, promise me this will go no further than you."

"Of course. No one will hear of this from me."

"No, I must have your word on this. I should never have mentioned it except that I thought you had a better knowledge of his friends, and perhaps any enemies. You must promise to mention this to no one."

She gave a little snort of exasperation. "Do you know how many affairs I've had?"

I was flustered at the change of subject. "Certainly not."

"Neither does anyone else. That's how discreet I am."

I threw her a sidelong glare. "I just saw you in a compromising position, in the middle of a crowded ballroom, with a very young man, so forgive me if I question your discretion."

Alicia twisted her lips in a grimace. "Good point. Perhaps I should be more careful. Fine. You have my word, but I'm afraid I can't be of any help. I can think of no one who had a grudge against Reggie. He rubbed along well with everyone. Well, except Graham, but I don't think that's altogether unusual with brothers."

Perhaps not, but her response still surprised me. "I don't recall any particular animosity between Reggie and Graham."

"I wouldn't exactly say it ran to animosity. Just that Reggie often complained Graham always hounded him about money. He felt Reggie spent it too freely."

I huffed. "I can't argue with him there."

Alicia gave my arm a squeeze. "Now I think it's time we parted company before people start to wonder what has us so engaged. We can discuss these things further tomorrow if need be." Her eyes twinkled with delight. "I must admit this conversation was definitely worth losing that young man!"

Chapter 15

The next morning Hetty and I stood at my doorstep, watching Delia and the girls climb into her carriage. I decided against going to the station with them to see them off on their train. This was difficult enough, watching them ride off with Delia— Lily, resigned, and Rose so excited it broke my heart. However, she had run back up the walk for an extra hug, her new kitten tucked in the crook of her arm. I think the hug was more for my sake than hers.

"They'll be back soon, dear." Hetty squeezed my hand in compassion.

I waved enthusiastically as the carriage pulled away. "Goodbye, darlings," I whispered, then turned to Hetty. "I suppose I'm being foolish, but she's my only daughter. And Lily is my only sister, and I'll miss them both terribly."

With an arm around my shoulders, she turned me back into the house. "Well, now you're left with your only aunt."

I paused in the doorway. "But you're not my only aunt."

"I know." She prodded me forward. "But it sounded so much more dramatic and suited to your current mood. Besides, I'm certain I'm your favorite aunt."

"Humph," I muttered, following her into the drawing room. "As if you would even participate in such a competition. Mother's sisters are dreadful." I stopped at the sight of an artist's easel in the place of the low tea table, a pad of paper where the canvas should be. "What's going on here? Are you planning to sketch something?"

She directed me over to the sofa. "In a manner of speaking, I suppose we are."

"We?" I seated myself on the sofa. "I'm afraid you have the wrong sister. I'm not a bit artistic."

"You have the skills for this, dear. It's time we tried to make some sense of the mischief going on around here. I thought if we put our heads together, and made some notes of the basic facts, we might be able to see some logic or a pattern—"

"That might lead us to the culprit. How clever of you." I warmed to the idea immediately. She truly was my favorite aunt.

Hetty was beaming, but she forced some severity into her countenance. "We must do something. You sent the girls away, but you may be in danger still. I'm hoping we can develop a plan of action."

"Well, I do plan to take some action already," I said, not without a little pride. "But I suggest we start with the facts, and I'll add my plans as we go along."

Hetty picked up a charcoal pencil. "I agree. First things first. We know someone is stealing valuable objects from homes around town." She wrote the word *Thief* at the top of the page.

"We might also make note of what was stolen," I began, only to be interrupted by the appearance of Mrs. Thompson in the doorway. Before she could even speak, Fiona brushed past her, the plumes on her tall toque bobbing in the breeze she created.

"Frances, I can't tell you how hurt I am by the way you've been neglecting me. All this excitement going on around you, and I have to learn of it from George." She sat on the sofa next to me and gave me an incredulous stare. "How can you just leave me in the dark? You must stop being so secretive."

"Have you left poor George at the breakfast table again?"

She made a dismissive gesture with her hand. "Oh, he doesn't need my company to eat. I, on the other hand, need to find out what's been happening."

"Had you been at the Roswell ball last night, I could have brought you up to date."

Fiona sighed. "We had a prior engagement. But from what I hear, you wouldn't have had time for me anyway. I understand you and Alicia Stoke-Whitney were thick as thieves last night. Are you sharing secrets with her instead of your best friend?"

Fiona had spoken lightly, as if she were teasing, but I could see she really felt hurt by my neglect. Unfortunately she'd never let me apologize. That would involve talking about unpleasant emotions, and Fiona would never admit that anything might disturb her serenity.

"Actually, if you wish to know what's been happening, you've arrived at the perfect time. Aunt Hetty and I were just about to review everything." I glanced at Hetty, who was waiting, not so patiently, at the easel. "I think explaining things to Fiona might help to clarify them in our minds, don't you?" I turned back to my friend. "You'd be doing us a great service."

"I suppose a fresh set of eyes can't hurt." Hetty never took long to catch on.

Fiona's smile lit her face. "Oh, then please carry on."

"All right then, we were just about to detail the various burglaries that have happened recently. The first item was stolen from the Haverhill home about three weeks ago. Then the Chestertons had a theft about three or four days later." I looked at Fiona for confirmation.

She shook her head. "The Haverhill reception was on the fifth of April, and the Chesterton musicale was on the thirteenth."

Hetty wrote this down. "Do either of you recall what was stolen?"

Again I looked to Fiona. "The snuffboxes were stolen from Mr. Haverhill, the necklace from Mrs. Chesterton."

"That's right, I remember now. The snuffboxes were taken from the library, but the necklace was actually removed from the lady's boudoir. That seems like quite a risk for our thief to take."

"If he moved swiftly, there's little risk involved." Fiona lifted her shoulders in a casual shrug. "At any gathering people excuse themselves for a short time. Who would be indelicate enough to ask where they're going? As for the stolen items themselves, they were all small objects. Easy enough to fit in a pocket, and leave the house with their new owner, undetected."

I turned my attention back to Hetty. "How does one dispose of stolen goods anyway?"

We all looked at each other with bemused expressions. What did one do with stolen goods? Especially items that could be recognized.

"Well," Hetty mused, "I suppose anything of gold might be melted down and sold somewhere, although who would buy a lump of gold?"

Again none of us had an answer.

I stood and took the pencil from Aunt Hetty and drew a horizontal line across the bottom third of the page. "Obviously none of us knows the answer to that question, and we'll never get anywhere by wondering about it. This is a question for Delaney, so that should be one of our action items."

I wrote the question under the line. "I'm sure to see him in the near future, so I can take on that task." I handed the pencil back to Hetty and returned to the sofa.

"Excellent," she said. "Now the third theft was Mrs. Stoke-Whitney's bracelet."

"On the seventeenth," Fiona added.

"And that brings us to the list of suspects Alicia and I prepared."

Both Fiona and Hetty turned to me in surprise. "That's
right," Hetty said. "You mentioned something about a list when
Capshaw was killed. What's that about?"

"When I returned to bracelet to Alicia, Delaney had us prepare a list of possible suspects—other guests who were near
Alicia just before she noticed the bracelet missing, and near me
shortly after."

"Well, that should certainly narrow the field. How many
names are on it?"

"There were only ten, but some of them are more coincidence than suspect." I turned to Fiona. "You, for example."

She placed a hand on her chest, eyes glowing with delight "I
am a suspect in a crime? How absolutely thrilling."

Hetty released an impatient sigh so I supplied the remaining
names on the list.

"Does George know he's a suspect?" Fiona clearly found
this amusing.

"I don't think I mentioned it, but it hardly matters. Delaney's
checking the names on that list against the guest lists for the
other two events where a theft took place, and George didn't attend either."

"Aside from Graham, do you know if any of these people
are short of funds?" Hetty asked.

Fiona and I answered her with blank stares. "That's a difficult question," I said. "The only reason I know of Graham's financial problems is through my close acquaintance with him.
The general population would assume he's well off. Just as I assume the rest of these people are."

Hetty nodded. "If that's the case, Graham has my vote for
chief suspect for two reasons." She held up two fingers. "He
needs money, and by leaving the bracelet in your reticule, he
could ruin your reputation."

Fiona stared in confusion. "Why would he want to ruin your reputation?"

"Inspector Delaney suggested it might improve Graham's odds of winning his lawsuit."

"Oh, please," Fiona muttered, dismissing the idea out of hand. "Inspector Delaney has no understanding of how society works. If Graham ruins your reputation, he ruins his as well. You are part of the same family."

Aunt Hetty wasn't ready to drop her pet theory. "Even though she's only family by marriage? And she's an American?"

Fiona shook her head. "It doesn't matter. Graham and Delia will be tarred with the same brush. Reputation is very important to Graham, even more so to Delia, and he would never want to disappoint her. He'd be more likely to murder you than ruin you."

That stung.

"Are you saying Graham would murder me for the money in my account?"

She shot me a look of exasperation. "Of course not. You take me too literally. I'm simply drawing a comparison as to how unlikely either action would be. Graham might file a claim to your funds, and while a few people may know about it, it's a private matter. He would never publicly draw the family name through the mud."

Fiona's argument was convincing, and I hoped Hetty was beginning to see things her way. Graham was very conscious of appearances. And I always had thought it was chance, not intention, that put the bracelet in my bag. I looked up at Hetty, still standing at the easel.

She held up her hands in surrender. "You know him better than I do. If you don't think it's possible, perhaps it isn't. But Graham is still the only one who needs money."

"As far as we know," said Fiona. "Besides, can't the thief be stealing for other reasons? Compulsion, or just for the thrill of it? That would mean all ten of us are still suspects, including George and me."

I shook my head. "Neither of you attended the first two events, so unless you have a confession to make, Fiona, let's move on to the footman, Mr. Capshaw, and I'll tell you why I suspect one of Lily's suitors."

Hetty wrote his name on the pad of paper. "I think it's safe to assume he was murdered because he had some knowledge he intended to relate to Frances."

"Would that knowledge have anything to do with the stolen bracelet?"

"If it were only about the stolen bracelet, Capshaw would have told Alicia. But he overheard me saying Lily's suitors were on the list of suspects. I even named them. So I believe he was coming here to give me some information about one of them, possibly that he's the thief. Capshaw was part of the staff at Alicia's ball. Perhaps he actually saw it happen."

Both women scoffed at my theory. "If he saw the theft, he would have told Alicia," Fiona said. "Don't you remember she asked the servants to help her look for it?"

"Then perhaps his information wasn't related to the theft, but I believe he knew something to the detriment of one of those men and planned to tell me. However, it's possible he visited the man in question before coming to me, offering to remain silent for a price."

I watched as realization dawned on both women. Fiona shook her head in regret. "A poor move on his part. So you think the gentleman in question hid in your yard and coshed him?"

"Cut his throat," I corrected, then felt guilty as she blanched. I suppose she didn't need all the details. "Delaney questioned Alicia's servants to learn if any of them knew where he planned to go before coming here. Alicia agreed to find out what Delaney learned, and pass that information on to me, when I visit her today."

"Good work, Frances." Aunt Hetty was scribbling notes on the paper. I also told them about obtaining Capshaw's references from Alicia, and my theory that a former employer might explain how Capshaw met one of the three men. I was warmed by the pride in my aunt's eyes.

"And I thought you were content to let everything flow around you. My apologies, Frances. I underestimated you."

"As did I," Fiona added. "At least I was unaware you had such powers of detection. I'm quite impressed."

"Well, I haven't actually detected anything yet. So far I'm only attempting to gather information."

"One must start somewhere," Fiona said. "And now that I consider the matter, you shouldn't visit Alicia alone. You are investigating a murderer after all. Whoever killed the footman has a secret he is desperate to keep. If you're determined to discover what it is, you may be next."

"Thank you so much for sharing that insight, Fiona. It does much to increase my confidence." I gave her a glare before continuing. "It's not as if I intend to catch the criminal myself. As I said, I'm only gathering information, which, of course, I will pass on to Inspector Delaney, while at the same time, I'll keep my sister safe from an unworthy admirer."

"Nevertheless," Hetty said, "I agree with Fiona. You shouldn't go to Alicia's alone."

I turned to my aunt. "Really? Who do you propose to go with me?"

Chapter 16

꧁꧂

"I must say, Fiona, I feel so much safer with you at my side."

Fiona harrumphed in response, as we descended from her carriage at Alicia's town house. "Laugh at me if you like, but should this horrid thief try to accost us, I assure you my footman would show you just how safe you are."

Indeed, I was quite assured, as I glanced up at her footman, a giant of a man, currently presenting our cards to the butler at Alicia's door. The butler bowed us inside, and escorted us to the drawing room where, once again, I found Alicia closeted with Inspector Delaney.

I was of two minds about this situation. I wanted to meet with Delaney and discover his progress on this case, but on the other hand, I didn't want him discovering me, calling on Alicia. I doubt he'd approve of me snooping about at his case, although I don't know what he could do about it.

No matter. I put on a pleasant smile, hoping Alicia wouldn't mention the reason for my call, and gave a nod to the detective who was now standing upon our entrance to the room. I introduced Fiona, and we all seated ourselves in an area of the draw-

ing room arranged for intimate conversation. We got the pleasantries out of the way—I confirmed that my sister and daughter had left for the country, and learned Delaney was just on the
point of departing.

"Then I'm pleased to find you still here, Inspector. How are
you getting on in investigating poor Mr. Capshaw's murder?"

"Still plenty of work to do, Lady Harleigh," he replied, revealing nothing.

"My aunt and I were discussing the possibility that the jewel
thief murdered that young man, and we wondered how one
would dispose of the type of articles he stole, as they would be
so easy to identify."

"Sadly there are many establishments in the city willing to
buy stolen goods." His eyes narrowed. "Just what exactly is
your interest?"

I countered with widened eyes, hoping to look as if I had no
particular interest at all. "Only that finding the goods might be
a way of finding the thief himself."

Delaney's countenance darkened. Oh, dear.

"It's good way for the *police* to find the thief. At least it can
be a start. Which is why we've been doing just that since the
first theft was reported." He rose to his feet as he spoke and
loomed over me. "I want to stress that this is something for the
police to do. Not a private citizen, and certainly not a lady like
yourself. Do I make myself clear?"

I fought the urge to shrink back in my chair. The man could
be horribly intimidating when he put his mind to it. My two
companions seemed to be absorbed in examining their finger-
nails so I'd receive no support from them. "You most definitely
do, Inspector. You may put your mind at rest. I simply wondered if we'd stumbled onto a possible line of investigation."

Delaney rolled his eyes to the ceiling. I could almost hear
him praying for deliverance from meddling women.

Not that I'd let that stop me. "Have you been able to learn if anyone from our list attended either the Haverhill or the Chesterton events?"

"The details of a police investigation are none of your affair, Lady Harleigh."

"Actually, I'm more concerned about my investigation. The three gentlemen?" I refrained from reminding him that I was paying for that investigation.

He conceded my point with an audible sigh. "I apologize for my lack of work on your investigation, my lady. However, I can tell you all three of the gentlemen were at both events. I wouldn't let your sister marry any of them just yet." With that he gave the three of us a nod, and bid us good day.

"Well." Fiona infused the single word with a wealth of disdain—but not until Delaney had actually left the room. I didn't blame her for not speaking up until he was out of earshot.

"Well, indeed," I agreed. "Two avenues of investigation that lead us nowhere."

"Yes, but at least you know the police are looking into it," Alicia said. "Did you really consider looking for the stolen items?"

I shook my head. "I never thought it through that far. It did seem finding the stolen items might lead to the thief. I should have realized the police were already doing that." I heaved a sigh at my own stupidity. "I suppose that is evidence of my amateur status as an investigator."

"I do believe Delaney is right on that point." Alicia's voice held a consoling note. "The police already know the usual and customary places to look for stolen goods, and they provide more of a threat in confronting the buyer."

I waved a dismissive hand "It was just a possibility. I'm more disappointed that we couldn't rule out one or more of Lily's suitors. Have you learned anything from your butler?"

"I have a little information for you, but not as much as you'd hoped. James mentioned only that he planned to visit an old friend he hadn't seen in some time."

My spirits sank. "That's it? No location? No name?"

"Sadly, no. But we have reason to believe his friend lived nearby. One of our maids asked if he was taking the train, and he replied that it wasn't far, so he planned to walk."

"So this friend might have been any of the ten names on our list, including Lily's beaux. That hardly narrows it down."

"It tells us nothing," Fiona insisted. "This friend of his might have been one of those gentlemen, or it might even have been you."

Both Alicia and I turned to her. "Well, he's not likely to say, *I'm going to visit Lady Harleigh, and sell her some information,* is he? He'd say, *I'm going to visit a friend.* In fact he might actually have visited a friend who has nothing to do with this."

I had to admit she was right. Capshaw's so-called friend might have been anyone, including me. But somehow I didn't think he meant me. "Alicia, does anyone know what time he left the house?"

"Not precisely, but Bradford, our butler, said he was gone by noon."

"And he arrived at my home about three. So he did go somewhere else before coming to me, and it was somewhere local."

"A park, or a café?" Alicia's face held the wonder of someone in the midst of a revelation. "If you were about to blackmail someone, would you march up to your victim's door, and reveal all in the privacy of his library, where he could just as easily shoot you as pay you off?"

"But then the so-called victim would have all the bother of a dead body to explain."

I found Fiona's tone a bit more acid than necessary under the circumstances. Alicia was only trying to help. I placed a restraining hand on her arm. "That's actually a good point. Capshaw might not have been concerned about his safety, but he wouldn't want to draw undue attention to himself. He wasn't a gentleman, so he couldn't just walk up to a gentleman's door and ask for him. At least not without a great deal of arguing with the butler, or footman, who answered the door."

Both ladies nodded in agreement so I carried on. "Capshaw would have sent a note, just as he did with me, arranging a place to meet. And it's very likely he'd feel more comfortable in a public place."

"If that's the case, then how do you proceed?" Fiona asked. "Ask each of the men on your list if they've had any interesting conversations in the park lately?"

I ignored the remark. "Now, if Capshaw was coming to sell me information, and it appears he was . . ." I looked to both my companions for agreement, and received nods in return. "And if he left Alicia's house three hours before he arrived at my home, then what he did in those hours before reaching my garden gate likely caused his death. Can we all agree on that?"

I received an emphatic nod from Alicia and a grudging glare from Fiona. "Go on," she urged.

"There are a number of things he might have done with that time, but most of those activities would not cause him to be murdered upon reaching my house. So I submit he spent that time blackmailing the very person he was coming to see me about. Can we agree on that?"

This time Fiona nodded in easy agreement. Alicia drew a deep breath. "That's a reasonable theory, but I have to ask if you really know who, or what, James was coming to talk to you about?"

"Of course I can't be certain, but I can only imagine it was about one of Lily's suitors. In which case, that narrows the list of suspects to three gentlemen, two of whom I'm dining with tonight."

Fiona's brows rose in surprise. "How do you intend to broach the subject?"

"I have absolutely no idea. However, my maid, Bridget, is walking out with Lord Ainsworthy's butler, so I can ask her to find out if he received any unusual notes, followed immediately by a trip to the park."

Alicia stared at me, aghast, while Fiona chuckled. "Ladies, I'm a babe in the woods. I'll ask Bridget to use her wiles to discover anything she can about the viscount's movements on the day in question. I suppose I'll attempt to do the same in my own way at the dinner party. Mr. Hazelton will be with me, and with his aid, I hope to pull this off without looking like a complete fool."

"I'm not as concerned about you looking like a fool, as I am about your looking like a corpse."

I winced at the blunt comment, but Fiona did not relent. "One of these men might be a murderer, Frances. You don't want to let on that you suspect either one of them, or you may put yourself in danger."

I blamed Fiona for my nerves that evening. I'm usually quite socially adept, and since my mother drilled me from the age of twelve, my conversational skills are second to none. So it had to be fear of giving away my suspicions that had me as nervous as a debutante.

We traveled in George's carriage to the home of my friend Lady Georgianna, who was giving this dinner. Her daughter was vying with Lily for the interest of two of the Season's eligible bachelors, Viscount Ainsworthy and Mr. Daniel Grayson. As I had a need to speak with both gentlemen, I was especially grateful to be invited myself.

I'd just briefed George on the necessity of these conversations and learned that he'd already done a bit of investigating on his own. He felt confident Mr. Grayson was living a blameless life, as he currently resided at the family home in London, with his mother and two sisters, acting as their escort. I wasn't

so sure *blameless* was the right word. I told George about seeing the young man with Alicia the night before but I had to
admit that didn't make him a thief or a murderer.

George had no news on Mr. Kendrick as of yet, and could
learn little about the viscount, beyond his general amiability,
and the fact that he was slow in settling his accounts.

George was in complete agreement with his sister on the danger
of revealing my suspicions to either man. "You must proceed with
caution," he said. "If your theory is correct, Capshaw threatened
blackmail to one of these men in the morning, and was dead by
the afternoon. That means one of them did the deed himself."

I looked up at him through the feathers curving over the side
of my head and resisted the urge to blow them out of the way.
"Are you saying one of them is a cold-blooded killer, or that
my theory is wrong?"

"If only I knew for sure. The premise seems reasonable to
me, so I'm leaning toward the former—cold-blooded killer. Be
careful. And make sure I'm nearby when you speak to them."

So maybe Fiona wasn't completely to blame for my nerves. I
scanned the room as we arrived. About twenty guests were
gathered here, chatting in groups of three or four. I saw Grayson
standing near a window, speaking with two gentlemen I didn't
recognize. George and I strolled over to the group to join the
conversation. It galled me to speak to the man after last night,
but I suppose it was all in the line of duty. He cast nervous
glances at me as we approached. Good. He deserved to be uncomfortable. I gave myself a "buck up" speech and jumped
right in when Grayson mentioned his despair that spring would
ever warm up.

"I'm perhaps not as fond of warm weather as you Mr. Grayson,
for I find these cooler temperatures perfect for long strolls in the
park. You live near Green Park, do you not?"

"I do," he agreed with a pleasant smile, "but as I prefer to ride rather than walk, I've ignored Green Park lately. I usually make my way over to Hyde Park for a run on the row."

"Ah, yes. In fact I believe I saw you there Thursday afternoon."

Grayson smiled and shook his head. "The park is far too crowded in the afternoon. I always ride in the morning."

I gave him a tight smile. "But I was certain it was you. Come now, you needn't feel badly that you ignored me."

"You must be mistaken, Lady Harleigh. How could anyone ignore you?"

I waved away his protest as if it were of no matter. "As I recall, you were with a lovely young lady. Completely understandable your attention would be on her."

"The only woman to hold my attention is your lovely sister," Grayson said, his gaze darting to his friends, in a desperate plea for confirmation. The two young men quickly turned their attention to another group nearby. "I assure you I was at Brooks Thursday afternoon. You must have seen someone else."

It was refreshing to see the arrogant man floundering a bit but I was finished with him. "I suppose if you were at Brooks, I must be mistaken." I glanced at George and received a wink in return. He'd follow up on the young man's whereabouts.

I let Grayson rattle on with George while I glanced around the room. Where on earth was the viscount? I was through with Grayson, and ready to move on. Luckily, Georgianna's daughter, Madeline, chose that moment to pass near our little group. I gave her a bright smile.

"Madeline, whatever has become of Lord Ainsworthy? Wasn't he planning to be in attendance this evening?"

Her smile was forced, more like a gritting of teeth. "Yes, we did expect him, but he sent his regrets yesterday. He had to leave town on some urgent business. We assume he's gone to his estate in Kent." Her eyes darted around the room as she took my arm and guided me a few steps away from George and Grayson.

Instantly I was all mother. "What is it, dear?"

"Is Lily well?" Her frown gave away her concern. "I heard she left for the country."

"I assure you, there is nothing terribly wrong with her. A slight cold. She didn't want to show a red nose around town, and since my daughter was going to Harleigh anyway, Lily thought she might spend a week there herself." I gave her a reassuring smile. "Your concern does you credit as a friend, dear. Thank you for asking about her."

I thought that was all, but her expression hadn't relaxed. "Is there something else?"

At these words, her countenance became even more clouded.

"Lady Harleigh, is she . . . that is, does she?" She heaved a sigh of frustration. "Does Lily have feelings for Viscount Ainsworthy?"

Ah, so that's what this was about. Oh, dear. How to answer? "Well, I'm not sure Lily's feelings extend beyond admiration for any of her suitors yet, but perhaps you cannot say the same?"

Madeline blushed a deep rose. "He is so handsome," she whispered.

"And he'll be just as handsome in a few months' time. Let me give you the same advice I gave Lily. Do not rush into a commitment. Hopefully at least one of you will take that advice to heart."

The butler gave a signal to Lady Georgianna, and we all processed to the dining room where I found myself seated between George and an elderly relative of Georgianna's. His name escaped me, but fortunately he was deep in a discussion about hunting, with Lord Grafton, at the head of the table. The poor woman seated between the two men would likely be listening to this conversation all through dinner.

Turning to my left I saw George gazing at me with an impish grin on his face. I knew immediately I was the object of his amusement. "I'm beginning to think I should start charging you a fee for all the entertainment I provide."

"I'm not laughing at you, Frances," he replied, and with a straight face, too.

"You are. And I'm not sure why. My line of inquiry with Grayson was rather effective."

"You were superb. Grayson was ready to admit to anything rather than snubbing you. Well done."

We were interrupted by a footman, serving the first course, Potage à la Reine. Delicious. When he had moved on, George turned back to me, changing the subject. "My sister deserted me again for your company this morning," he observed.

"She thinks you do that intentionally, you know—tell her something about me so she'll rush off, and leave you to enjoy your breakfast in peace."

"Ha!" We both looked around the table to see if anyone had heard his exclamation. George continued, lowering his voice. "An excellent idea, and one I would have conceived eventually, but so far I'm innocent of her charges. I hope she didn't disturb your breakfast."

"Oh, no, we were up early to see the girls off with Delia. By the time Fiona arrived, my aunt and I were going over the main points of the recent criminal activity, trying to come up with a common thread."

His expression of interest told me he considered this a worthy occupation. "And did you find one?"

"Sadly no. We did have one unanswered question though, about the disposal of stolen goods. Later, Fiona and I paid a visit to Alicia, while Delaney was there. When I asked him about it I thought he was going to have some sort of fit."

George lowered his soup spoon and stared at me. "He seemed such a calm sort. What exactly did you ask him?"

"Just whether finding the buyer of the stolen goods would lead one to the thief."

"I see. And you gave him no reason to believe you intended to seek out that buyer yourself?"

"I did not. He came to that conclusion without any encouragement from me. I fully understand anyone who buys stolen goods would be just as dangerous as the thief himself. I am not so foolish as to go looking for him." I didn't think George needed to know I had been just that foolish earlier today.

"I knew you had a good head on your shoulders," he said, returning to his soup. "That type of work is best left to the police."

"But are they doing it? You said yourself, Alicia's case was probably closed, and with this murder to solve, are they even looking for the thief anymore? I still need to learn if one of Lily's suitors is involved. Oh, I did find out from Delaney that all three have been on hand every time there was a theft. So all three are still suspects."

George's gaze drifted up and to the side. "There might be another way," he murmured, almost as if speaking to himself. He turned back to me, a slight smile about his lips. "These were crimes of opportunity, so the thief would not have had a buyer ready and waiting for the goods. Fencing stolen goods is no easy task, and the thefts were recent, so there's a chance our man may still be in possession of some of these items."

"An interesting possibility, I agree, but how on earth can you find out if it's true?"

His smile widened. "Leave that to me."

The teasing man! Though I worked on him all through dinner, he would give me no more of an answer, so I had no choice but to give up and enjoy the rest of my evening. My high hopes at the start of it had become seriously deflated by the end.

George had confidence that Mr. Grayson was innocent of any crime, and despite my general opinion of him, I had no reason to think otherwise. My idea of questioning these gentlemen, and finding a link to poor Capshaw, had turned into an exercise in futility. It's not as if I were the police and could interrogate them. Ainsworthy wasn't even here. And I might have just given him away to one of Lily's competitors. Not what I would call a successful evening. But perhaps George would have better luck. I wondered just what he was planning.

Chapter 17

With last night's encounter, I was on my way to eliminating
one murder suspect, and determined today would go as well.
With that in mind I rose from bed before Bridget brought in
my morning coffee. Alicia had kindly given me the copied letters of reference for Mr. Capshaw and I learned from the society pages of the *Times*, his most recent employers had just
come up to town two days ago.

Mr. and Mrs. Rockingham, an older couple, rarely left their
home in Derbyshire, so my luck must be improving, as they
had conveniently turned up, and were staying in the house of
Mrs. Rockingham's sister for a fortnight. I had just penned a
letter, asking them if I might call at their earliest convenience,
when Bridget slipped through the door. Upon not finding me
in bed, her head swiveled round as if I'd disappeared on her.

I raised my pen in the air. "Over here, Bridget."

She let out a little "Oh!" of surprise at seeing me at the es-
critoire, then scurried over to set up the coffee on the little
desk. "Couldn't sleep, my lady?"

"Actually, I slept quite well. I just woke early, and decided to get some work done, rather than rolling over." I picked up the delicate porcelain cup and took a long sip of coffee. "Ah, that's what I needed!"

Bridget worried her lower lip. "You should have rung for me, my lady. I would have been happy to bring up your coffee earlier."

"I'm just now out of bed, Bridget. There was no point in troubling you with an early bell. Now put that tray down, draw up a chair, and tell me if you learned anything from Mr. Barnes last night. The viscount didn't attend the dinner party. It's said he's visiting his estate."

"Right you are, my lady." Bridget placed the tray on a table by the door, and returned to my side, although she didn't take a seat. "He left very suddenlike. Day before yesterday, he went to his club about noon, as usual, came back early in the evening to get ready for some event, and asked his valet to pack a bag for him. Said he was going to the country the following morning, and he'd be gone a few days."

That seemed to agree with my knowledge of the viscount's movements. Two days ago we met him at the charity fashion show around two o'clock. If he'd left the house at noon, he might have gone to his club first. We also saw him at the Roswell ball that evening. He must have known he was leaving town by that time, yet we heard nothing of it. "Odd that Lily didn't mention his plans to me. I wonder if he didn't tell her. And if not, why not?"

Bridget's expression stated she couldn't enlighten me on that point. "Did Barnes say anything about Ainsworthy's actions on Thursday—the day of the murder?"

Her eyes rounded as she placed a hand over her mouth. Good Lord, she looked as if she were going to faint. I jumped up, led her over to the bench at the end of the bed, and seated the both of us. Bridget stared into my face, shaking her head. "I thought this was only about stealing some jewelry. Did the viscount murder that poor man in the garden?" She looked away, wringing her hands. "Oh, poor Barnes."

That took me aback. "Poor Barnes?"

"He's going to need a new situation. And if His Lordship's arrested for murder, he won't be able to give Barnes a character."

I placed a calming hand over hers. "Let's just take one step at a time, shall we? You shouldn't jump to the conclusion that the viscount is a murderer. What did Barnes tell you?"

"Only that His Lordship seemed irritated about having to leave London. He didn't mention anything special about Thursday. Barnes is very sharp and likes to talk. If he'd noticed anything strange about the way His Lordship was acting that day, he would have told me."

"Very good," I said, in what I hoped was a soothing voice. "So Thursday was just an ordinary day. We can assume Ainsworthy went to his club around noon, came home to change his clothing some time later, then left for whatever entertainment he had on that evening."

Bridget nodded. "That'd be about right, my lady."

"Then Friday started with his usual routine, until he decided he needed to go to the country. Did he tell Barnes he had business there?"

"Well, at first he didn't give any details, but when Barnes asked if His Lordship was going to his estate, he said that he was, that he'd take the morning train, and he should only be gone a few days."

"Did he take his valet?"

"No, and that seemed a bit strange to me, too. His Lordship dismissed the staff at the manor several weeks back. Before he even came to London. I guess he didn't expect to spend much time there, so he just has a caretaker couple in place—a maid of all work and a man to do the heavy work. I asked Barnes why he wouldn't take someone to wait on him, but he said that was just the viscount's way. It wasn't so long ago His Lordship was just a plain mister and taking care of himself. He wasn't used to having people to do for him."

I considered everything she told me. Ainsworthy would have been away from home at the pertinent time on the day of the murder, but he'd come home unruffled and apparently, unbloody. He sacked the staff of his country home as soon as he'd arrived in England. That is rather unusual behavior, but perhaps he didn't plan to spend much time at his estate. If not, it was a reasonable thing to do.

Then why did he suddenly decide to go there?

"So Barnes didn't say whether the viscount received a letter from the country, or some other communication, that would have necessitated the visit?"

Bridget shook her head. "Barnes thinks His Lordship is considering marriage though, and might be going to his estate to hire the staff back. But that's just him thinking, my lady. The viscount didn't say that himself."

Two thoughts occurred to me. One, was that it was a reasonable explanation for Ainsworthy going to his country house. The other, was that Lily was going to kill me if he proposed to Madeline instead of her. But what if it was Lily he wanted to marry? I felt a moment's panic. What if he'd already proposed and been accepted? What better time to go the country and prepare his household to receive his bride?

I drew a calming breath. No, Lily could never have kept something like that to herself. I was losing my perspective. I needed to look at this as a disinterested party.

The only reason a man rushes at breakneck speed into marriage, is because he needs money, and if Ainsworthy dismissed his staff, that might also indicate a lack of funds. But did that fact increase the odds of his being the thief? Not really. When you're a titled aristocrat in need of money, you simply live off credit until you marry it. I'd have to make sure to warn Lily, but as far as criminal behavior, I didn't see that in the picture.

His Lordship was probably innocent. However, I could verify one more thing.

"Do you know which club Viscount Ainsworthy belongs to, Bridget?"

She shook her head. "Barnes mentioned it. I know it started with a *B*, but I don't remember the name."

"That's all right. It's either Brooks or Boodles then. I'll ask Mr. Hazelton to make some inquires around both of them to see if the viscount was there on Thursday. If so, then I think we can take him off our list of suspects."

After my conversation with Bridget, I sent Jenny to find a messenger to take my note to the Rockinghams, then got dressed for my day. I wrote a short letter to Rose, so she wouldn't forget me, with all the fun and frivolity she was supposedly having in the country. I wrote an even shorter one to Lily, telling her she might want to think twice about the viscount as a potential husband since money was definitely a factor in his search for a bride. I could have sent a message to George, but decided to pay him a visit instead.

At half-past ten, the butler showed me into his breakfast room. As George's home was much larger than mine, it was no surprise the footprints were nothing alike. For example, I had no breakfast room, and upon seeing his, I immediately wanted one. Light poured in from the south-facing windows, where the buttery yellow draperies had been pulled back. The small room glowed. What an excellent place to start one's day.

"I love this room," I said, smiling at George, who stood to greet me. He led me to a seat next to his, at the head of the table. "Now I know why Fiona comes here for breakfast so often."

"I'd like to say she comes here for my charming company, but then we would both be wrong." He tipped his head toward the sideboard. "She comes for the food."

I turned and was amazed by the number of chafing dishes crowded on the sideboard. "All this for one man?"

"What I don't consume, the staff eats. In fact, I think they resent the mornings when Fiona stops in for breakfast." He gave me a grin. "You know she's always reducing, so she won't have anything more than toast served at home. Poor Robert has to eat at his club. When she comes here, she's ready to indulge in a big meal." He picked up a plate from the sideboard. "Can I tempt you to indulge? I usually just help myself, but I'd be happy to prepare a plate for you."

He didn't have to ask me twice. "I'll help myself." I stood and took the offered plate, choosing a few items from the chaffing dishes. "So," he said when we were both seated again, "aren't you risking your reputation by calling on a single gentleman?" He arched one dark eyebrow. "What if someone had seen you on my doorstep?"

"I never risk my reputation, as you well know. And I was never at your doorstep. I slipped out the back from my garden gate and in through yours. You had the doors open to your drawing room, where I found your maid, who called your butler, who led me to you." I brandished my fork like a wand. "And voilà! Here I am."

George set his own fork down with a clang. "Good Lord, you could be a spy." He leaned back and took me in with a glance. "While I like the idea of you sneaking around just to see me, I have the feeling your reasons are far from romantic."

I chuckled at that. "Yes, I'm afraid you're right. I have two reasons for coming, neither of which could be considered romantic. The first is to ask if there's been any progress with the anonymous letter."

"Ah! I do have some news on that front." He took a sip of coffee and dabbed at his lips with his napkin. "My friend managed to see the letter which is roughly three sentences that verify what Inspector Delaney told you. Reggie's death was not from natural causes and the police should look to the wronged wife."

I frowned. "The wronged wife?"

"A direct quote."

"How dramatic." I felt my shoulders slump as I let out a sigh. There was no feigning indifference. I was worried. "You might as well tell me the worst. What will the police do?"

He placed a hand over mine. "Chin up now. They aren't coming to arrest you yet."

"Yet?" A twinge of fear slipped up my spine.

His wink was barely perceptible. "Probably never."

It took a moment to absorb the words and in that space of time, anger replaced my fear. I pinched his hand. Hard. He jerked it away with a yelp.

"This is my life, George. Stop playing with me and tell me what you learned."

I glared at him while he rubbed his hand. "Good Lord, that smarts! We once had a nursemaid who did that when my brothers and I misbehaved."

"Was it effective?"

"Rather." He gave me a sheepish grin. "All right, the good news is that the Guildford police have found no evidence to support this letter. The doctor thinks it's all hogwash, the earl is in London and unavailable for questioning, and none of the local constables are willing to knock on the door of Harleigh Manor and ask the countess for her opinion on the matter. So they will have to give up any hope of ordering an autopsy."

"Goodness, how did your friend learn all this?"

"A few pints at the local pub works wonders."

Relief flushed through my veins. "Then it's over?"

"As far as the police are concerned, it's over, but since the letter was unsigned, they won't be able to tell the writer the accusation was false." He shrugged. "There may still be some whispers around Guildford."

"That also means we'll never know who wrote it."

"Someone who knew you were the *wronged wife?*"

I shot him a look or scorn. "It seems everyone in society knows I was the *wronged wife.*"

"But the letter was posted in Guildford so . . ." He paused to frown at me.

A flush of shock heated my skin. "Graham?"

George gave me an incredulous stare. "I was about to say, disgruntled housemaid. I thought you'd decided Graham wouldn't want to start a scandal."

"No, I suppose that was just an impulsive reaction. Graham would abhor the scandal and Delia would be worse." I had to chuckle at the thought. "If she thought I'd murdered Reggie, she'd do all in her power to cover it up."

"Considering they had the most to gain from Reggie's death, why would they question the cause? Since the letter is no longer an issue, I wouldn't be too concerned about the writer."

"I agree. As I have enough worries already, I'll have to be satisfied I'm no longer a murder suspect."

"Is there something I can do to lessen your worries?"

I sighed in frustration and told him about my conversation with Bridget. "Would you be able to confirm that Ainsworthy was at his club on Thursday as well as Grayson?"

"I believe so. Confirming the exact time might be difficult, but since he was there for several hours, chances are he was playing cards, which means I'll have a few people to help sort out a time line."

"Thank you, George. At the risk of sounding pushy, how soon can you check on this?"

"I have some business this morning, but I should be able to go this afternoon. If you'll be home later, I can stop by to report in."

I beamed. "That would be perfect. I hope to pay a call on the Rockinghams today, but I doubt that will take long." At his look of surprise, I explained their relationship to Mr. Capshaw, and how I thought they might be able to help.

I preened a bit when I saw George's look of amazement. "You really did miss your calling, you know, but what do you intend to do with any information you glean today?"

"Assuming they actually have any knowledge of Capshaw that connects him to one of my three suspects, otherwise known as my sister's suitors, I will of course pass it on to Inspector Delaney."

"Hmm. From that little light in your eye, I'd say you are savoring the idea of passing on information to him."

"I am," I admitted. "He believes me to be quite useless, and I'm eager to prove him wrong, however childish that might be." I sighed as I sank back in my chair. "Unfortunately, I'm much less confident of my suspects. We both feel quite certain Mr. Grayson is not our culprit. The evidence seems to be pointing away from the viscount as well. That leaves us with only Mr. Kendrick, and a more unlikely villain I've never met."

George cocked his head as one brow jerked upward. "You find that unfortunate? I'd have thought exonerating Lily's gentlemen would be the very definition of fortunate."

The truth of his words hit home. "Good heavens, George, you're right. Their innocence of this crime is precisely what I'd been hoping for." I shook my head. "What on earth is wrong with me?"

He gave me an indulgent smile. "You've been taken by the fever. You're embroiled in a mystery and wish to solve it. With your three suspects absolved," he raised his hands, palms up, "where do you turn?"

"Without my three suspects, I'm left with the perplexing question of just what did Capshaw want to tell me, if it had nothing to do with those three men?"

"Perhaps you're not yet convinced of their innocence?"

"Perhaps I will be when you tell me what you discovered last night," I said, with a sidelong glance.

"Ah! I wondered when it would come to that."

I gazed at him, shaking my head. "I can't believe you made me ask. Surely you realize I'm burning with curiosity."

George set down his fork and leaned back in the chair, never taking his eyes from mine. "If I tell you I found the absence of any evidence incriminating Leo Kendrick, would that satisfy you?"

"You know it wouldn't, or why would you even ask?"

His only reply was a blank stare. Teasing man. "All right then, let me see if I can work it out for myself. Last night you determined three things if I remember correctly. First, stolen goods are difficult to dispose of, unless one has a ready buyer; second, the thief was stealing whatever was at hand when he had the opportunity; and third, therefore he had no ready buyer."

So far I was only repeating what George had told me himself, but the re-telling helped me to understand what was in his mind, and therefore, what his actions might have been.

"If the thief was unable to dispose of everything, he must still have some of the items hidden away." I pointed my fork at George. "So you went looking for the thief's cache. What did you do, break into Mr. Kendrick's lodgings?"

He maintained a stony expression, but I saw the slightest glint in his eyes that told me I was right.

I was also horrified. "You broke into his lodgings?"

George didn't flinch. "That is the logical place to look. Don't you agree?"

Words failed me. I simply stared at him, most likely with my mouth gaping open in an unattractive manner. It took several moments to come to my senses. "George, you cannot mean you snuck into another man's house without his knowledge or permission. Surely it's a crime to do so."

"In most cases, I believe it is, which is why it's imperative one not be caught."

I was still wearing my fish face—goggle-eyed and open-

mouthed. Who was this man sitting at the table with me, casually eating breakfast? "I can't believe this is something you
learned working for the Home Secretary."

"That's precisely where I learned it." He rose from his seat
and pushed the door closed. Turning back, he gave me a mischievous smile. "The security of the country was at stake, Frances.
Sometime I had to do things that weren't strictly legal. Though
I don't work for the government any longer, that work has put
me in contact with several men in high places, and occasionally
I'm asked to do a favor for one or another of them."

"Like Haverhill, for example?" I narrowed my eyes. "George,
is this some kind of political espionage?"

He frowned. "I doubt it. Since the Conservatives took
power they've done their best to make their Liberal counter-
parts look as bad as possible. That's not unusual, but I'd rather
not allow them more ammunition. The theft probably had
nothing to do with politics. But if the opposition party found
out about—these items, they could show Haverhill in a very
unfortunate light."

I searched his face for any signs he was joking. How absolutely incredible. "So does that mean you're authorized to
take action that would otherwise be unlawful?"

"That's rather a sticky point. When people ask for my help,
they want results and rarely ask questions. How far I wish to
test the lawfulness of my actions is up to me. If I'm ever caught,
I'll no longer be of any use to them. Which is why you must
understand this is to go no further. Not Fiona. Not Lily. No
one else must know."

I was still having a difficult time giving credence to his
words, but I nodded in affirmation. "Yes, yes, of course. But
weren't you taking a dangerous risk last night?"

"Not really. Kendrick himself told me he'd be out, and I
knew his valet always takes his master's absence as an opportunity to go to the pub and enjoy a pint."

As I absorbed this information, I assessed my feelings about it. I noted much less horror, and a growing fascination with George's work. I wasn't sure I wanted to know what that might say about me. "If you found nothing to implicate Mr. Kendrick, what will you do next?"

His smile spread and a mischievous glint lit his eyes. "That's where you come in."

"Me?" Nothing could have shocked me more. "What can I do?"

"You can give Bridget the night off, or rather request that she get Barnes away from home for an hour or two."

My mouth fell open. "Ainsworthy? You are looking at him next?" Another thought hit me. "Wait, how do you know Bridget is stepping out with Barnes?"

"It's all part of the job, my dear, and yes, I am looking at Ainsworthy next. The question is—can you help me?"

I can't explain it, but suddenly it became my fondest wish to help George with this mysterious and exciting—well, criminal enterprise. Though it wasn't exactly criminal, was it? He didn't intend to steal anything; he was only looking for stolen goods.

"I'll do my best," I replied. "I'm not sure what to tell Bridget, but I'll try to encourage her to get Barnes out of the house. I can tell you, when we meet this afternoon, if I was successful."

With that settled, I retraced my sneaky steps back to my own house, and found a response from Mrs. Rockingham. It turns out, her husband would be away from home all afternoon, but she'd be available to receive me at my convenience. Since I had absolutely nothing to do at the moment, I decided now was convenient. It was nearly noon, so once I changed my clothes, and had Jenny order a cab, I'd arrive at the correct time for a "morning" visit. It seems I was about to do some investigating of my own.

I met Mrs. Rockingham in the drawing room of her sister's town house on Hamilton Place. Fortunately for me, the sister was out paying calls. Unfortunately, I'd given no consideration as to how I'd pose my questions to Mrs. Rockingham. Why was I such a ninny? I should have fabricated some sort of story in advance. As we greeted one another, I assessed her to be upwards of sixty, not a tall woman, but of sturdy build, and with a face that held the wrinkles of someone who'd smiled a great deal in her lifetime. She did not strike me as the type of woman who would willingly engage in a conversation about murder.

I was wrong.

After the usual opening pleasantries, she informed me she'd read about Capshaw's murder in the paper. "At my age, I'm not unused to hearing about the death of people I know, but to read one of them was murdered, well, that came as a shock."

A shock indeed. Imagine a woman of the upper class not only reading the paper, but admitting to doing so, and discussing what she'd read. Heavens! Not only that, but she recognized the name of someone who'd left her employ several years ago. I liked this woman already.

"I'm so relieved you mentioned that, Mrs. Rockingham. I have a small interest in the resolution of that crime, you see, and was floundering for a way to introduce the subject."

"Indeed?" I could see her wondering what manner of woman she'd invited to her home and decided I'd better embellish a little. I hoped Delaney would forgive me. Or better yet, never find out.

"Has Inspector Delaney contacted you since you arrived in town?"

"Contacted me? A police inspector? No, of course not."

"I was afraid of that. The police don't seem to be as interested in Mr. Capshaw's murder as they might be if he were of a different class." I let out a little sigh of frustration. "In fact, they don't seem to have taken much action at all, and if something isn't done soon, the murderer may get away with his crime."

I could see her curiosity growing. "You do sound as if you have an interest."

"Yes, I do. My younger sister is in London for the Season, or rather she was. She had three suitors, and the police believe one of them may have had something to do with Mr. Capshaw's murder."

Mrs. Rockingham gave me a hard look. "Don't mince your words for me, Lady Harleigh. Are you saying a *gentleman* is suspected of murdering James? Why?"

"The police believe he knew something to the gentleman's discredit. Unfortunately, we don't know which of the three, if any, committed this crime. But until we do, well, the cloud of suspicion will hang over them all."

"Of course." She shook her head, most likely wondering what the world was coming to. "I hope your sister is well out of the way."

"She's retired to the country until the murderer has been found."

"Very sensible." The older woman gave me a nod of approval. "How is it you think I can help?"

"Since we think Mr. Capshaw had some damning information about one of the gentlemen, it stands to reason he must have come into contact with one of them at some time in the past. Mr. Capshaw worked at your home in the country for several years, so I can't help but wonder if one of the men visited your neighborhood, or perhaps even your home, while Capshaw was in your employ."

"Yes, yes. I follow you though I'm not sure I can help. James was with us for ten years but we didn't entertain a great deal during that time. I hate to think something nefarious might have been going on in my own home, but,"—she shook her head—"why don't you give me their names?"

I complied, naming the gentlemen one at a time, but the lady just continued shaking her head. "No, I'm not familiar with any of them. We live a rather retiring life, and right now I'm quite glad of it. I'm sorry, my dear, but I'm afraid I can't help you."

I could see from her face that her answers had been honest as was her regret at not being able to help. I thanked her for her time and expressed my wishes that we would meet again while she was in town. Then I collected Bridget, and set off for home, feeling so defeated I didn't even bother asking the Rockinghams' maid to find me a cab.

For the next few blocks, I pondered the fruitlessness of my actions thus far. I still didn't know how Capshaw could have come into contact with any of the three gentlemen. It appeared they all could be innocent of any wrongdoing, and I'd sent Lily away for nothing. Well, not for nothing. Someone had broken into my house, and a man was killed in my back garden. I was just no further ahead in finding out who did it or why.

"Why on earth was that young man murdered?" I asked Bridget, who simply shook her head. Probably disgruntled at my decision to walk. "And what could he have wanted to tell me?"

We'd just approached Hyde Park Corner. I paused, glancing to my left at a queue of cabs along the curb. I was wondering if I should have Bridget engage one, when I felt a hard shove from behind. Losing my balance, I stumbled into the street, flailing my arms in an attempt to latch on to something that would keep me upright.

"Careful, Lady Harleigh!" A strong hand gripped my right arm and hauled me back just as two horses, pulling a cab, trotted past me. The driver shouted at me as he maneuvered the vehicle out of the way, but all I cared was that I was back on my feet, rather than lying under his wheels.

Bridget came to my side in an instant. "My lady, are you all right?"

It took me a moment to realize I was still clinging to the arms of the man who had rescued me. "Yes," I said. As I straightened myself, and took Bridget's arm, I looked up at the man. "Mr. Kendrick!"

Kendrick flagged down a cab, bundled us inside, and climbed

in himself. "Allow me to see you home," he said, while Bridget looked me over for signs of injury. "You gave me quite a scare," he said. "I saw you on the corner and was just about to greet you when suddenly you took a tumble right toward those horses. Did you trip on something?"

"I suppose I must have done. Thank goodness you were there to catch me."

I didn't hear his answer. My mind was too busy reliving the last few minutes. Someone had pushed me into the street. Without Kendrick's quick action, I would now be severely injured, possibly dead. It might have been an accident, but the hand at my back hadn't felt like an accident. I could not ignore the possibility that someone had tried to kill me.

Chapter 18

Light flooded through the windows when I awoke the next day. Bridget had set my coffee on the bedside table and was in the process of opening the draperies. I stretched and wondered why I still felt so tired. Then I remembered. The crimes—not even close to being solved. The attempt on my life. The argument with George and Aunt Hetty. And the sleepless night, due to, well all of the above.

When Bridget helped me into the house yesterday afternoon, Hetty had appeared from nowhere and immediately began fussing over my appearance. It seems I'd lost my hat in the fall, so my hair was in disarray, and my sleeve was torn. I suppose that was enough to tell her I hadn't been out for a casual walk, especially since I returned in a cab.

She clutched my arm and led me into the drawing room when all I wanted was to lie down in my own bed. Poor Mr. Kendrick, abandoned in the foyer, watched helplessly has the two women took me into their care. I called out my thanks to him and he made a hasty retreat.

Then the interrogation began.

"What on earth happened to you?" she said, helping me to one of the cozy, overstuffed chairs.

Bridget answered for me. "She tripped, ma'am, and almost fell into the street right in front of a pair of horses. Mr. Kendrick saved her from being trampled."

"Oh, my word!" Hetty glanced from Bridget, to me, and back. "Go to the kitchen, Bridget, and order some tea. In fact, you should stay there and have a cup yourself. You look quite done in. I can take care of the countess for now."

Bridget nodded and hurried from the room. Hetty stood over me. I raised my eyes to meet hers. "You tripped?" she asked.

"Bridget assumed I tripped. In fact, everyone assumed I tripped. I certainly couldn't prove otherwise, so I didn't argue the point. I just wanted to get home."

"So you didn't trip."

"No." I looked into her worried eyes and made myself sit up in the chair. "I was very definitely, very firmly, pushed by a strong hand between my shoulder blades. Kendrick caught me before I actually hit the ground. By the time I regained my feet, and looked around me, I had no way of knowing who did it. No one else had noticed. I didn't see anyone I recognized. Whom should I have accused?" I shook my head. "It was quite hopeless."

Hetty raised a shaking hand to her cheek as she lowered herself into the chair next to mine. "Could it have been Kendrick?"

I was saved from responding, by the arrival of Jenny with the tea service. Once she'd placed everything on the table, Hetty sent her off, and poured a cup for us both, adding some brandy from her supply, which I'd noticed was now in a crystal decanter. She let me have a few sips, so we could regain our composure, before continuing with her questions.

"You said you didn't recognize anyone in the crowd. Whom did you expect to see?"

I waved my free hand while the other clung to the teacup like a lifeline. "I don't know, maybe someone with the word *villain* written on his forehead? That would certainly make this easier."

"What about Mr. Kendrick? Why was he there?"

"He mentioned on the ride home he was on his way to a meeting. Since it was his quick action that saved me, it's hard to imagine he's also the one who pushed me."

Hetty frowned. "Have you considered Graham?"

I sighed. I really did not want to consider Graham. "Yes. I'm ashamed to admit it, but Delaney planted that seed in my mind and, as I fell, Graham was the first person I thought of." I met my aunt's gaze and saw concern and fear for me in her eyes. "He wasn't there, Aunt Hetty."

"Would he have to be? Couldn't he have hired some thug to do away with you? To make it look like an accident?"

I'd just begun to sputter some sort of answer, when Jenny arrived at the door again, asking if I was at home to Mr. Hazelton.

Hetty's resounding *yes* nearly drowned out my *no,* and caused obvious confusion for Jenny, who hovered in the doorway, unsure what to do.

"I don't want him to see me like this," I hissed.

Hetty's brows shot up. "Really? While that's very interesting, I don't much care at the moment. I think we could use his support." She rose from her chair and nodded to Jenny. "Please bring him in."

To her credit, Jenny waited for my nod before leaving to fetch George. I glared at my aunt. "Just because I had a little fright, doesn't grant you the right to take over my household."

"A little fright, you call it?"

"Someone had a fright?" George strolled into the room, tall, broad-shouldered, and ready to take on all manner of problems, and my irritation at Hetty vanished. It was comforting to have him near, which, in an odd way, was also discomforting.

I set down my tea and stood to greet him. It was a struggle not to throw myself into his arms and beg him to make all my troubles go away. Something of that struggle must have shown on my face. His smile faded and his brow furrowed as he took in my disheveled appearance. "What happened?" he asked, his voice gentle.

"Someone tried to kill Frances this afternoon," Hetty blurted.

"What?"

"Oh, good heavens, Aunt Hetty, must you be so dramatic?"

"Well, I didn't see any point in beating around the bush."

I shifted my gaze to George, who was standing beside my chair, his hands fisted, and a vein throbbing in his forehead. Oh, dear.

"One of you tell me what happened, right now."

I glared at Hetty until she sat down. I followed suit, giving George a summary of my afternoon, beginning with my fruitless visit to Mrs. Rockingham, and ending with Hetty's suspicion of either Kendrick or Graham being responsible for the attack on my life. At some point, as I related my adventure, George had seated himself on the edge of the chair on my other side, and taken hold of my hand. I looked down at our clasped hands and marveled again how glad I was to have him nearby. I'd forgotten—well, actually I'm not sure ever knew, how nice it was to have someone hold your hand in times of trouble, and tell you everything would be all right. As I looked into George's eyes, I felt sure that's what he was about to say.

"It wasn't Graham," he said.

Hmm, no warm feelings from that statement.

"How can you be so sure?" Hetty's tone was stubborn.

"Because while I was checking on Ainsworthy's alibi, I ran into Graham at Boodles less than an hour ago. He couldn't be in two places at once."

Hetty dismissed that pronouncement with a wave of her hand. "Frances already said she didn't see Graham in the crowd, and when you arrived, I was just explaining that he didn't have to be there to be responsible."

"That's true, I suppose, but Kendrick was on hand. Why not him?"

"Because he saved her. Graham is much more likely."

George scowled. "Graham may be angry with her now, for turning off the flow of funds, but he gains nothing by killing her. Fighting her in court is his best hope."

I was growing a little tired of this back-and-forth, in which I had no part. Not to mention a little disconcerted at hearing the man who was supposed to be my support, defending my brother-in-law. "While I'm not as quick to dismiss Graham as you may be, for the sake of moving forward, who else do you suppose might want to do me in?"

George sat back, releasing my hand, and ran his own through his hair. "Unfortunately I can't put a name to him. Grayson's alibi for the time of Capshaw's murder is good, but while Ainsworthy did go to Boodles that day, I haven't been able to determine how long he was there. So he's still a suspect, as well as Kendrick, and there's always the possibility of someone we haven't even considered. But whoever it is, I think you must be getting close to the murderer. He knows you're looking for him and wants you to stop."

I glanced at Hetty, who seemed to be considering George's words, then back at him. "But I told you, Mrs. Rockingham was unable to help me." I raised my hands palms up. "All my leads have gone nowhere. I'm not close to naming the murderer at all."

He wagged his index finger at me. "You only think that because you don't know who you're looking for."

"Yes, that's what I just said."

"I'm beginning to understand." Hetty's voice held a note of triumph. "You are unknowingly getting closer to discovering who the murderer is. It doesn't matter that you have no new evidence. He believes you do."

"Oh, heavens. I see what you mean. The murderer knows Capshaw was coming to see me. Perhaps he also knows I went to visit Mrs. Rockingham, but he isn't aware I received no information from either of them."

"Well, he knows you didn't get anything from Capshaw," Hetty pointed out. "He saw to that. But the fact that you visited the Rockinghams seems to have made him nervous."

"So Mrs. Rockingham must have some information. I just didn't ask her the right questions."

We all fell silent, wondering what the right questions might be. George was the first to break the silence. "Or you didn't ask about the right man. Perhaps we're focusing on the wrong suspects."

"But we all agreed Capshaw was coming to tell me something about one of Lily's suitors."

George shrugged. "That was a theory, but in truth, we have no idea what the man was coming to tell you. Just because we can't think of another reason for him to meet with you, doesn't mean there isn't one. Kendrick and Ainsworthy are still suspects, but Ainsworthy couldn't have pushed you into the street. And if Kendrick had, he wouldn't have bothered to save you. You said those three men were part of a larger list. What list, and who else was on it?"

"Goodness, I kept meaning to tell you, but I was always distracted. It was a list of suspects who may have stolen Alicia's bracelet. I know your name was on it, and Fiona and the three young men, but now I can't remember the others."

This garnered me a look of outraged amazement. "I was on the list?"

I patted his hand in a conciliatory manner. "Only because we spoke with each other during specific hours of that evening. And the list is Delaney's, not mine, so don't hold it against me." George gave me an ironic smile. "But now that you mention it," I added, "Delaney would have all the other names."

"That's good, because we should put all this in Delaney's hands now."

"What? You just admitted I was getting close to exposing the murderer."

"And he came after you. Frances, you're placing yourself in a dangerous position. You're no longer looking for a thief. The man's a murderer. Let Delaney talk to the Rockinghams and draw the man's attention away from you."

After a pause, Hetty spoke up. "I have to agree with Mr. Hazelton, Franny. This has become far too dangerous."

I glared at my traitorous aunt. "But you were the one who urged me to do something."

"That was before your life was threatened. That changes everything. If you keep pursuing this murderer, you may end up leaving Rose without a mother."

While I thought it terribly unfair to bring Rose into this business, I had to agree it was wrong to take such a risk, so I backed down, and sent a message with the kitchen boy to Delaney's division in Chelsea. He arrived a few hours later, and between the three of us, we brought him up to date. He said he'd make arrangements to interview Mr. Kendrick but agreed the culprit might not be one of the three suitors.

As it was getting late, Delaney thought it best to call on the elderly couple in the morning, but he'd make sure a constable patrolled that area all night. I felt a twinge of guilt that I hadn't even considered the safety of Mr. and Mrs. Rockingham. If someone was willing to murder me because of information I supposedly gained from the Rockinghams, why would he hesitate to murder them?

So with no criminal to pursue, my sister and daughter off in the country, and my social engagements canceled at the insistence of Inspector Delaney, for my own safety of course, I found myself with nothing to do this morning. I slept late, ate a leisurely breakfast, spent an excessive amount of time with Bridget, dressing my hair, and myself, and here I was at noon, wandering through the house like some forlorn ghost, looking for any task I could take on. Unfortunately I was too agitated to settle on anything.

I finally decided to retire to the library where I could try to focus my mind on reading the morning mail, or perhaps the newspaper might distract me. I sat down behind my desk where my eyes landed on Lily's sketchbook. She hadn't been in my house above ten days, yet I felt her absence strongly. I smiled as I paged through her drawings. She'd sketched each of her suitors—very good likenesses, too.

I studied the face of each man. They were young and handsome. It was clear Lily had caught them unawares. These were no posed portraits. Her swift hand had captured each man's essence. One, rather serious and thoughtful, another mischievous, and the third simply seemed contented just to be in her presence, which made me wonder what they'd been doing before she picked up her pencil.

Of course my mind was drawn back to the case. I hoped I was wrong, and none of these men were guilty. Not a one of them looked capable of murdering a man, but a handsome face could hide a multitude of sins. And I still struggled to understand why Capshaw had chosen to give *me* some information—not Alicia, not Delaney. Somehow these three men were significant. One of them was the link from Capshaw to me.

I picked up the sketchbook and made my way out the back of the house. As I crossed George's garden, I spotted him through his library window, and knocked on the glass. He jerked around in surprise, but recovered quickly. He motioned me over to the drawing room and met me at the French doors.

"I would admonish you for sneaking around like a felon, but under the circumstances, that's probably the best choice. What brings you here?"

We'd walked back to his library, and I placed Lily's sketch-book on his desk, then turned to face him. "I still think Capshaw planned to tell me something about one of Lily's suitors." I held up a hand before he could protest. "It may not follow that any of them murdered Capshaw, but he has some damning information about one of them, and so does Mrs. Rockingham."

George listened with a furrowed brow. "Do you believe Mrs. Rockingham lied to you when she said she didn't know them?"

I shook my head. "Not necessarily. She may not realize she knows one of them." I flipped the sketchbook open. "But if she saw his face, she might."

I watched as he stared at the page, considering my suggestion. "An alias?"

"Perhaps, but it's also possible that while she may not recognize the name, she might well remember the face. We should show her these sketches."

He gave me a warning look. "Delaney should show her these sketches. I'll place a call to his division and leave a message."

I couldn't help rolling my eyes. "Oh, George, don't be so tiresome. It could take hours to get a message to Delaney, and even longer before he can come here and pick up the book. He planned to call on the Rockinghams this morning. If we hurry, we might meet him there."

"You promised to stay home and out of trouble today."

"Yes, yes, I know." I stepped over to the bell pull and rang for a servant. "But if you're with me, and we're meeting up with Delaney, how could I be safer?"

A maid came to the door before he could answer, clearly surprised to see me there. "Mr. Hazelton will need his carriage as soon as possible." She turned from me to George, and when he gave her a short nod, I knew I had won.

* * *

Fortunately Delaney was still at the Rockingham home. Unfortunately, he looked more than a little irritated upon seeing me there.

The Rockinghams were seated together on a divan, Delaney in a hard-backed chair opposite them, his notebook and pencil in hand. Mrs. Rockingham brushed away my apology for intruding on them. "Nonsense, my dear. You said you were working with the police, so I'm sure the inspector doesn't mind." This earned me another glare from Delaney, and I felt my cheeks burn. To make amends, I addressed him directly.

"Inspector, I have some sketches the Rockinghams ought to see." I showed him the pages in question, watching his expression change, as he considered the possibilities. I knew he wouldn't require an explanation.

George and I seated ourselves on a second divan between the Rockinghams and Delaney. I found George's hand and squeezed it, as Delaney handed the sketchbook to Mr. Rockingham. "Would you be so kind as to look at the sketches on those three pages and tell me if you recognize any of those men?"

Mrs. Rockingham slipped on a pair of reading glasses, and the couple perused the pages with moderate interest, but no apparent recognition—until they turned to the third page.

"Oh! This one I know. Yes. He looks older, but of course it's been several years since I've seen him." She pulled off her glasses and turned toward her husband. "How long would you say, Trevor, since he worked for us?"

Worked for them? Delaney, George, and I were riveted to the exchange between the couple.

"Hmm, not so sure I know the fellow," Mr. Rockingham said. "You say he worked for us?"

Mrs. Rockingham handed the reading glasses to her husband and urged him to look again at the sketch. "That's Thomas. I'm sure of it. Don't you remember?"

Mr. Rockingham, at least a decade her senior, adjusted the glasses, then moved the picture away from him, before giving a firm nod. "Ah. It is Thomas. As you say, he's a little older in this sketch. He left us some ten years ago. Found a position in South Africa of all things."

Delaney reached forward and took the sketchbook. "So this man worked for you—"

"He was a footman," Mrs. Rockingham supplied.

"Up until about ten years ago," Delaney continued. "Did James Capshaw also work for you at that time?"

"Well, yes, but their employment overlapped by only a few weeks. In fact, Thomas trained James in his duties, just before he left us."

My mind reeled from the shock of this revelation, yet I still wasn't quite sure what had been revealed. The sketch was of Ainsworthy. That he had posed as a footman ten years ago was preposterous, so did that mean the man we all knew as the viscount was an imposter? If so, Capshaw must have recognized him at Alicia's ball.

"You say he went to South Africa when he left your employ?" I asked.

"I believe he actually became a clerk in a mining operation owned by a gentleman, but I don't recall the man's name, assuming I ever heard it in the first place."

Delaney had pocketed his notebook and was closing the sketch pad. He stood and nodded deferentially to the older couple. "Thank you for your time. You've been of great help to us."

George and I said our good-byes and followed Delaney from the room. "Allow us to drop you wherever you're going, Inspector," George suggested. "And you can tell us what you make of all this."

Delaney agreed and the three of us climbed into George's carriage. Delaney gave the driver instructions, then settled in the seat opposite us.

"Ainsworthy, or the man we know as Ainsworthy, isn't at his home in town," I said. "According to his servants, he's gone to the country."

Delaney nodded. "Yes, that's what I was told as well and, with the Rockinghams in town, I can understand why he'd wish to avoid them at all costs. Yet someone made an attempt on your life, so either he was still in town until yesterday, or someone else is trying to harm you."

I let out a groan at his words. "Just how many people do you think wish to kill me, Inspector?"

His lips curved into a smile. It might be the first time I'd seen him with a genuine smile. "I don't know the number, my lady, I only wish to ensure that none are successful."

"Since that's my goal too, I plan to be in attendance on Lady Harleigh, at all times, until you've found the killer."

"But if Ainsworthy murdered Capshaw, then Kendrick is innocent. Who else is there?"

George turned to me with a grave expression. "Perhaps someone who was paid to follow you, and assure you met with an accident."

As I really couldn't argue with that possibility, I turned the subject. "How do you intend to pursue Thomas, Inspector?"

"If I may keep this sketch, my lady, I'd like to duplicate it, and distribute it so we can search for him in town. Then I must set someone to the task of finding out what happened to the real Viscount Ainsworthy. I find it highly unlikely he sent Thomas home to England to impersonate him while he stayed in South Africa. So I fear he may well be deceased."

I nodded my agreement, distressed by the thought. "But did he die at the hands of this man, Thomas, or by some other means?"

"That is indeed the question," George concurred, "but regardless of how it happened, Thomas found a way of improving his lot in life, and might have got away with it, if not for Capshaw." He turned to Delaney. "Do you intend to send any-one to the viscount's country home?"

"Yes. As he is unaware we've learned who he is, I think that's the most likely place for him to be, until the Rockinghams quit London. I'll go there myself on the next possible train. Once I have him in custody, and back in London, we will, I hope, find out what happened to the real viscount."

By this time we'd reached the Chelsea Division. As Delaney departed the carriage, he charged George with the task of watch-ing over me, and me with the task of staying out of trouble.

As soon as the door closed, George gave me a mischievous smile that made me wonder if we were about to disappoint De-laney on both counts. I eyed him with suspicion. "What are you thinking?"

"That perhaps I should have a look around Ainsworthy's house after all." He took my gloved hand in his. "Can you arrange to give Bridget the evening off?"

With all the excitement yesterday, I'd completely forgotten to arrange anything with Bridget, allowing George access to Ainsworthy's house last night. I ignored the gentle pressure of his hands, refusing to be distracted. "But why is that necessary now? If this Thomas is the thief, and he probably is, the police will recover the stolen property."

"Ah, you forget my client wants me to recover his valuables. Not the police."

"Oh, yes, of course. So you intend to break into Ainswor-thy's house tonight?"

"It may be my only chance. Once Delaney has Thomas in custody, the police will be going through it themselves."

I didn't respond immediately. An idea was taking shape in my brain. I wasn't sure if I could pull this off, but it was worth a try.

George misunderstood my hesitation. "I don't want to leave

you unprotected, Frances, but I won't be gone long. I can station two of my footmen on the street to guard your house."

I brushed off his concern with a shake of my head. "That won't be necessary, George. I'll just go with you."

"Absolutely not."

The look of shock on his face was almost comical, but I was in no mood to laugh. "You must take me with you. Perhaps you were right when you said I was taken by the fever, but I've never felt such a sense of purpose as when I was trying to solve this crime. Then you and Hetty took it out of my hands."

"But you did solve the crime. You provided the essential clue to the police. It's not as if you could have arrested this Thomas fellow yourself and brought him to justice. In the end you would have had to turn your information over to Delaney, no matter how far you'd taken this. You did your part."

"I don't feel as though it's finished. I understand I can't bring Thomas to justice, but retrieving the valuables he stole, well, that is a sort of justice. Please take me with you, George. You said yourself breaking into Mr. Kendrick's house wasn't dangerous. Why should Ainsworthy's be any different?"

"The danger will be in having a novice along." George still held my hands. He shook them as he spoke, emphasizing his words.

"You can't dissuade me with that argument. Bridget will remove Barnes from the house, and the few other servants will either be in the kitchens or in their rooms in the attics."

"Or moving from one place to the other."

"Using the servants' stairways. They'll have no idea we're there." I locked eyes with him. "Please, George? We are partners."

He looked away first, heaving a sigh. "I'm sure I'll regret this."

"You'll take me?"

"You'll follow my every order?"

"Without question."

The carriage had stopped in front of my door. George released my hands, allowing me to gather the sketchbook and my bag. "Then make your arrangements with Bridget and meet me in my garden at midnight."

"Midnight? Are you insane? I'd never allow Bridget to be out at so late an hour."

George raised his eyes heavenward. "Whatever was I thinking? Meet me at eight."

"Perfect."

Chapter 19

❧

"Wait here," George whispered through the open window. "I'll make certain no one is around and come back to help you inside."

With that, he disappeared into the darkness of Ainsworthy's house, and I was left in the shadows outside. The street was a hundred feet or so to my left, the mews about the same distance to my right, and someone's home just a few feet to my back. That rather unnerved me. The mews was empty, the street, nearly so, with only the rare carriage rumbling past. My black wool mourning dress and cloak made me all but invisible from that distance. But the window in the house behind me was little more than an arm's length away, and if anyone looked out, I would be very visible indeed.

For the first time tonight my confidence wavered, and I began to question my sanity in joining George in this venture. I'd had no problems in convincing Bridget to dine out with Barnes tonight. Hetty had been thrilled I was spending the evening with George, and had been conveniently in her own room when I left, giving her no chance to see my ensemble. I thought it perfect for sneaking around in the dark.

George too had been dressed in black, when I met him in the garden, and hesitated only long enough to confirm I truly wanted to go with him. The carriage ride was swift and silent. George's driver dropped us at South Audley Street, near Mount Street, about a block away from the viscount's house. The air was misty, but not so much that we needed an umbrella. George finally spoke as he helped me from the carriage.

"Remember," he said, pulling me close and speaking in a low voice, "you agreed to follow my instructions without question."

I nodded, and we set off down Mount Street on foot, walking arm in arm, as if we were on our way home for the evening. I'd felt perfectly confident then, rather excited even, until George pulled me off the walk, and into a dark passage between two houses. When we stopped, he raised a finger to his lips, pushed open a window, and hoisted himself inside.

He'd probably only been in the house for a minute or two, but standing here, exposed, it felt so much longer. I was beginning to worry in earnest when I saw him approach the window. I released my breath only to gasp it back in as the window sash behind me was raised.

Oh, dear God! There was no time to follow George through the window as he made a cowardly disappearance behind the wall. With my heart pounding, I turned toward the window in the house behind me, to see the curious face of a young boy.

"Hello," he whispered. "Are you lost?"

Ah, a friendly child, about six years old, I'd say. And since he had a mouthful of something likely pilfered from the kitchen, it was doubtful he'd call for a parent or servant to send me on my way. I gave him a smile. "Lost? No, I'm not lost. I'm hiding."

"That's funny. I'm hiding, too. I'm supposed to be in bed, but I got hungry." He held up a fistful of biscuits. "I snuck them out of the kitchen, but I didn't want to get crumbs in my bed so I brought them in here." His smile faded. "Would you like one?" he asked, clearly hoping I'd say no.

"Oh, no. I'd hate for you to still be hungry after you went to so much trouble."

As he stuffed one of the treats in his mouth, I stepped closer to the window, resting my arms on the ledge.

"Are you Lord Ainsworthy's friend?" Crumbs flew at my face as he spoke.

"Yes. We're playing hide-and-seek right now. I don't think anyone will look for me outside, do you?"

"Well, you left the window open. That might give you away."

I glanced at the window as he gobbled the last biscuit. I turned back with a serious expression. "Perhaps I'd better find another place to hide then. And you had better get back up to bed before someone catches you."

With a worried frown he brushed crumbs from his chin. "You won't tell on me, will you?"

"Not if you go right now."

He brought down the sash with a quiet thud, gave me a smile and a wave, and scurried away. I leaned back against the house for a moment to collect myself.

George's head popped back out the window. "Well done," he whispered.

I stepped over to Ainsworthy's window, noting its height. "How do you propose I do this?"

"I don't believe you'll be able to climb in," he said, eyeing my narrow skirts. "I suggest you try sitting on the ledge, if you can, and I'll pull you inside."

This turned out to be more easily said than done as the window ledge was several inches higher than my posterior. I suffered the indignity of several false tries, when George finally placed his hands on my waist and whispered in my ear, "On the count of three, hop."

One, two, three, and I was on the ledge, swinging my legs through the window. Once I was again on my feet, I took in my surroundings. George had lit a gas lamp and turned it down low. From its soft glow, I could see we were in the viscount's study. The walls were paneled in dark wood, with a bookshelf built in to the wall behind a large, tidy desk. On the opposite wall hung a portrait of some Ainsworthy ancestor, under which was placed a round table and two armchairs. There was a low upholstered bench under the window, which had assisted my entrance. The last wall held a door and two more paintings.

"Go through the desk," George instructed. "I'll check for a safe."

"You never told me what I'm looking for," I said, as I moved behind the desk.

"Yes, I suppose there's no keeping it from you now," he replied, looking behind one of the smaller paintings. "A packet of letters. And a key to a safe would be helpful. At least it would indicate a safe is in this room. If we're fortunate, we won't have to search any other part of the house."

"We're already fortunate in finding the window open." I moved the chair back from the desk. It had a set of three drawers on either side, leaving an opening for one's legs. I sunk down to my knees, and felt along the sides of the opening, finding a set of keys on a hook. Standing up, I held them out to George.

"Good fortune had nothing to do with the window. I came by earlier today, and made sure it was closed, but unlocked." He took the keys, looked them over, and handed them back to me. "The two small ones are probably for the desk. Unlock the drawers first, and then I'll look for a lock that fits the third key."

I stared at him, the keys dangling from my fingers. "You've already been in the house? Why are we here now, then? Is this just a farce to appease me?"

He gave me a look of such complete incredulity that I instantly saw how ridiculous my question was. I held up my hands in surrender. "Forgive me. I did not mean to suggest you staged this housebreaking for my amusement."

He leaned over the desk toward me, wearing an expression

of exaggerated patience. "I stopped by today, asking for the viscount. Barnes of course told me he was away from home, so I asked to leave a note. I watched where Barnes went to fetch paper and pen, which was this room. When he left me alone to write my note, I slipped back here and unlocked the window." His brows drew together in a frown. "And just what happened to following my orders without question?"

Heavens, he was thorough. "It starts in a moment," I said, unlocking the desk drawers. "First, what do you mean I'm looking for letters? What kind of letters could cause Haverhill such trouble?"

He took the keys and stepped over to the second small painting. "The trouble lies in who wrote them."

The first drawer did indeed hold a file of letters, but they all belonged to the viscount. All were either addressed to him, or were copies of letters from him, and appeared to be of a business nature. As I scanned through them, it became clear the business was not going well. As the Rockinghams said he owned an interest in a mining operation in South Africa. But it was not producing. The large number of dunning letters indicated he'd stopped paying his suppliers. There were a couple of references to "my clerk, Thomas Martin," which drew my eye.

So Thomas now had a surname, and he'd worked for Ainsworthy. The next letter threatened seizure of the mine for non-payment of debt. A letter from the family solicitors announced the death of Ainsworthy's uncle and that young Ainsworthy was now the viscount.

I opened the next file to find a letter in a different hand. The salutation was to "My Dearest Gordon." The signature read, *Claire*. Gordon was Haverhill's given name but his wife's name was Anne not Claire. These must be the damning letters. The remaining pages in the file were folded. I was just removing them from the drawer when I heard a muffled sound from across the room. George was replacing the large picture on the wall.

"Did you find the safe?" I whispered.

He nodded, moving back to the desk. "The safe, and a few gewgaws that might be the missing snuffboxes. No letters."

I held up the small cache of letters. "I believe this is what you're looking for."

He took the letters, scanned the first one, and nodded. "Excellent work, Frances." He folded the pages in half and stuffed them into his coat pocket. "And now we leave."

I didn't move. "He was having an affair. I can't believe you'd help him cover it up."

George came around the desk and replaced the files in the drawer. "We don't have time to discuss that now, I'm afraid. We can't risk being here when Barnes returns. Remember, Delaney charged me with watching over you." His lips quirked in a half smile. "He'd think me derelict in my duty if we were both arrested for breaking and entering."

I cursed the "following orders" clause in our agreement, while I watched him lock up the desk with all Ainsworthy's and Thomas' secrets inside. He was right, though. We could not be caught here.

We turned off the lamp, George helped me through the window, and within minutes, we were back in the carriage, heading home. I was the first to break the silence.

"Was protecting Haverhill really worth the risk you took? I doubt an affair would ruin his career."

"He wasn't having an affair. Claire Allen is his half sister." In the darkness of the carriage, I barely saw his shoulders life in a shrug. "His father had the affair."

"Claire Allen, the actress? Heavens, she's wonderful."

"Indeed. She's also Irish, or half-Irish, and an outspoken advocate for Irish Nationalism. If word got out she was his half sister, not only would that embarrass his mother, but it would call into question his motives as a proponent for Home Rule."

He laughed at my look of utter amazement. "Truly. The opposition could play this up beautifully. Put it around that she and her cronies influenced him. He'd lose all credibility and any hope of another Home Rule bill."

"Do you suppose she does influence him?"

"The fact of her probably does. Because of her, he recognizes Ireland as its own country. One that should rule itself."

"As an American, I can hardly argue with that sentiment."

We made the rest of the trip in silence, each with our thoughts and each, I believed, with a sense of accomplishment.

The following morning, I realized George took the task of watching over me quite seriously. He arrived at my breakfast table, which in my house, was the dining room table, along with the morning mail. "I wish I'd known you wanted company for breakfast, George. We'd have come to your house."

Hetty held a forkful of eggs. "Why? Is there something special about breakfast at your house?"

I indicated he should take a seat while I answered for him. "The quantity and variety of food is quite impressive. Will you join us, George? Do you take coffee or tea in the morning?"

"Coffee, please," he said, seating himself at the end of the table between Hetty and myself. He dropped a document case by his feet.

I poured a cup of coffee and handed it to him, nudging the cream and sugar in his direction. "Did you bring work with you?"

"I did. I promised not to let you out of my sight until this Thomas fellow is in custody, but unfortunately I have some documents to work through. Perhaps I can use your library for that a little later."

"Are you serious? You intend literally to watch over me until we hear from Delaney?"

He raised an eyebrow. "That is exactly what I intend. Someone broke into your home a few days ago, while I was next door, and I had no idea of it." That he managed to say this without laughing at the irony amazed me. "I won't take the risk of something like that happening again. I'm afraid you'll have to put up with my company, at least for the day."

"Well." I'll admit it. I was flattered, and gratified and, of all things, I could feel myself blushing. I hid my face in my coffee cup and wondered just when I had started enjoying George's company so much.

"Since you're both here," Hetty said, drawing George's attention away from my embarrassment, "perhaps you can bring me up to date on this whole situation. Just how did this man manage to impersonate a viscount and did he cause all the other trouble? Was he also the thief and did he break into this house?"

As much as I wanted to share with her the little I'd learned about Thomas Martin last night, I had no way of explaining how I'd come by that information. I offered a little prevarication instead. "I don't think we'll know all of that, Hetty, until he's in custody. However, it does appear he worked for Ainsworthy in South Africa, came here in the guise of the viscount, and probably killed Capshaw because he knew who Thomas really was."

"The more I think about it," George said, leaning back in his chair, "the more I understand why he felt it necessary to resort to theft. He might not have had access to the funds from the estate—death duties would have been levied, debts paid. Even if he knew he could live off credit until the funds were available, he might not have understood how to arrange it."

"Yet if he wanted to put up a credible front, he would have to dress the part, and live the part he was playing," I continued. "And to do that he needed ready money."

"But what about breaking into this house?" Hetty asked. "Why take such a risk when he could simply steal something else?"

"I don't believe he did break in. He paid a visit to Lily that day and had to wait for her. Do you remember? You and she had gone to the library and were expected back at any moment."

I remembered how George had been left alone to wait at Ainsworthy's home and knew what happened as surely as if I'd been there. "Mrs. Thompson probably asked him in and let him wait in the drawing room. As we were all out of the house, he took his chance. It would only be the work of a moment to slip up to my room and search for my bag. When he found it empty, he became careless, and left the room in complete disarray. If I remember correctly, he was back on the street, with his horses when you returned to the house."

"So he broke the window to make it look like the work of a housebreaker. Why, that little sneak." Hetty looked even more outraged than when we thought someone had broken in.

George provided the voice of reason. "A good possibility, but we won't know the whole until he's caught."

"Which I hope will be today. Since you don't want anything to eat, George, may I show you to the library?"

With a nod to Hetty, George picked up his document case, I picked up my letters, and we moved to the library. "Have you returned Haverhill's letters?"

"This morning," he said.

"Good. Now I must tell you what else I found last night." We walked into the warm, paneled room. "Business letters, pertaining to Ainsworthy's mine in South Africa."

George raised an eyebrow as we seated ourselves in the arm chairs opposite the desk. "Diamonds or gold?"

"I don't know. I could only tell it wasn't profitable, and Ainsworthy was going into debt, but that's not the interesting part."

"Go on."

"The letters were filed by date, and the last two were copies of letters Ainsworthy supposedly sent out."

"Supposedly?"

I brought the letters to mind, wondering how to explain my suspicions. "They were different in tone, more desperate, and the signature, though it was Ainsworthy's name, was definitely not his writing."

"So someone else signed the man's name. What do you surmise from this?"

"That Ainsworthy was dying, or perhaps already dead, and Thomas—oh, he has a surname by the way. It's Martin."

George gave me a nod, and what I suspected was a condescending smile, but I was still pleased I'd learned this bit of information.

"Anyway, I believe Mr. Martin was trying desperately to keep the mine going. After all, if their creditors found out Ainsworthy was dead, Martin would be out of a job, possibly out of money, and stranded in a strange country."

George shook his head. "I assume his plan didn't work?"

"Sadly, no. The next letter stated the creditors would be seizing the assets of the company. But there was one more letter from a different source."

"Ah, the one notifying Ainsworthy of his inheritance."

"Exactly." I leaned back in my chair and gazed at George. "I must say, if it were only the thefts, if he hadn't murdered Mr. Capshaw, I'd feel some sympathy for Thomas. He was in rather desperate straits."

This time George's smile wasn't condescending. It was rather sad. "Others have been in desperate circumstances and not turned to crime."

"I know that, and I don't mean to say I condone what he did, just that I understand."

"Even though he ransacked your bedchamber?"

"Clearly he needed to learn the finer points of breaking and entering." I rose from my seat. George followed suit and caught my arms before I could move. "You have a beautiful heart,

Frances. This experience might have hardened it. I'm glad to see that hasn't happened."

Heat rose to my cheeks. "Well, you had best get on with your business, George. Go ahead and take the desk. I'll just sit over here by the window and read my letters."

He smiled and released my arms. Moving behind the desk, he began pulling papers from his document case. I settled into the window seat and opened the first letter, an invitation. "Ah, Florence Carrington is having a party to celebrate her husband's birthday next week."

George grunted something in reply.

"Her parties are quite something. I do hope Lily is back in time to attend. Do you think you'll go, George?"

When he didn't reply I glanced up to see him scowling at me over the rims of a pair of spectacles. "Why, I didn't know you wore spectacles!"

The scowl deepened. "Are you going to read all of your correspondence to me?"

I smothered a laugh. "Apologies. You'll not hear another word from me. I'll be quiet as a mouse."

With that I turned back to my post. Oh, the next was a letter from Lily. I managed not to say this aloud, and tore open the seal, wondering how Lily had been spending her time. By the time I read the second paragraph, I was in a panic. "Oh, my heavens!"

"That doesn't sound like a mouse, Frances. It sounds more like you saw a mouse."

"George, this is terrible. This letter is from Lily and she tells me Ainsworthy is at Harleigh."

One look at his face told me he was as horrified as I. He rounded the desk and was beside me in an instant. "When did she write that? Is he actually staying at Harleigh?"

I looked back at the letter in my hand. "No, he's staying in Guildford, at the White Horse. She writes, '*He has some busi-*

*ness in Guildford and stopped in to pay his respects. I know you
didn't wish me to see him, but Delia asked him to return for
dinner tonight.'* The letter is dated yesterday."

My heart pounded as I looked up at George. "Could he really
have had business in Guildford?"

"I suspect his business is seeking your sister's hand in marriage. He still has no idea we know of his subterfuge, and may
believe that with her fortune, he can continue to live as the viscount."

"What can we do?"

"I'll go to my house and call the police right now and find
out where Delaney is. If he's already left for Kent, perhaps they
can contact the Guildford police, and have Thomas arrested."

I followed him to the door, then turned back as Hetty called
to me from the dining room. I explained the circumstances to
her, and we both sat in anxious silence until George returned.
When he did, my spirits sank even lower at the sight of his grim
expression.

"What did they say? What can they do?"

He sighed. "Delaney left on an early train this morning for
Kent, to Ainsworthy's estate near Maidstone. They can send a
message to that constabulary, but by now Delaney would have
already checked in with them, and would be off searching for
Thomas. Now they have to search for Delaney. It could take
some time to find him, then get him on a train to Guildford.
Meanwhile, they'll contact the Guildford constabulary, and
alert them that there's a warrant for the arrest of a Thomas Martin, posing as Viscount Ainsworthy, in the hopes that they'll
detain the man until Delaney arrives."

"In the hopes? Wouldn't they be rather in a hurry to arrest a
murderer?"

George shook his head. "They'll have only a verbal description of the man. They may well wait for Delaney to identify
him, rather than arrest the wrong aristocrat."

This was ridiculous. "We can identify him. For goodness' sake, we can go to Guildford."

"I suggested that."

"And?"

"They may still choose to wait for Delaney and the warrant."

My frustration was beyond words. "And how hard will the other constables look for Delaney? Will they simply wait until he reports back to their offices?"

He put up a hand to stop me. "It doesn't matter. I'll go to Kent and find Delaney myself. I consulted a train schedule after speaking to the police. The next train leaves in an hour. With luck I can find him and bring him to Guildford by tomorrow morning."

"Then Hetty and I will go to Guildford now."

George's expression turned thunderous. "You'll do no such thing. He's a murderer."

"And Lily, and Delia, and my daughter don't know that. He's called at Harleigh. He's dined at Harleigh. Who knows what he might be doing to turn Lily's head. I must go."

George ran his fingers through his hair in agitation. "Then I'll go with you and leave it to the police to contact Delaney."

"No."

The single syllable startled us as if it had been a shot. We both turned to Hetty. I'd completely forgotten she was even in the room.

"If there's a chance the Guildford police will insist on waiting for Inspector Delaney, there's no time to lose in bringing him there. You must find him. Frances and I will go directly to Guildford and try to convince them to act immediately. If they won't, then Frances is right. Someone has to alert the ladies at Harleigh to the danger they may be in."

I took hold of George's arm. "If we can't convince the police to take action, then I'll insist on one of them accompanying us to Harleigh, where we can lock the doors, and wait in safety for you and Delaney to arrive. I promise you we will not court danger."

In this manner Hetty and I worked on George until he finally agreed. Then he was off to catch his train. His carriage would return for Hetty and me in three quarters of an hour to take us to the station. We both rushed to pack a small bag each.

"I thought travel by train was supposed to be swift," Hetty grumbled, as we finally stepped onto the platform at the Guildford station.

"That's true only if you refer to the time the train is actually in motion." I skipped out of the way of a porter, pushing a cart piled high with trunks and bags. The trip had been absurdly long considering we were now only thirty miles from home. But missing the first train, then waiting for another, which was delayed for who knew what reason, took a toll on our patience, and a significant amount of our time. It was now nearly four o'clock, and we still had to look for transport to the constabulary.

I took Hetty's arm, guiding her through the station, and out to the street where omnibuses and cabs lingered. Since I had no idea where the police were headquartered, I asked a porter to fetch a cab for a ride so short, we could have walked it faster.

Finally we were talking to a young constable who, upon hearing the name Viscount Ainsworthy, had us wait while he spoke to his superintendent. I wondered if these were the same men who, only days ago, were investigating me as a murder suspect. I didn't have long to dwell on that thought as the constable returned momentarily, with another man in his mid-forties, sporting a trim mustache, and wearing a plain dark suit, rather than a uniform. He introduced himself as Superintendent Jessop and asked us to come back to his office. Once we were all seated, he gave us the bad news.

"I'm afraid your man has fled," he said.

The blunt words pounded at my brain, but did not penetrate. I stared at him stupidly. "Fled? Are you certain? Have you looked at the White Horse? Checked with the proprietor?"

Jessop nodded at each question. "Paid his bill, packed his bags, and left several hours ago. The ticket master at the station didn't recall seeing him, but the description we have of the man is rather vague. It's possible he purchased his return ticket when he arrived a few days ago, so by now, he could be on his way to just about anywhere." He gave me a hard look. "We contacted the Chelsea Division with this information. What's your connection to this man?"

"I'm Frances Wynn, my late husband was the Earl of Harleigh. My sister-in-law, the countess, is in residence at Harleigh, along with my young sister and daughter." I told him about the letter I'd received from Lily. "They have no idea he's a criminal, and if he's not at his rooms at the White Horse, he may be at Harleigh at this very moment."

Jessop's brows rose at this. "Would the countess have invited him to stop there? Is there some connection?"

His calm demeanor only made me more frantic. Did he not see the urgency? I took a breath to steady my voice. "Under the guise of Viscount Ainsworthy he was courting my sister, while they were both in London. I can think of no other reason for his coming to Guildford, and to Harleigh, other than to continue advancing his suit. They don't know who he is, and would have no reason to turn him away. Simple courtesy alone might induce the countess to invite him to give up his rooms and stay at Harleigh. Please, you must send someone there."

My voice broke on a sob with these last words. Jessop excused himself, and I used that time to regain my composure, while Hetty patted my shoulder. He returned after several minutes, with two other men dressed in drab suits and overcoats. Jessop introduced them as Inspectors Collins and Redding.

"They're ready to accompany you to Harleigh. If our man is in residence, then he still has no idea we're looking for him. He'll consider himself in no danger, and should be easy to arrest."

Eager to be off, Hetty and I stepped toward the door. Jessop raised a hand to stop us. "Your rank can hold no weight in this matter, my lady. While you're with the inspectors, please follow any instructions they give you. Do you understand?"

We assured him we did, and swiftly followed Collins and Redding out to the street where a hired hack waited to take us to the manor. Once we were moving, my thoughts were all of the residents of Harleigh. I vaguely heard Aunt Hetty explaining our history with Thomas Martin while I tried to assure myself everything would be fine once we arrived. There was no reason for Thomas to depart from his gentlemanly persona. No reason for him to become violent. No reason for him to hurt anyone. Still, I could not ease my mind.

I have no idea how long it took to reach the manor house. It felt like hours, yet I'm sure it was less than half an hour. Twilight was just settling in. I barely waited for the carriage to stop at the top of the drive before thrusting open the door. One of the inspectors, I believe it was Redding, held my arm, forcing me to wait while Collins lowered the steps, then assisted me to the ground. As he turned to assist Hetty, I glanced up at the manor and saw the shadows of scaffolding along one side. Would they never be finished working on this behemoth? When we were all four collected, we made our way up the wide front stairs, while Inspector Collins gave me instructions.

"Don't do anything to raise suspicion. If you see the man we're looking for in the house, just address him as Ainsworthy, and we'll take matters from there. Don't go near him, or give him any type of warning."

I nodded my understanding just as the door opened. Crabbe must have heard our arrival, and ushered us into the dim foyer with a warm welcome. His face, however, bore a solemn expression which did nothing to ease my concerns. I chose not to introduce my companions, but only asked after the countess, while Hetty and I handed our wraps to a waiting footman. The inspectors kept their outerwear.

"She is in the drawing room, my lady. I'll announce you."

We were just a few steps behind Crabbe when he threw open the doors to the drawing room. I had only a glimpse of Delia as she jumped to her feet. "Lady Harleigh and guests, my lady," Crabbe announced.

I stepped past him and glanced around the room. Delia looked shocked to see me there, and even more so to see the people following me. But she was the only occupant in the room.

I rushed forward. "Delia, where's Lily?"

Her lips moved soundlessly as her eyes darted from me, to Hetty, then to the two inspectors. The color drained from her face.

Oh, dear. "Delia, what's wrong? Where's Lily?" I took her arm, guiding her to a chair where she promptly buried her face in her hands.

"Oh, Frances! I'm so sorry. Lily has left with the viscount. I fear they've eloped."

Chapter 20

It took a good twenty minutes, and a glass of brandy to calm Delia into any coherence, and another half an hour to pull the story out of her. Ainsworthy had been calling on them over the past few days. He returned early this afternoon with a new motor car and offered to take Lily for a drive.

"A motor car? But they're terribly expensive. How on earth does he come to be in possession of one?"

Delia stared at me. "I could hardly ask such a thing. The two young people were so eager for the drive. I saw no harm in it. But now it's been hours since they left, and it's getting dark. I can only imagine they've eloped."

"Why would you jump to such a strange conclusion?" Hetty's tone indicated she considered the idea ridiculous. "Automobiles are notoriously unreliable. It's much more likely the thing broke down somewhere on the road."

Wonderful. "Thank you for that reassuring image, Hetty." I turned back to Delia, intending to question her further, but Inspector Collins spoke first.

"Do you know where he planned to take the girl, my lady? Or which direction they took?"

The way Delia stared at the man one would think the sofa had just spoken to her. She turned to me with a stony expression. "Who are these men, Frances?"

Good Lord. How to explain? "Viscount Ainsworthy is not who he says he is, Delia. These are inspectors with the Guildford police. They came here to arrest him. I can tell you the whole story later, but for now just answer their questions, so they can find him."

"Arrest him? Whatever for?"

"Delia!" I was on the verge of shaking her. "He's a dangerous man, and every moment Lily spends with him puts her further at risk. Now if he told you where he planned to go, for heaven's sake, tell us."

"Well!" Delia glared at me in all her injured dignity. "He told me they would simply drive about the countryside. I believe he brought a picnic lunch with him. They turned right at the end of the drive, about five hours ago, and I haven't seen them since. I've been pacing about this room for the last hour, wondering if I should contact the police myself. Your sister has had me worried sick, Frances. I fear she's well and truly ruined herself."

Delia gave a sad shake of her head at the end of this pronouncement, but for my part, Lily's reputation was the least of my concerns. She was alone with a murderer. They must be found. I felt Hetty's hand on my arm. "He has no reason to hurt her, Franny. Don't think the worst."

She was right. There was no need to panic, and I had no time for it right now. In order to be of any value to Lily, I had to keep panic at bay. I turned to the inspectors. "If they turned right, they weren't heading to the train station or toward town. Perhaps my aunt is right, and the automobile has simply broken down."

One of them nodded in agreement. "We'll light the carriage

lamps, and do our best to look for them, my lady." With that, they were off, and I turned to Delia, a thousand recriminations on the tip of my tongue. I bit them back. It was far too easy to blame Delia, but while she'd been lax as a chaperone, to say the least, she had no idea the viscount was so wicked. Her talk of worry and pacing the room rankled when I'd seen her myself, stitching at her embroidery as we'd entered. But I had to remind myself Lily's presence was forced on her.

"I'm truly sorry about Lily, Frances. You must know I never wished her any ill."

"Of course you didn't, dear. I suppose now, all we can do is wait for the police to find them." I smiled with more confidence than I felt. "Hopefully very soon."

"I'm sure Crabbe has made rooms ready for you. I'll have a maid take you upstairs so you can freshen up before dinner."

The maid answered the bell and showed us up to two guest rooms as Lily had been given my old room. Hetty pulled me into a hug at my door. "Try not to worry, dear. I'm sure Lily will be just fine. He has no reason to hurt her, and she is far more resourceful than you think."

I hoped, rather than believed her to be right. "I'm going up to the nursery to check on Rose first, then I'll come back to change for dinner."

"I'll just go to my room and rest awhile then." Hetty squeezed my fingers, and we parted at her door.

I spent the better part of an hour with my daughter and nephews, listening to them recount everything they'd been doing for the past few days while Rose's kitten slumbered in my lap. But even while their chatter had me laughing, I couldn't escape my worry over Lily. Where had she and Thomas gotten to?

And for heaven's sake, what was wrong with Delia? What was she thinking sending Lily off alone with the viscount—or Thomas? I was having a hard time remembering that. But even if he were a titled aristocrat, Delia would know better than to let them spend an afternoon together unchaperoned. And to say she saw nothing wrong with it? Was she just a disaster as a chaperone, or was her negligence deliberate?

I pondered the matter as the children's voices rose and fell around me, but could divine no reason why Delia would wish to ruin Lily. I determined to question her at dinner where I'd have Hetty to back me up. Before returning to my room, I gave Rose a kiss, promising to come back up before she went to bed. I brought in a taper from the hall and lit the paraffin oil lamp on the dressing table.

"Still no gas up here."

I jumped at the unexpected voice. Delia reclined in a chair by the glass doors to the balcony, a taper in the sconce beside her cast an earie glow. "Goodness, Delia, you startled me. Why are you waiting here? Am I late?"

She seemed not to have heard me. "No gaslight. Drafty rooms. Crumbling walls. Did you notice the scaffolding outside when you arrived?"

"I'd be surprised if it was missing," I replied. "It seems to have become a fixture," A maid had unpacked the skirt and blouse I'd brought, and laid them out on the bed. Not entirely suitable for dinner, but at least they were clean. I decided to go about the business of changing my clothing. Delia clearly had something to say to me. She could do the talking.

"We're taking down the stone balconies on the west wall on this floor and replacing them with railings. We can't afford to repair them, and they're just too dangerous to use."

"That seems like a wise idea," I said, unbuttoning my blouse.

"The whole place is crumbling down around us and we simply can't keep up with the repairs."

"It's always been an expensive proposition, maintaining a home like this." I pulled off my blouse, and began working on my skirt. "I can't begin to tally the pounds I've spent on this place. I think it was the roof that needed replacing when I first came here."

"This once great estate is the sole legacy of the Wynn family, and we're losing it piece by piece because we can't afford to keep it up." Her voice was soft, defeated.

I gave up on unfastening my skirt and turned to face her. Were we really going to discuss finances now? "Delia, you have my sympathy, but I'm not in funds any longer myself."

"It's a shame you weren't able to control Reggie. You brought a great deal of money into the family, and Reggie squandered it before I was able to stop him."

Actually he hadn't, but I wasn't about to quibble. After all, he had squandered a fair portion of it. As I pulled on the clean blouse, the rest of her statement tickled my consciousness. "What do you mean, before you stopped him? When did Reggie ever stop spending money?"

She smiled. "Well, he certainly quit spending it after he died, didn't he?"

"Delia! That's a terrible thing to say. Reggie was feckless and irresponsible, I agree, but I know you didn't wish him dead for all that."

"Oh, I did more than wish him dead. You may as well know now, I made sure he took a very heavy dose of his heart medicine."

I shook my head, confused. "But he had a heart attack. How would his own medication cause that?"

She shrugged. "Because he rarely took it and I gave him a triple dose."

My fingers froze on the buttons of my blouse. "You couldn't have." I scarcely knew what I was saying, I just needed to utter any words that would negate what she was admitting.

"Someone had to stop him." She lurched forward in her

chair and pointed a finger at me. "You had no control over him. For heaven's sake, he was never even here with you. I can hardly credit that you miss him."

"He was my husband!"

"And he spent his time dallying with other men's wives. He was a terrible husband, and an unworthy earl. He should have been a custodian of the earldom of Harleigh, but he let it fall into ruin, and this house into rubble, all for want of funds."

She pushed up from the chair and walked toward me, anger twisting her face into a grimace. "He never cared about the title and he never cared about Harleigh Manor. I hoped when he married you he'd finally step up to his responsibilities, but instead he used your money to fund his escapades."

I felt moisture on my cheeks, and realized I was crying, as the horror of her words struck me. "Why are you telling me this? You've kept your secret for this long, why force it on me now?"

She sighed. I could see the anger leaving her body, not that she relaxed, but simply calmed, her face set in firm lines. "Because I'm afraid we're going to have to dip into your family's deep pockets again, and I wanted you to understand how desperate we are. I won't take no for an answer."

She pulled a pistol from behind her back, and my heart pounded a frantic beat. "Oh, for heaven's sake, Delia! Put that away! I'll give Graham the money in my account, for all the good it will do you."

"That's nowhere near enough. I can't believe Graham even bothered trying. We need a sum that will tide us over until his investments start paying off. Or until the boys are old enough to find their own heiresses. Otherwise we'll lose the estate. Without this, we're nothing."

I couldn't take my eyes off the gun. She waved it around with the flow of her words, making me wince at each pass.

"What do you hope to gain from killing me? Once I'm gone, you'll never see another penny from my father."

"Oh, I don't know. He wouldn't want his granddaughter to live in poverty, and since she'll be living with us, I think your father will be inclined to provide for her support."

My stomach roiled. The movement of the pistol fogged my brain. I desperately needed to understand what she was talking about, so I could say, or do, the right thing to make her put that damn pistol down. "Why would Rose be living with you?"

"Well, dear, I'm afraid no matter what happens between the viscount and the police, your sister will be ruined. Either that man will be arrested while in her company, or she'll have run off with a known criminal. After that, no court would give her custody of a young child."

She stepped toward me, placing herself between me and the door to the hallway. As she advanced, I backed away, moving toward the glass doors, and the balcony outside. Perhaps if I ran out and screamed someone would hear me.

Delia continued her explanation during this maneuver. "I'm sure your parents will try to gain custody themselves, but Rose is British, and Graham is a peer, and we'll pull every string we must to keep her with us. Though we'll encourage them to continue her support." She shook her head. "I'm sorry, Frances. It's not personal. I just can't see us getting by any other way."

"Delia, listen to me. No one knows you killed Reggie." I held up my hands, imploring her to wait, while the words rushed from my lips. "The police questioned the doctor. He was certain it was a heart attack."

Delia's brow furrowed in confusion. "Why did the police question the doctor?"

"There was an anonymous letter. They suspected me of killing him, but I wouldn't let them do an autopsy. Delia, we'll work something out. I'll get the money you need. You don't have to kill me."

Delia's jaw dropped as she stared at me, her face blank. "I don't believe it," she muttered. "How could everything have gone wrong?"

Did she seriously expect an answer? I had no idea what she was talking about.

She let out a miserable laugh. "And you have no idea what I'm talking about, do you?"

My first thought was if she could read my mind, it was going to be all the more difficult to get that pistol away from her. Then I realized she was simply reading the compete bafflement on my face. I gave a little shake of my head.

"Nothing worked out the way it should have." She flung her arms out in frustration, but never lost her grip on the pistol. "Reggie wasn't used to taking digitalis. He should have become sick before his heart stopped. The doctor should have suspected he was poisoned. And I was prepared to point the finger at you."

"Me?" I squeaked.

"Then I would have been rid of the both of you and had Rose in my care. But nothing ever works for me!" She slapped the pistol against the side of her leg, punctuating each syllable.

I was in awe of the tantrum she was throwing, but I must confess myself utterly devoid of sympathy. "You planned to murder Reggie, then see me hang for the crime?"

"We would have pleaded for leniency," she said with a shrug. "You would probably have been committed to an asylum."

Suddenly everything became clear. "You wrote the letter to the police. You told them to look to me—the wronged wife!"

"And that didn't work either!"

I could see anger and frustration was making her even more deranged, but I didn't care. I was furious and lunged forward, ready to throttle her. Despite her possession of the pistol, she darted aside, toward the balcony.

"So then you arranged for me to have an accident, didn't you?"

"What else could I do, Frances? I didn't know the police had acted on my letter. I thought they ignored it. When Lily told me about her accident on the bridge, I could only wish it had been you going over that rail. And then I thought why not? It took a little work, but I found a man in Guildford who would do just about anything for the right price. And he didn't ask any questions. I'm pleased to hear he at least made an attempt."

The little witch! As I advanced further she backed away. "An accident would certainly be more convenient. However will you explain that I've been shot?"

She looked down at the pistol in her hand.

Oh, dear. Stupid question. Smiling, she took aim. "I'll think of something."

I dropped to the floor as she fired, lodging a bullet deep in the wall behind me. On all fours I barreled into her legs, knocking her out the balcony door. She screamed as she fell and the door slammed shut as her outstretched arm banged against it.

I pushed myself up from the floor as the room spun about me. Oh, my Lord, I couldn't be sick now! Hasty footsteps sounded behind me, as I reached for the door handle, my breath coming in gasps. Should I just lock it or check on her? Something was very wrong about the way she fell.

I opened the door and stepped forward.

"No!" Hetty's arm circled my waist, pulling me back into the room.

In an instant I saw why. The candle, burning in the sconce on the wall, threw off enough illumination to see that where the balcony had been, was now simply space, air, nothing. Scaffolding stood to both sides of the doorway, but there was no balcony. I looked down, and in the darkness, I could barely make out the shape of Delia's body, twisted over a huge pile of stone.

Hetty pulled me away from the door. I clung to her as she walked me back to sit on the bed, my head spinning. "She might still be alive," I said hopefully, thinking of the Delia I had known, and trying to reconcile her with the crazed person who had just attacked me. "It wasn't a long fall."

"Once your head clears, we'll go down and find out." Her voice did not hold much hope.

Chapter 21

❧

Delia did not survive the fall. The distance hadn't been great, but landing on the broken chunks of stone, from the old balcony, had ensured her death. I tried to stop my tears by reminding myself that this was the fate she had chosen for me. Still, they flowed for some time.

Hetty sent a servant to Guildford to inform the police and send a telegram to Graham. The children were already in bed and we asked the nurse to keep them upstairs should they waken. I felt my eyes water again as I realized someone would have to tell the boys about their mother in the morning.

Before a constable could arrive from town, Lily returned with one of the inspectors. I'd completely forgotten their names by then. She rushed into my arms, and I was so relieved to have her back safely, I almost neglected to tell him what had happened here. I gave him the briefest summary, and Hetty took him up to my room to review the scene, leaving me alone with my sister.

"My God, are you all right?" Her eyes searched my face, perhaps looking for signs of a breakdown.

I gave her a helpless gesture. "Still a little shaky at the moment, but what about you? What happened with the viscount?"

She guided me over to the divan, then curled up next to me, resting her head on my shoulder. "I didn't want to go for a drive alone with him," she said. "I knew you didn't want me to see him, and it bothered me that he pursued me here. He and Delia had one or two private conversations in the study that I didn't care for either." She wrinkled her nose. "Oddly enough, there's a hole in the floor of my room, and I could hear them quite clearly."

"Really?"

She nodded her head against my shoulder. "Delia encouraged his suit." She sat up and turned to face me. "With him pleading, and her insisting, I didn't see any way out of it, so off we went for the bloody drive."

I grimaced at her language, but was just too weary to correct her.

"We drove five or six miles out into the countryside," she continued, "and ate a picnic luncheon he'd brought with him. Then he made some advances I didn't appreciate. I insisted he take me back home, but then the motor car wouldn't start." Her eyes goggled as she shook her head. "I let him work on it for far too long before I realized he might be doing this deliberately. The sun was setting by then, and I knew if we had to stay out there all night, my reputation would be ruined."

I pushed some loose curls behind her ear. Poor dear. "Did you accuse him of planning this?"

"I did. Then he became angry, which made me angry, and the next thing I knew, I'd hit him over the head with the champagne bottle." She paused and looked up at me, biting her lip. "We'd both had quite a bit of champagne."

"I see. I'm thankful it didn't slow your reflexes."

"No, I suppose it didn't." Her voice held a note of pride. "Well, he slumped against the motor car, and I started walking home. Perhaps an hour later, the two inspectors drove up in a carriage, saying they were looking for me. They took me up, and we returned to find the viscount."

"Was he still where you left him?"

"He was not." Her eyes grew wide in outrage. "Which proves the motor car would start, and he'd been trying to trick me. Can you believe that?"

"Hmm, I'm afraid I can believe that and more. How did you find him?"

"Well as there were no turn-offs from the road, we just followed it for several miles, until we found him pulled off by the side. This time the motor car truly had broken down. You should have seen his face when he saw me with the inspectors. He thought someone had come to assist him."

"You do know he wasn't really Viscount Ainsworthy, don't you?"

She nodded, eyes wide with amazement. "Yes, Inspector Collins told me what they knew of him. You don't suppose he murdered the real viscount, do you?"

I shook my head. "The police will eventually find out what happened to the real viscount, but I don't believe Thomas murdered him."

"But he did kill that footman, didn't he?"

I told her the story, and how her sketches had helped to identify the fake viscount as Capshaw's killer, until Crabbe came to the door, and announced the coroner and another constable. Hetty came back from my room with the inspector, and the three men went outside to view Delia's body.

Hetty seated herself in a chair next to me and placed a hand on my knee. "How are you holding up, dear?"

"As well as can be expected, I suppose." I rubbed my hands over my face. "I'm still trying to take in the fact that Delia murdered Reggie. And she would have murdered me."

"I know you considered her a friend, dear, but I've been

wondering for the past hour if she wasn't the author of the anonymous letter the police received."

"She admitted she sent it." Hetty's lips compressed in anger as I gave her that part of the story.

None of us slept much that night, what with police coming and going, first to examine, and remove Delia's body, then to take statements from all of us, regarding both Thomas and Delia. It was very early in the morning when the last constable left us. Hetty snored softly in her chair, and Lily was curled up next to me on the sofa. I woke them both and urged them upstairs for a few hours' sleep. I bunked in with Lily as I could not face going back to my room.

The next week was like the uneasy wakefulness after a nightmare. It took a few days before I stopped jumping at sudden movements and noises. Graham had come home, and after a long consultation with him and the chief inspector, we decided to call Delia's death an accident. No mention would go into the report about her attempt on my life, and I never said a word about her confession of killing Reggie. She was gone now. There was no way to punish her further, and in this way the horrible truth would never reach the children, or Delia's parents.

After showing the inspector out, Graham invited me back to the library for a drink. We both needed it. We were building a link between us—more than a truce, not yet a friendship. Perhaps just a mutual understanding of what the other must be suffering.

Graham strode to the tantalus and poured a healthy tot of spirits into two glasses. "I'm selling Harleigh," he said.

I was stunned by his announcement. "I wasn't aware you could sell the estate. Isn't it entailed?"

"Not all of it." He turned and handed me a glass. "Do you recall where the ruins are?"

I nodded. "Reggie and I took a picnic luncheon there once, long ago."

He gave me a wry smile. "That was the original house which stood on the original holding that was conferred with the title. The rest of the property the family purchased over the centuries. So yes, I can sell most of the estate."

"Including the house?"

"Especially the house. The last thing I'd want to do is hand the curse of feeding this white elephant over to my son."

"I see." While I couldn't fault his decision, my mind reeled at the thought of the money I'd put into this house. He was right though. It would always demand more. It *had* become a curse. Still, I worried he was acting on emotion rather than reason.

"I understand why you'd wish to rid yourself of this burden, and why you can have no desire to live here, but this might not be the best time to make such an important decision."

Graham finished off his drink in one swallow and returned the glass to the tray. "I made this decision almost a year ago. Delia and I argued about it nearly every day since. She didn't want to give this place up. It meant everything to her."

He turned back to face me, his expression grim. "Two weeks ago I engaged an estate agent. I fear that may be what pushed her over the edge."

I saw the pain in his eyes and searched my mind for some words to relieve it. Delia had jumped over that edge long before she attacked me, but Graham had no idea she'd caused his brother's death. Perhaps I had an obligation to tell him one day. But not today. He was in enough pain.

I placed a hand on his arm and gave it a squeeze. "I don't hold you responsible for Delia's actions, Graham. Don't take that weight on yourself."

He blinked several times before turning away.

* * *

We females returned to London the day after the funeral, with a promise from Graham to follow us a few days later, bringing the boys. It felt good to be home, sleeping in my own bed, with the knowledge there would be no break-ins in the future.

That thought made me wonder what had happened with Thomas Martin. Though Delaney had come to Guildford to take his prisoner back to London, I never saw him and I'd heard nothing from George while we were at Harleigh. My curiosity was relieved the next morning when George paid a call, with Delaney in tow. It was nearly noon, but fatigued from the previous week's events, we still lingered over the breakfast table. It took an invitation from each of us to convince the inspector to join us.

George, who needed no urging, dropped himself into the chair next to mine, and took my hand. "Forgive me for not waiting for a more suitable hour, but I needed to find out how you were faring."

"Well enough," I said. There'd be time later to relay all that had happened at Harleigh. After his investigations on my behalf, he deserved to know Delia had murdered Reggie, at the very least. As for the rest, if I didn't tell him I'm sure Hetty or Lily would. I wondered if he'd react with another proposal.

Hiding my smile, I turned to Delaney. "Have you news of Thomas Martin?"

"He's made a full confession," he said, pouring a cup of coffee. "It ties with the reports we received from South Africa. Seems the real Ainsworthy had died of typhoid fever, several weeks before notice of his inheritance arrived. Thomas was living in the viscount's lodgings, and selling off his belongings to raise the fare back to England, when he received the notice. I understand both men were similar in build and coloring, and there was Thomas left in a foreign country without a job or funds. Ainsworthy's creditors had seized the mining company.

The viscount was dead as were his closest relations. I suppose the temptation to impersonate him was just too strong."

I considered Thomas' situation. "He must have felt he had nothing to lose, and everything to gain."

"Imagine his disappointment when he arrived at the viscount's solicitor's office to find the coffers nearly empty, and the estate entailed." George's voice was tinged with a grim irony.

"That must be when he decided he needed a wealthy heiress," Lily noted with a scowl. "And to keep up appearances, he started stealing small items and selling them."

"As for the thefts, did you happen to learn why he left the bracelet in my bag?"

Delaney nodded. "He overheard Mrs. Stoke-Whitney instructing two servants to search for it and decided it was best to be rid of the thing. As he planned to call on Miss Price, there would be a chance of retrieving it."

"If he had no money, how did he manage to purchase the automobile?" Hetty asked.

"Who would not accept a bank draft from a viscount?" Delaney shook his head. "Everyone took him at face value. Everyone believed the lie." His gaze landed on me.

"Except you, my lady."

I frowned across the table at him. "What do you mean?"

"You were having him investigated before any of this trouble started. Your instincts were correct."

I only wished my instincts had been as good when it came to my in-laws. I pushed the thought aside and smiled at my guests. "Goodness, Inspector. A compliment from you is a rare thing indeed. But I must confess it's something any good sponsor would do for her charge."

"Only the best sponsors would do it," Lily argued. "Which is why you should consider my suggestion to bring out other young ladies. Even though you didn't find me a match."

"Oh, so you've turned your back on Mr. Kendrick, have you? You know he's quite the hero in my eyes."

The russet color in her cheeks gave me my answer.

"Well, perhaps when you write home, you might mention the possibility to some of your friends in New York. One or two of them may wish to visit next Season."

"It is only April." A sly smile curved her lips. "There's still a great deal left of this Season."

"I suppose that's true, and now that I think about it, Madeline was very taken with Ainsworthy too, more so than you, I'd say. Her mother might be persuaded to mention my services to the right people—very discreetly, of course." I thought of the bank draft my mother sent me for sponsoring Lily. Could I actually make my own way in the world? Better still, could I steer these young ladies away from disastrous marriages? The very idea made me smile.

"I just might be able to make a go of this," I said, marveling at the possibility.

I turned toward George when he squeezed my hand. "One can't help but admire an independent woman."

My cheeks grew warm with a blush. I wasn't ready for marriage again, nor was I completely independent. I fell somewhere between the two, with a fair mix of responsibility and freedom. I was in a place where anything could happen. And when such a man lived right next door, who knew what would happen next?